"I THINK YOU OUGHT TO LET ME GO."

"Aunt Lydia informed me that you had a friend— of the masculine gender," Jaime said, ignoring her plea. "Is that right?"

"She had no right to—"

"And did you?" he demanded harshly. "You are my wife. Perhaps it's time I put in my claim," he said, one hand finding the curve of her nape and compelling her face down to his.

"You told me you didn't want me!" Miranda protested, trembling as she felt his lips move along the curve of her cheek.

"Correction." He moved his head in a negative gesture. "I believe I said I didn't want to make love to you. At least not then. Now, I do!" With a lithe movement, he imprisoned her beneath him.

Miranda was unable to evade his embrace even had she wanted to.

HARLEQUIN
PREMIERE AUTHOR EDITIONS

These books may be available at your local bookseller.

Don't miss any of our special offers. Write to us at the following address for information on our newest releases.

Harlequin Reader Service
P.O. Box 52040, Phoenix, AZ 85072-2040
Canadian address: P.O. Box 2800, Postal Station A,
5170 Yonge St., Willowdale, Ont. M2N 6J3

ANNE MATHER

SCORPION'S DANCE

Harlequin Books

TORONTO • NEW YORK • LONDON
AMSTERDAM • PARIS • SYDNEY • HAMBURG
STOCKHOLM • ATHENS • TOKYO • MILAN

First Harlequin edition published December 1978
Second printing May 1982

ISBN 0-373-80659-0

This HARLEQUIN PREMIERE AUTHOR EDITION
published April 1985

Original hardcover edition published in 1978
by Mills & Boon Limited.

CHAPTER ONE

MIRANDA could remember clearly the first time she saw Jaime Knevett.

It was on the occasion of her tenth birthday, and as a special treat, Lady Sanders had agreed to a birthday party on the lawn, out of sight of the house, of course. Miranda could recall the excitement with which she had anticipated her birthday. Until that time, birthdays had been very little different from any other day, with perhaps a trip to the pictures in the evening, after her mother had finished the preparations for dinner.

But that was hardly unusual in the circumstances. After all, housekeepers' children should be seen and not heard, or so she had always been led to believe, and no one could deny that Lady Sanders had been kind to her mother when her father died so suddenly, leaving his wife with a three-year-old daughter, and no visible means of support.

Her father had been a farm worker and their cottage was tied to his job. Naturally, when he died the cottage was required for his replacement, and Miranda's mother had been desperate when Lady Sanders, who incidentally owned the estate on which their cottage stood, had suggested she should come and live at the Hall. Her housekeeper was getting near retirement age, Lady Sanders explained, and reliable help was so hard to find these days.

By taking in Lucy Gresham and her fatherless little daughter, Lady Sanders assured herself of 'reliable help' for numerous years to come, but it was only as she got older that Miranda got more cynical. At ten, she was still young enough to take kindness at its face value, and at three she had no opinion at all.

Lady Sanders was a widow. Her husband had been killed in a road accident a year after Miranda was born, and the less charitable people in the village had been heard to express the opinion that it was fortunate he had only wrapped his own car round the tree and not someone else's. It

seemed the late Lord Sanders had imbibed rather freely, and
it was chance rather than good fortune which had kept him
alive as long as it did.

After his death, Lady Sanders assumed the running of
the estate with an assurance that revealed she had been
doing so surreptitiously for years. She had one son, the new
Lord Sanders, and she was determined that his inheritance
should in no way suffer through the death of his father.

Miranda saw Mark Sanders rarely during her formative
years. The local prep school, followed by succeeding board-
ing schools, took care of his education, and in the holidays
his mother took care never to let him out of her sight. Mrs
Gresham explained that Lady Sanders worshipped the boy,
and now that her husband was dead, she had no one else. It
seemed a lonely existence to Miranda who, in spite of the
strictures impressed upon her at home, led quite an active
social life outside. She had friends in plenty, and she pitied
the pale-faced youth she occasionally glimpsed playing by
himself on the lawns.

A week before Miranda's tenth birthday, Lady Sanders
gave a dinner party. It was the beginning of June, the night
of the Hunt Ball, and Mrs Gresham had worked solidly for
over a fortnight getting the Hall ready for Lady Sanders'
guests who were staying overnight and going home the following day. There had been such an orgy of cleaning and
polishing, and even Miranda had been roped in to fetch and
carry for the domestics hired for the purpose. The meal itself had taken hours to prepare—smoked ham and melon,
delicately-battered scampi, roast duckling, with peas and
new potatoes, and Mrs Gresham's special orange sauce, and
peaches soaked in brandy. The wines, too, had been specially chosen, chilled to perfection, and Miranda had been
enchanted by the sight of the table, its silver and crystal
gleaming in the light of half a dozen scented candles.

The dinner party was a success, and in gratitude for the
work she had put in, Lady Sanders had suggested that as
it was Miranda's birthday the following week, perhaps Mrs
Gresham might like to organise a small party for her.

In later years, Miranda was to speculate upon the character of a woman who chose such a way to reward her housekeeper, but at that time the idea of a party had been so ex-

citing to her that she had not stopped to think that perhaps her mother might have preferred less work rather than more.

In any event, the party was arranged, and in spite of lowering clouds which had hung around all morning, the afternoon skies were clear. Miranda helped her mother, and old Croxley, the gardener, carried a trestle table out on to the lawn at the back of the house, and when it was set with sandwiches and pastries, cakes and jellies, and a huge jug of orange juice, to her eyes it looked every bit as good as Lady Sanders' dinner table had done. Seven little girls had been invited, and Miranda was to occupy the seat at the head of the table, immediately behind the iced sponge cake with 'Happy Birthday, Miranda' written in tiny hundreds and thousands.

The guests arrived and Miranda opened her presents with trembling fingers. There were books and crayons and handkerchiefs, and her best friend, Judith Masters, whose father taught at the village school, gave her a pretty pearl pendant that Miranda insisted on wearing at once. They played games and Mrs Gresham had packets of sweets for prizes, and then it was time for tea.

Miranda presided over the table proudly, aping the odd occasions when she had peeped through the dining room door and seen Lady Sanders taking lunch with some of her friends from the Rotary Club. It was her first party, and she was determined it should be a success. Then it began to rain ...

Only a few spots at first, rather large spots that dropped just over Miranda's head, and spattered on the carefully arranged inscription on the cake, making the decorations run together and partially obliterate her name.

Miranda jumped to her feet at once, disappointment bringing an anxious frown to her forehead. Her mother had gone back into the house, leaving her in charge, but surely she must see the rain from her windows. She looked back towards the kitchen, but there was no sign of either her mother or Croxley, and then when one or two of the other girls told her to sit down again, to stop worrying, that it was probably only a shower, Miranda turned her face skyward to see a cloudless arc of blue.

Then a huge drop of water fell in her eye, and she gasped and brought her hands to her face, as a veritable shower sprayed over the table and its occupants, bringing them all to their feet, gulping and protesting and giggling helplessly. Miranda didn't giggle. Her reason told her it couldn't be raining. The sky was clear; and besides, the leaves of the laurel hedge that shielded the kitchen garden from sight of the Hall were dry.

And yet the shower just kept on coming, and her guests were so bemused by what was happening that they paid little attention to its source. But Miranda's sharp eyes noticed how the shower arched over the hedge, and with an exclamation of fury, she dashed towards the bushes.

Immediately there was smothered laughter, and the shower ceased as quickly as it had begun. Miranda paid no attention to that. With furious hands she tore aside the twigs and branches that held her back and burst through the hedge like a veritable virago.

Beyond the hedge was the tap which Croxley used to operate the sprinkler system on the lawns in dry weather. Presently not needed, the sprinkler had been stored away in the garden shed, but someone had got it out. Someone who was presently disappearing round the corner of the house, a tall dark figure who was as unfamiliar to Miranda as she must be to him.

She set out in pursuit, and then halted uncertainly, looking down in dismay at the pretty flowered dress her mother had made her specially for the party. Pushing through the hedge had torn the hem, and it was streaked with dirt as she was. Her hair, rust-coloured, and always unmanageably straight, had come loose from its braids and was presently straggling untidily about her shoulders, and the pearl pendant had disappeared, probably broken in the struggle.

Her friends were shouting to her from the other side of the hedge, and Mrs Gresham, alerted by their excitement, had come to see what was going on. Miserably, Miranda forced her way back through the hedge, and suffered the stifled giggles and compassionate glances of the other girls.

'*Miranda!*' Her mother was not prone to unwarranted sympathy. 'What on earth has been going on?'

At once half a dozen voices attempted to regale her with

their version of the story, but Mrs Gresham waited until
Miranda herself could explain. Half expecting her mother to
disbelieve her, or alternatively find excuses for what had
happened, Miranda was surprised to discover that Mrs
Gresham seemed as angry as she was. Listening to what had
happened, her face went first red, and then white, before
she turned and walked silently into the house.

Miranda stared after her worriedly, but the other girls
clustered around, demanding to know what had happened,
and she allowed herself to be swayed by the importance the
incident had granted her. She accepted their sympathy as
her right, and basked in their admiration of how she had sent
whoever it was packing. She scarcely looked at the table, but
when she did, she felt a lump rise in her throat at the sight
of the ruined cake and waterlogged sandwiches. Only the
jelly repelled the moisture, green and yellow islands in a
transparent sea.

Miranda was still standing there surrounded by her
friends when her mother came back again, but she was not
alone. With her was Lady Sanders—and a boy of perhaps
fifteen or sixteen. He was tall for his age, thin, with angular
features that were not enhanced by the dark pigmentation of
his skin. His hair was thick and black, blacker than any
hair Miranda had seen before, and she wondered what
nationality he was. But she had no hesitation in identifying
him as the instigator of that artificial rainstorm.

She glared at him and was infuriated to discover that she
could still see amusement in those darkly-lashed eyes, although his face bore an obediently solemn expression. She
wondered who he was, and what he was doing at the Hall,
and found herself praying that he was an intruder and that
Lady Sanders was about to have him arrested.

'As you can see, my lady, the table is ruined,' her mother
was saying, as they walked across the lawn together, accompanied by the abominable boy, and Lady Sanders nodded
her head in agreement, and murmured some words of
regret.

Then they turned to the group of girls, and belatedly
Miranda remembered that she should have washed her face
and hands and combed her hair before appearing before
anyone. As it was, she stood there, with the group of other

girls, looking like a tattered parrot among so many pigeons. Lady Sanders saw her, exchanged a look with the boy at her side, and ignominy of ignominies, she started laughing. And when she laughed, the boy laughed, and that set all the girls giggling and laughing all over again. Only Mrs Gresham didn't laugh, but that was small comfort to Miranda. With a sob of humiliation she brushed past all of them, rushing across the lawn and into the house, not stopping until she reached the sanctuary of her own room. She would never forgive them, she thought, not her friends, not Lady Sanders, and most particularly not that black-haired beast who had ruined the only party she had ever had ...

Of course, she got over it. She could even laugh about it in time, only never in Lady Sanders' presence. That day was a turning point in her life, the day she began to realise the differences between the people of Lady Sanders' world and her own.

She learned that the boy was a distant relation of the late Lord Sanders, son of his cousin, Patrick Knevett, who had estates in Brazil, and who had scandalised his family in 1947 by marrying an Indian girl of Portuguese extraction because she was expecting his child. The boy had been brought up in South America, which would account for the deep tanning of his skin, and had been staying with Lady Sanders while his father made arrangements for him to finish his schooling in England.

During the years that followed, Miranda saw him several times. Because his home was such a long way away, he usually spent Christmas and Easter at the Hall. On the few occasions when Lady Sanders chose to confide in her housekeeper, she explained that he was company for Mark, three years his junior, and much in awe of his older cousin.

Miranda herself succeeded in passing the examination which took her to the grammar school in the local town, but when she was sixteen she left school with eight 'O' levels, much to the disappointment of the headmistress, who had been expecting great things of her. However, further education on a housekeeper's pay was simply not on, and she got a job in the town library and settled down quite happily. She loved books, and working in the library enabled her to read everything that was published.

She had had boy-friends before she left school, and she continued going out with different boys and not going steadily with any of them. She had seen too much of the struggle her mother had had bringing her up to want to put herself into the same position, and she gained the reputation of being frigid and mercenary, which wasn't strictly true. It was simply that she wanted more out of life than a mortgaged semi, and a parcel of children she couldn't afford.

Then, when she was eighteen, she was invited to the Hunt Ball.

She had been going out with a young farmer, Dennis Morgan, whose father owned some land on the outskirts of the village, and because his land was used by the Hunt, he had been invited.

At first she had demurred, realising that Lady Sanders would attend the Ball, but surprisingly her mother took a stand.

'Why shouldn't you go?' she demanded, her work-worn hands kneading together. 'You've been invited. I don't see what it has to do with her ladyship.'

But Miranda noticed she didn't tell her employer that her daughter was attending the ball, and no one could have been more surprised than Lady Sanders when she saw her housekeeper's daughter dancing with the son of one of the local landowners.

Miranda was enjoying herself. Her gown was new, and she was aware that it suited her. The years between that disastrous party and now had wrought a great change in her. Her hair was no longer so red, but had toned to a deep chestnut streaked with golden lights, and its straightness was used to advantage by careful cutting. Shoulder-length, it swung in a silken curtain from a centre parting, accentuating the wide depths of eyes that were translucently green. She was tall, too, but not thin, and her breasts swelled provocatively above the deep *décolletage* of her gown. The gown itself was green, almost exactly matching the colour of her eyes, layers of chiffon over a clinging chemise-like underskirt. What she was unaware of was that another pair of eyes, very similar to those of Lady Sanders', were watching her with more than casual interest.

The evening was well advanced before a slender, pale-faced young man chose Dennis's temporary absence to ask her to dance. Miranda knew who he was, of course. She had seen him frequently about the Hall in the past couple of years, just as he knew her; although he doubted he would have believed how beautiful she could be, dressed as she invariably was in denim jeans and shirts, or plain uniform dresses for work. But tonight she was sparkling, and Mark Sanders recognised that she was easily the most interesting girl in the room.

Miranda, prepared to dislike him, found her sympathies aroused by his diffidence, and his barbed humour had nothing coarse about it. He knew everyone there, of course, and his wry comments and dry wit made her see them all in a different light. Old Squire Matthews, who used to terrify her when she was a child by cracking his riding crop against his boot, was just a foolish old man who couldn't face a kill sober; the Falconers of High Garth, much respected in the village, couldn't stand the sight of one another outside of public occasions like this; and Canon Bridgenorth and his wife, who lived far beyond their means, would likely retire on social security.

That his comments were vaguely malicious did not really disturb her. Gossip was rife in a village like King's Norton, and he was only relating what her mother had suspected for years. Besides, she thought, he was only trying to put her at her ease, and she was flattered that out of all the girls there, he should have chosen to dance with her.

Dennis was waiting for her when the dance was over, and he was not best pleased by what had happened. 'You're not interested in that pansy boy, are you?' he demanded, unable to ignore her flushed cheeks and the unaccustomed light in her eyes, and Miranda turned on him angrily.

'He's not a pansy boy!' she declared hotly. 'He's very nice actually. A gentleman—something you might not know a lot about.'

Dennis looked affronted, and immediately she was contrite. 'I'm sorry, Dennis,' she exclaimed at once, realising she had been rude. After all, without Dennis's invitation she would not be here. 'It's just that—well, I liked him.'

Dennis allowed himself to be placated. He didn't want to fall out with Miranda. He was half in love with her, and he had been beginning to hope that she might care for him. He knew her reputation. He knew she had never had a steady boy-friend, but he was hoping to change all that.

However, Dennis was to be disappointed. Within a week, Mark had started dating Miranda, much to his own and her mother's disapproval.

'You're a fool!' Mrs Gresham told her daughter, never one to mince words. 'He's not for the likes of you. Lady Sanders would never let her son marry the housekeeper's daughter!'

'Why not?' Miranda was still riding on cloud seven. All the girls in the library had seen Mark's super sports car when he came to pick her up after work, and all her friends envied her her good fortune. All except Judith, that was. The schoolmaster's daughter sided with Miranda's mother in disapproving of the affair, and had jeopardised their friendship by accusing Miranda of dating Mark because he had money. Miranda had denied it emphatically, but deep inside her she wondered if she would find him half so attractive without his sports car and the Hall behind him.

Now Mrs Gresham sank into her comfortable rocking chair by the fire and folded her hands. 'You're not thinking seriously enough,' she said with a sigh. 'Oh, I suppose I can't blame you. You and I have always had to work for every penny we earned. But that young man—he's too like his father for my liking. And I don't want him smashing up that flashy car of his while you're inside it.'

Miranada shifted restlessly. 'Mark wouldn't do that. He drives fast, I know, but he's always careful.'

'When he's sober,' remarked her mother dryly. 'I doubt you've seen him drunk yet. But it has been known. And that's without—well, you know what I mean.'

'Sex?' Miranda paced impatiently about the kitchen. 'Is that what you mean? We don't have sex. I—I wouldn't, even if he asked me.'

Her mother looked sceptical. 'What do you know about it? What do you know what you'd do faced with such a situation? Miranda, it's no use talking. You'd never understand in a million years. But believe me when I say that there comes a time in every woman's life when a situation gets completely out of her control ...'

'Oh, Mum!' Miranda sighed. 'I do know the facts of life, you know. I know about—body chemistry.'

'Is that what you call it? They called it something else in my young day. But never mind. So long as you always remember that so far as Lady Sanders is concerned, you're just one of the long line of girls her son will date before he settles down and marries someone *suitable*.'

Miranda flounced out of the room. There was more than a grain of truth in what her mother had said, she knew that, at least so far as Lady Sanders was concerned. But she couldn't honestly believe that Mark was like his mother. He was too kind, too attentive, too much fun.

Then, two days later, she had an experience of how much fun he could be. They had been to a nightclub in the nearby town and were driving home in the early hours. Miranda, who had taken driving lessons as soon as she was seventeen and bought herself an old Mini to get to and from work, had realised Mark was drinking too much and offered to drive them home, but he had scorned her caution.

'I'm not drunk!' he had protested mockingly. 'What's the matter? Chicken?'

Miranda had shaken her head and climbed into her seat obediently. Perhaps she was being over-cautious, she thought. Perhaps she was thinking too much about what her mother had said. Whatever her private feelings, she had maintained a composed façade, and this seemed to infuriate Mark. Instead of driving with extra care, he seemed to delight in taking unnecessary risks, and Miranda's palms were moist with sweat when they breasted a hill on the wrong side of the road and saw the headlights of an approaching car directly ahead of them.

She scarcely remembered the details of what happened afterwards. She knew Mark screamed and took his hands off the wheel, and somehow she threw herself across him and wrenched the wheel towards her. The sports car slewed dangerously across the road, but it missed the oncoming vehicle and ploughed half through the bushes on the left-hand side of the road.

Miranda was trembling violently when she brought the car to a halt, but Mark was shattered. Shaking, he had buried his head in his hands, and not until the irate driver of the other car came to ask what the hell was going on did he lift his face to reveal he had been crying. It was left to Miranda to explain how the steering had apparently gone out of control and she let the man assume that Mark had saved them. As it happened, he did know who Mark was, and in consequence was prepared to accept her explanation.

After he had left them and they were alone, Mark pulled her into his arms and buried his face in her hair. 'I'm sorry, I'm sorry,' he said, over and over again, and although she was still shocked, Miranda had comforted him like a child.

It was only when his lips strayed across her face to her mouth and his hands fumbled grotesquely at her clothes that she drew back from him, feeling curiously repelled. Suddenly their positions were reversed, and she was no longer in awe of him. It was another turning point in Miranda's relationship with the Sanders family.

Several days passed before she saw Mark again. She knew the girls at the library imagined that the young earl had walked out on her, but somehow she didn't really mind. To find that your idol had feet of clay was always a chastening experience, and Miranda was glad of the breathing space to gather her thoughts.

Then, just when she had come to the conclusion that it was all over between them, she found him waiting for her one evening, outside the library. Ignoring the raised eyebrows that greeted his appearance, she got into the car and gave him a long speculative look.

'I know,' he said, without turning on the ignition. 'I needed time to think. I guess you did, too.'

Miranda bent her head. 'What was there to think about?'

'You. Me. Us!' He regarded her intently. 'Miranda—will you marry me?'

Miranda was staggered. She had expected anything but this! 'Me?' she whispered. 'Marry you? Are you serious?'

'Never more so in my life,' he replied gravely. 'I care about you, Miranda. Enough to want to look after you for the rest of your life.'

'But—your mother—' she stammered helplessly.

'Leave my mother to me,' he said, and strangely enough she thought she could.

But was this really what she wanted? she wondered daz-

edly, as Mark set the car in motion. For days now she had
been battling with the realisation that she did not really
love him at all, that his wealth and social position had
blinded her to the weaknesses in the man himself. Now,
suddenly he was asking her to marry him, giving her the
chance to get out of the rat-race once and for all, and she
was hesitating. His mother would be furious, she knew, and
her own ... How could she go on being housekeeper to her
own daughter's mother-in-law?

But she needn't. Miranda could see to it that she never
had to work again. She *could* do that; *if* she married Mark.

It was a tempting proposition, made the more so by the
thought of what everyone in the village would say. Miranda
Gresham, the new Lady Sanders! Mistress of the Hall!

Her breathing quickened. What was happening to her?
she thought disgustedly. How could she consider Mark's
proposal seriously when only hours before she had felt
almost a sense of relief to know herself free of him? What
had changed? He was still the same man, and she was still
the same woman. Except that now she had something con-
crete to contend with ...

Yet it was what came after the wedding that she would
have to live with. Could she do that? Did she care for him
enough to contemplate the intimacies of marriage without
any qualms? There was no one else, and there were times
when she believed there never would be. She had never been
madly attracted to any man, and she had come to the conclusion that she simply did not have it in her to feel deeply
about anyone, except her mother. How could she be sure she
would ever feel any differently than she did today? And
how could she throw this opportunity away on the fleeting
chance she might? She was not mercenary, she consoled
herself, just practical; but how practical might she have to
be?

As expected, Lady Sanders disapproved of their engagement, although perhaps disapproval was too mild a term to
use to describe the words she said to her son when he
apprised her of the situation. The row they had could be
heard in the kitchen, and Miranda had tightened her lips
and closed the doors, and tried to ignore that she was the
cause of the quarrel.

Her own mother had taken the news rather differently. She had said little beyond repeating that Miranda was a fool and that a man like Mark Sanders didn't have it in him to make her happy.

The wedding was arranged for a week before Christmas, and the young couple were to fly out to Barbados afterwards for two weeks in the sun. Miranda got used to the other girls envying her her good fortune, and to having her picture in the paper alongside Mark's, and to parrying the reporters' questions about her rags-to-riches story. She found it harder to quieten her own conscience when it came to justifying her reasons for accepting his proposal.

Defeated, Lady Sanders gave in gracefully, outwardly at least. She was seen to accompany Miranda to her own dressmaker in London, pictures were taken of them shopping together, and just occasionally all three of them appeared together at some official function or other. Miranda was an apt pupil, and while she didn't like Lady Sanders, she could respect her, and they adopted a kind of armed truce with one another. Lady Sanders recognised that Miranda was not some impressionable debutante she could mould to her own design, but a girl with definite ideas of her own. Nevertheless, she was experienced enough at dealing with people to know exactly how to approach her future daughter-in-law to get the required result. She never gave up hoping that Mark might come to his senses, but in the event that he didn't, she was determined to hold on to her position in the household.

Surprisingly Miranda grew less apprehensive as the wedding neared. Mark was behaving particularly well, never demanding too much of her, never drinking excessively, never driving too fast; reassuring her that her first opinion of him had not been misplaced. Until the Rotary Club Ball in December ...

The Ball was an annual event, and as Lady Sanders was a prominent member, naturally she was expected to attend. Her son and his fiancée were invited, too, and Miranda spent hours in her room beforehand, preparing for the last official gathering before their wedding. The wedding itself was only two weeks away, and a sumptuous function it was going to be. Lady Sanders had taken over all the

organisation because, as she explained, no one could expect
Mrs Gresham to pay for the kind of reception their friends
would expect.

But before that, there was this evening, and Miranda was
determined that Mark should feel proud of her. Her gown
was made of velvet, rich cream velvet, that brushed against
her skin with a kiss of silk. Her hair was about her shoulders as usual, but she had threaded it with seed pearls,
which matched the pearl necklace and ear-rings Mark had
given her as an engagement present. Excitement had heigh-
tened the colour in her cheeks, and her lips were parted in
anticipation. She had never looked more attractive, and she
knew it.

Her mother viewed her appearance without enthusiasm.
These past weeks Mrs Gresham seemed to have aged considerably, and Miranda wondered if she was unhappy at
leaving the Hall to retire into the comfortable cottage on the
green that Mark had acquired for her. She was fifty-three,
after all. Surely she couldn't want to work all her life.

But Mark and his mother were waiting for her, and pick-
ing up her evening cloak, Miranda said a reluctant goodbye
and walked along the passage which separated the housekeeper's and kitchen quarters from the rest of the Hall.

Another door, set beneath the curve of the stairs, brought
her into the main hall of the building. Here, panelled walls
stretched up two floors to a magnificent carved ceiling, and a
massive fireplace was flanked by portraits of earlier members
of the Sanders family. The floor was polished, and briefly
Miranda could remember her mother working on her hands
and knees to keep it so, although now she had an electric
polisher. There were skin rugs, and long damson-coloured
curtains, and two huge armchairs which almost blocked
the heat from the glowing log fire. The hall had an almost
mediaeval charm, and Miranda had always responded to its
austere beauty.

She thought the hall was deserted, and with a glance up
the wide carved staircase, she made her way towards
the library where Mark and his mother usually enjoyed a
drink before dinner. But before she reached the leather-
studded door, a man rose from the depths of one of the
armchairs by the fire and said: 'Good evening, Miranda.'

His sudden appearance startled her, and because he was not Mark or his mother she thought for a moment he must be the ghost of one of their ancestors. But no Sanders was ever so dark or so big, and her hands clenched tightly as she realised who he was.

'It—it's Mr Knevett, isn't it?' she asked, unwilling to speak to him at all but equally unable to ignore him. It was five or six years since she had seen the brutal violater of her childhood tea-party, and then only from a distance. She couldn't recall that he had ever spoken to her, not even to apologise for what he had done. And now he spoke to her as if he knew her! How dared he? And what was he doing here anyway?

CHAPTER TWO

As if in answer to her unspoken question, Jaime Knevett flexed his shoulder muscles, and said: 'I seem to have arrived just in time for the wedding, don't I?'

He spoke English without a trace of an accent, as well he might, she thought broodingly. He had attended school in England, after all, and his father was English. But he didn't look English. He looked Brazilian, or Portuguese, with that straight uncompromising nose and those fine lips. And yet there was something about his eyes which was wholly alien to either of those nationalities.

'You're—staying?' she asked now, not quite knowing what to do, and he inclined his head gravely. Belatedly, she saw he was wearing a fine mohair dinner jacket, and his shirt front was an intricate mass of pleated lace which contrasted wildly with his hard, wholly masculine features. Was he to attend the ball with them? And why hadn't Mark told her he was coming?

'I gather you don't approve,' he observed dryly. 'Haven't you forgiven me yet?'

Miranda felt the wave of colour sweeping up her neck to her face. 'I really don't know what you mean,' she protested, but patently he didn't believe her.

'I think you do,' he told her insistently, his hands sliding into the pockets of his jacket to leave his thumbs hooked outside. 'But never mind. You're almost a member of the family now.'

'Not your family, Mr Knevett,' she retorted, and saw the faint smile that lifted the corners of his mouth.

'You may call me Jaime,' he said, refusing to argue with her, but she determined he should never have that satisfaction.

Lady Sanders' appearance curtailed any further conversation between them. Black lace became the older woman very well, although her eyes flicked almost enviously over Miranda in her cream velvet. Mark was evidently well pleased with his fiancée's appearance, and his hand curved possessively about her waist as he asked Jaime whether he didn't envy him his good fortune.

Jaime's reponse was as enthusiastic as he could have wished, but Miranda was aware of the cynicism in the older man's gaze, and hated him for it.

The ball was a glittering occasion in the county, and because the Sanders were there, the press were out in force. Miranda was forced to face so many flashbulbs that her head began to feel as if it was exploding, and she hardly noticed who took advantage of Mark's diverted attention to draw her away to dance. It was such a relief to escape from the pressures of being Lord Sanders' fiancée that she didn't particularly care who engineered it.

But once on the dance floor, with Jaime's arms linked about her waist in the manner of the young people present, she had to press her palms against the soft material of his jacket to keep some breathing space between them.

'What's the matter?' he inquired softly. 'We're only dancing.' But Miranda could not relax.

Her breathing was unaccountably quicker, and she looked round determinedly at the other dancers, endeavouring to dismiss the hardness of Jaime's thighs close against her own. There were lots of young people present, all dancing in the way they were dancing, the girls often with their arms looped about their partners' necks, so why she should feel so uncomfortable she had no idea. But she did. It was not as if he was attracted to her, and certainly she despised him. But he possessed a certain animal magnetism which drew the eyes of many women in the room, and she told herself it was this physical manifestation which was causing her intense awareness of his man's body against hers. She had never felt like this with Mark, but then Mark was so much thinner, less muscular somehow, and he had never held her so closely when they were dancing.

'Do you—do you intend to stay in England long, Mr Knevett?' she asked, attempting a casual conversation, and he looked down at her with slightly raised eyebrows.

'I didn't think you cared,' he drawled, and she pressed vainly against the iron bands that encircled her. 'As a matter of fact,' he continued, 'I intended to return home next week, but Mark's persuaded me to stay until after the wedding.'

Of course. Mark would. Mark had always admired his older cousin, however remote their relationship might be. But Miranda wished that he hadn't with a strength that far outweighed the importance of that distant childhood humiliation.

'My aunt tells me you've been working in the local library,' he said, and realising she could not cause a scene here, on the dance floor, Miranda forced herself to look up at him. He was taller than Mark, and her gaze crossed his face, noting the firm line of his jaw and the lean flesh stretched across his cheekbones before reaching his eyes. But those dark brown depths derided her and she wished she dared say something to wipe that mocking amusement from his face. Apparently he agreed with his aunt and could see no reason why Mark should choose to marry someone socially inferior and so obviously unsuitable.

'What do you do, Mr Knevett?' she responded coldly. 'When you're not making sport of the working classes? Or is honest toil abhorrent to you?'

His expression scarcely registered her taunt. 'As it is to Mark, you mean?' he countered provokingly, and she realised she had fallen into a trap of her own making.

'Mark works,' she defended her fiancé hotly. 'The estate——'

'——is run by a very efficient bailiff,' he interrupted her mildly. 'You see, I do know about such things, but I doubt you do.'

Miranda wished the band would get to the end of this particular waltz so she could return to the safety of Mark's protection. Every minute she spent with Jaime Knevett seemed to deepen the antagonism between them. She didn't like him, it was true, but he was her fiancé's cousin, and she suspected Lady Sanders would still use any method within her power to prevent her son from taking such an irrevocable step.

'As a matter of fact, I'm a doctor, or I shall be when I've completed my training.'

Miranda realised Jaime was speaking again and gathered her thoughts. 'I beg your pardon ...'

'I said—I'm a doctor,' Jaime repeated, lowering his head so that she could hear him more clearly and in so doing bringing his lips within touching distance of her hair.

The faintly alcohol-scented fumes of his breath fanned her forehead; a not unpleasant sensation, it made her aware of the other scents about him—the soap he used, the spicy tang of his after-shave lotion, the clean male smell of his body. His hair, as straight as her own, needed no artificial preparation, and lay thick and smooth against his head.

All this her senses told her, sensitising her fingertips against his chest, her breasts swelling against his hardness. A wave of heat began in the pit of her stomach and spread to the outermost extremities of her body, firing her blood and quickening the tell-tale beat of her heart. Dear God, she thought weakly, what was the matter with her? She felt quite faint. Surely she was allowing her imagination to run out of all control.

He had noticed her sudden lack of colour, however, and he said sharply: 'Are you feeling all right?'

Miranda managed to nod. 'Yes. No. That is—it's very hot in here, isn't it?'

'Is it?' His eyes compelled hers. 'Shall I take you back to your fiancé? Or would you rather step out into the corridor for a few minutes?'

Either seemed wholly unsuitable. How could she step outside with Jaime and run the risk of being spotted by scandal-hungry reporters? But equally, how could she go back to Mark like this, her legs unwilling to support her, and trembling like a leaf?

'There's an ante-room behind the dais,' Jaime observed quietly. 'The band use it in the interval. You could go in there for a few moments, if you'd rather not run the gauntlet of the press.'

The ball was being held at the Fleece, the largest hotel in the town, and the ballroom was used for conferences on other occasions and there were several ante-rooms adjoining.

The size of the hall and the press of people made it possible to slip unnoticed into the ante-room. Miranda stood there in the semi-darkness, unwilling to put on the light, and took several restoring gulps of air. She had expected Jaime would leave her, but he leaned against the wall just inside the doorway, watching her with dark inscrutable eyes.

'Better now?' he inquired, after she had expelled her breath on a shuddering sigh, and she looked at him uncertainly.

'I suppose you'll tell Mark,' she said.

'Tell Mark? Tell him what?'

'About me. About this.'

'What about this?' He straightened away from the wall. 'Why should you think he would be interested?'

Miranda shook her head. 'I—don't know.'

'Don't you?'

He didn't sound wholly convinced, and she flinched when he put out a hand and touched the creamy pallor of her cheek, his thumb probing the quivering contours of her mouth. When her lips parted, the pad of his thumb rubbed against the vulnerable barrier of her teeth, and then withdrew with an abruptness that left her with an aching pang of regret.

'Come!' he said. 'We will be missed. The band has stopped playing.'

Humiliation such as she had never experienced before washed over her. With trembling fingers she smoothed her hair, checked the neckline of her dress and then swept past him out of the ante-room. But she didn't get far before cruel fingers caught her wrist, and she was jerked round to face—her *fiancé*!

'Mark—' she began in surprise, and then checked at the thunderous expression contorting the normally pleasant features of his face. 'Mark, what is it?'

'Little *tramp*!' he muttered against her ear. 'What the hell have you been doing?'

If Miranda had been pale before, she was bright scarlet now. She looked round desperately for Jaime, for once needing him, requiring him to explain.

'I—we—Jaime—'

'Jaime, is it?' Mark sneered. 'That didn't take long, did it? My God, I should have listened to my mother when she warned me—'

'Warned you!' Miranda stared at him aghast, praying that no one could hear what they were saying above the sound of the beat number the band had started to play. 'Mark, I don't know what you mean!'

'You bloody little fool! Don't you understand? Haven't you guessed? Mother asked Jaime to come, not me! She invited him to the Hall, she asked him to stay for the wedding. And not because she dotes on him, because she doesn't. But because she knows what a sexy swine he is, and how a little tart like you wouldn't be able to resist his flattery!'

'*No!*' Miranda put a shocked hand to her mouth. 'No, that's not true! Mark, I swear to you——'

'What do you swear?' he taunted, swaying a little as he spoke, and she realised to her dismay that already he had drunk more than was good for him. 'That you weren't attracted to him? That you didn't spend the whole of the last dance gazing up at him, moon-faced? That you haven't been missing for a quarter of an hour since the dance ended?'

'I felt faint——' she began desperately, and Mark nodded vigorously.

'I bet you did,' he muttered. 'And to think I thought you were saving yourself for me!'

Miranda looked about them despairingly. Reason told her that Mark didn't mean all the things he was saying, but that didn't make them any the less painful. Painful too was the realisation that he might be right about his cousin, and that hurt most of all. If she could only get him out of here, away from all these people, she might to able to convince him he was wrong.

'Mark, we have to talk,' she said, in a low forceful tone. 'Now—do you want it to be here, where everyone can see us? Hear us?'

Mark looked at her suspiciously. 'What do you mean?'

'Oh, Mark!' She stared at him appealingly. 'Can't you see? You're reacting exactly how they want you to react! I've done nothing to be ashamed of. Don't you believe me?'

Even as she said the words, she wondered if she was being strictly honest. But this was a dirty game she was involved in, and she had to use the cards as they were played to her. Her own reactions to Jaime Knevett she would take out and examine at some other time, but right now she had to make Mark understand how he was being manipulated.

Mark was breathing heavily, the amount of alcohol he had consumed befuddling his brain, making it difficult for him to think clearly. He wanted to believe her. He had never cared for any girl the way he cared for her. In fact, girls had never figured too prominently in his life until she came along. He had much perferred fast cars and horse racing, and the company of his friends. But he was tired of those pursuits, and it had been a novelty taking out someone of whom he knew his mother disapproved. She had always chosen his friends for him, but he was sick and tired of that arrangement. Miranda had been a heaven-sent opportunity, a chance to escape from his mother's cloying possessiveness.

'All right,' he said heavily. 'Let's go to the car. We can talk there.'

Miranda would have chosen anywhere but there, but she had no choice in the matter. So long as Mark was prepared to talk, there was a chance she could persuade him he was wrong. And unless she wanted the break-up of their engagement, and the subsequent gossip that would arouse, she had to go along with him.

It was cold outside. Avoiding the main corridors of the hotel meant leaving her cloak behind, and Miranda was shivering when they climbed into the sports car. She had seen Mark's mother watching them as they left the ballroom, and the look on her face had confirmed Miranda's worst fears. Lady Sanders would not give up while there was still a chance she might be able to split them up.

Mark put his keys in the ignition and started the car, and Miranda looked at him in consternation. 'What are you doing?'

'Car's cold,' he said. 'We'll warm up the engine, then we'll talk.'

'But Mark ...'

She bit into her lower lip anxiously, and he gave her a derisive stare. 'What's the matter? Think I'm too drunk to drive or something?'

She sighed. 'Frankly, yes.'

Mark shook his head. 'You worry too much. I know exactly what I'm doing.'

Miranda wished she could be sure. Staring out of the

frosted window, she wondered where Lady Sanders thought they had gone. Perhaps she would send Jaime to look for them. *Jaime*! Miranda's lips tightened. How she would like to see him humiliated just once in his life!

Mark had stopped at the traffic lights and was looking at her in the light cast by the street lamps. 'You're beautiful,' he said, as if he had just realised the fact, and she forced a faint smile although her lips felt stiff and unresponsive.

Then the lights changed and they were moving again, faster now as the outskirts of the town were left behind them, and the open road invited greater speed. Miranda fastened the safety belt and gripped the seat tightly with her fingers. She would not ask him to slow down, she told herself fiercely. If he killed them both now, she would at least have the satisfaction of knowing that Lady Sanders had not won. She felt curiously fatalistic, and it was almost a shock to see the lights of the village ahead of them and to know that they had arrived safely.

'Wh-where are we going?' she ventured, speaking for the first time when he drove past the turning to the Hall, and he heaved a half regretful sigh.

'You'll see,' he said, and slowed to a standstill before the cottage he had bought for her mother.

Miranda caught her breath. 'Here?'

'Why not? It's mine, isn't it?'

'Well, yes, but——'

'The decorators have been here all day. The place is bound to be warm. It's as good a place as any to talk, isn't it?'

Miranda made no reply, and he thrust open his door and climbed out. As she joined him, she wondered how many pairs of curtains twitched as their owners espied the visitors to the cottage, and she cringed at the thought of her mother being regaled with the information.

Inside, as he had said, it was warm, and there was the pungent odour of new paint. Central heating had been installed, and the radiators still retained an atom of heat. But it was the gas fire in the living room which really dispelled the draughts, and illuminated the shadowy corners of the room. Mark had not put on the light as there were no curtains as yet at the windows, but the firelight was enough.

Two planks were fixed horizontally between two pairs of steps and the painters had spread the planks with an old piece of carpeting they had found to make a seat. Mark sat down on the planks and beckoned to Miranda to join him. She looked doubtfully at her cream gown and then at the grubby carpeting. Obviously it would stain, but if Mark was prepared to risk it, so must she.

'So,' he said, turning sideways to look at her. 'Here we are.'

'Yes.' She sought about desperately for some way to begin this. 'Mark, I want you to know——'

She broke off suddenly when he leaned towards her and pressed his lips to the side of her neck. It was a totally unexpected caress, and her tension melted.

'You—believe me?' she breathed.

'Let's say I'm prepared to be persuaded,' he responded, his voice thickening somewhat. 'You can tell me first what you were doing with that half-breed cousin of mine!'

Miranda caught her breath. 'Mark! Don't say things like that.'

'Why not? It's true.' His lower lip jutted aggressively. 'Is that why you found him so attractive? They say women like that sort of thing!'

Miranda sighed. 'Mark! I've told you what happened. I felt faint and—and Mr Knevett suggested I stepped outside for a few minutes, that's all.'

'All?' Mark's lips curled even as his fingers probed the nape of her neck before sliding down to linger suggestively on the swelling mounds of her breasts. 'And what did you do while you were—outside?'

'Nothing!' Miranda's unease returned in full measure. 'What do you think we did? What could we do?'

'I could think of a lot of things,' replied Mark with a sneer. 'This, for instance,' and he slid his hand inside the neckline of her gown to cup the rounded softness of her breast.

Miranda froze. His hand inside her gown aroused nothing but a feeling of distaste inside her, and the derisive twisting of his mouth revealed that he was aware of her

SCORPION'S DANCE   29

revulsion.

'What's the matter?' he demanded, leaning towards her. 'Don't you like me to touch you? Don't you want me to see how desirable you are?'

'Mark, this has gone far enough——'

'No, damn you, it hasn't,' he snapped violently. 'Not half far enough!'

With a muffled exclamation his arms were around her, forcing her back on the planks until her shoulder blades were digging painfully into the wood. Then he threw himself upon her, his lips wet and slippery against the shrinking coldness of her flesh.

Miranda was so shocked that for minutes she could do nothing but lie there. Then, as his intentions became clear to her, she began to struggle desperately, digging her nails into his arms, fighting in any way she could to escape his revolting caresses. He was no longer the gentle man she had imagined him to be, but a drink-crazed beast who cared for nothing but his own sexual appeasement.

And she was no match for him. Slender though he was, he had no difficulty in overcoming her frantic efforts to evade him, and tears were streaming down her face when she heard his groan of defeat. Not understanding, she was too shocked and shaking to move when he rolled off her, buttoning his clothes and muttering to himself in tones of distress.

Blinking, hardly capable of coherent thought, she propped herself up on one elbow, staring at him through the wild disorder of her hair. Holding the bodice of her gown together with trembling fingers, she thought at first he had come to his senses, but the ravaged face he turned to her disabused her of that fact.

'M-Mark!' she got out unsteadily, but his face just contorted more savagely.

'Don't speak to me!' He spat the words at her. 'Don't speak to me!'

Miranda pushed back her hair with an unsteady hand and got to her feet. 'Mark, you're drunk——'

'Drunk, am I?' He lurched a step towards her, and then shaking his head, he stared broodingly down at the floor.

'Drunk! Huh, that's a laugh! God, I wish I was!'

Miranda was trying to understand what he was saying, but her mind wouldn't work very well. Yet common sense told her that something had happened to bring Mark to his senses, and she desperately wanted to find some good in this awful mess.

'Mark, you'll feel better in the morning——'

'Will I? Will I?' He glared at her. 'What do you know about it? What do you know about anything?' His breathing had quickened again, and as she watched him she saw to her astonishment that there were tears in his eyes.

It was a revealing moment, and compassion swept over her, dispelling the revulsion she had felt for him. 'Mark, let me help you——'

'You! Help me?' His laugh was bitter. 'I don't need your help. I don't *want* you. I don't *need* you. I never did. Don't you understand, I don't need anyone!' And with a muttered oath he flung himself across the room and out the door.

Miranda stared after him blankly, not immediately comprehending the import of what he was saying. But suddenly she knew, suddenly she guessed why he had not finished what he had started. He couldn't! That was what was eating him up. He couldn't love anyone.

She turned back to the fire, her hands pressed to her mouth, and as she did so she heard the sound of the sports car starting up outside. With a cry, she turned and darted to the door. He couldn't go! He couldn't leave her here like this, without even a coat to cover her torn gown.

But he had. The tail lights of the sports car were already disappearing into the light mist which had fallen when she reached the door, and she stood there watching them until they disappeared from sight. Then she turned and went back into the cottage.

There was no phone, so she could not even ring her mother to ask someone to come and get her. But equally, she could not spend the night here. Apart from anything else, her mother would worry about her, and besides, she wanted to get home, to close the door of her own room and shake away the horrifying implications of the night's revelations.

She turned out the gas fire, and running combing hands

through her hair, walked to the door. The freezing air made her hesitate, and on impulse she went back and gathered up the piece of carpeting to hold like a cloak about her shoulders. Her dress was light, and therefore noticeable, but she couldn't help that. It was a quarter of a mile to the turn off to the Hall, and another half to the Hall itself.

Miranda had scarcely gone two hundred yards, however, when the headlights of a car picked her up, and she bent her head in agony, praying it was no one she knew. The village attracted a fair number of evening commuters to its two public houses, and it was after closing time.

The car slowed, but she hurried on determinedly, aware of the dangers of a casual pick-up, but when a window was rolled down and a harsh voice said: 'Miranda!' she was forced to turn and look.

The car, a red Daimler, was familiar to her. It belonged to Lady Sanders. But Mark's mother was not driving, she was not even in the car. Jaime Knevett was behind the wheel.

His raking gaze swept her dishevelled appearance, and even in the shadowed street lights she knew she must present a ragged figure. She was reminded of that other occasion when he had seen her torn and bedraggled, and she thought with a rising sense of fury that indirectly he was again the cause of her distress.

'Get in!' he said, but she just returned his stare, determined not to be beholden to him for anything. 'I said—*get in*!' he repeated forcefully, and telling herself it was because she was cold and the Hall was still a good distance away and not anything to do with the bleak fury in his eyes, she complied. Gathering her mist-dampened skirts about her, she huddled into the seat beside him, and he leant across her to slam the door with controlled violence.

'Now,' he said, his profile hard in the gloomy light, 'what in God's name has been going on?'

Miranda cast him a sidelong glance. 'I'd like to go home,' she said pointedly, but he ignored her, tossing the disreputable piece of carpet into the back and shrugging out of his own jacket to wrap it about her shoulders. Miranda wanted to protest that she needed nothing from him, but the jacket was so blessedly warm and soft after the scrubby pile of the carpeting that she gave in without argument.

'If we have to stay here all night, you're going to tell me where you've been,' he intoned grimly, and she had the feeling he meant it.

'Don't you know?' she demanded, drawing an unsteady breath. 'Or didn't your imagination stretch that far?'

'What do you mean?'

Miranda's composure was slipping. She didn't want to sit here discussing what had happened with him. It was still too raw, too vulnerable, and to consider breaking down in front of him was too frightful to be borne.

'Please,' she said tremulously, 'I want to go home. Can't you restrain your curiosity until the morning? I'm sure Mark will be only too happy to regale you with the details!'

'Mark?' His heavy black brows drew together. 'Mark is responsible for—this?'

His fingers flicked the tangled strands of hair that clung to the mohair of his jacket, but she flinched away from his touch with the nervous mobility of fear. Immediately his eyes narrowed, and uncaring of prying eyes, he switched on the interior light and saw what the masking shadows had concealed. Miranda's face was pale and haunted, and there were bruises around her throat, just visible above the en-compassing shoulders of his jacket. Wordlessly, he tugged the jacket out of her resisting grasp and spread the lapels to reveal the scratches on her arms, and the torn material of the bodice of her dress. Miranda spread her arms crosswise over her breasts, but she had the feeling he was not seeing her as a woman at all, but as the victim of some sexual attack.

With a savage oath, he wrapped the jacket around her again and switched out the light. Then he drew several deep breaths before saying quite calmly: 'I'll kill him!'

'No!' Somehow from the depths of her being, Miranda managed to articulate the words. 'It's not what you think. He ... didn't. That is ... he tried to, but ... he didn't.'

Jaime rested his forehead against the steering wheel. 'Where is he now?'

Miranda shook her head. 'I don't know.'

'You mean he just left you? He put you out of the car ...'

'Oh, no, *no*!' Miranda had never felt so weary in her life. 'We ... went to the cottage. Mark ... he bought my mother a cottage, you see. Back there.' She gestured feebly. 'We went there.'

'But he left you?'

'Yes.' She gulped despairingly. 'Can I go home now?'

He straightened, flexing his shoulders. 'In a moment. There's one more thing.'

'What?'

'Why did you assume that I might know what had been going on?'

Miranda sighed. 'Perhaps I was wrong. Perhaps you didn't.'

Jaime's mouth was a thin line. 'Nevertheless, I think I deserve an explanation.'

'Oh, can't it wait?'

'No.'

Miranda shifted restlessly. 'Why should I give you explanations? You're on their side, not mine.'

'I am not on any side,' he declared coldly. 'And what is all this talk of sides? You're marrying Mark, aren't you? You'll marry him anyway, whatever he's done.'

Miranda gasped at the callousness in his voice. 'Why should you assume that?' she demanded, but he merely shook his head.

'I'll take you home,' he said, starting the motor. 'Perhaps we'll find your fiancé is there, waiting to make amends.'

But Mark was not at the Hall. Only Lady Sanders awaited them, pacing impatiently about the polished floor, and gasping in horror when she saw Miranda's dishevelled appearance. Miranda had not wanted to confront her future mother-in-law like this. She had wanted to slip round the side of the building and let herself in through the kitchen as she had always done. But Jaime's hard fingers around her wrist had prevented this, and her strength was too depleted to put up much of a struggle.

'My God, what's happened!' Lady Sanders grasped her shoulder, and then dropped her hand aghast when Miranda winced painfully. 'There's been an accident, hasn't there?' Her eyes lifted to her nephew's face. 'Jaime ... tell me! Tell me! Where's Mark?'

Unhurriedly, Jaime unfastened the studs at his wrists, and folded back his cuffs. 'I thought you might know that, Aunt

Lydia,' he remarked levelly. 'I haven't seen him.'

'You haven't? But ...' Lady Sanders gestured towards Miranda. 'Then how ...' She broke off to moisten her upper lip with her tongue. 'Miranda! Where is my son?'

Miranda wished the floor would open up and swallow her. She had had just about enough, and she swayed on to her heels. 'Mark ... Mark left me at the cottage,' she was beginning, when Jaime interrupted her.

'Don't you want to know how Miranda got into this condition?' he inquired, the mildness of his tone belying the glitter of his eyes, but Lady Sanders was in no state to look for hidden meanings.

'I ... well, of course,' she said agitatedly. 'If it has any bearing on the matter.'

'Oh, it has bearing on the matter,' retorted Jaime tautly. 'Believe me!'

At last, his aunt seemed to gauge the tenor of his mood, and took a moment to give him her full attention. 'Well?' she demanded. 'What happened?'

Jaime's nostrils flared. 'Your son did this,' he said coldly. 'Your son attempted to rape his own fiancée! Now why do you suppose he did that?'

Lady Sanders gasped, one hand going automatically to her throat. 'You can't be serious!'

'Oh, but I am,' declared Jaime heavily, and Miranda felt Lady Sanders' eyes going over her with almost tangible distaste.

'How do you know?' Mark's mother countered swiftly. 'Who told you that? You said you hadn't seen Mark.'

'Miranda told me——'

'Oh, please ...' Miranda began to protest again, but they both ignored her.

'So you'd take her word against the word of my son,' Lady Sanders was saying now, and Jaime swore violently.

'We don't have any word but Miranda's,' he retorted. 'But you don't imagine she did this to herself, do you?' and with forceful fingers he plucked his jacket from her shoulders.

It was like a scene from some Victorian melodrama, thought Miranda, an hysterical sob rising in her throat. Behold, the villain's perfidy! Will wicked Sir Jasper win the day? The difficulty was in deciding who was the wicked

Sir Jasper. Was it Mark, the victim of his own inadequacies? Or was it Lady Sanders, whose overriding ambition for her son blinded her to his faults? Or could it possibly be Jaime Knevett, whose motives were as enigmatic as he was? Miranda was too tired to figure it out.

Lady Sanders plucked with nervous fingers at the diamond necklace circling her throat. 'That still doesn't explain where Mark has gone, does it? What was this Miranda said about the cottage?'

'We went to the cottage,' said Miranda dully. 'My mother's cottage. There—there was a scene. Mark left. Afterwards, Mr Knevett found me walking back to the Hall.'

'How convenient!' Lady Sanders' voice was taut with malice, but her nephew intervened.

'Convenient?' he asked. 'Convenient for whom?'

'Oh, Jaime!' Lady Sanders waved away his questioning. 'Don't get involved in all this.'

'But I am involved,' he insisted harshly. 'However, I do believe no useful purpose is being served by standing here arguing about it. I suggest we allow Miranda to go to bed. She looks—exhausted. We can talk again in the morning.'

'But what about Mark?' cried Lady Sanders, aghast. 'Aren't you going to look for him?'

'If you want me to, of course I will,' he replied gravely. 'Now, if you'll excuse me, I'll escort Miranda to her part of the house.'

'That's not necessary—' Miranda began, but he ignored her, dropping his coat about her shoulders again and urging her forward with his hand in the small of her back.

Miranda was glad to escape from the accusation in Mark's mother's eyes. It had been a long evening, a strange evening, and one she never hoped to repeat. But it wasn't over yet.

Jaime opened the door and accompanied her along the corridor towards the kitchens. But Miranda halted so far along, and turning to him said stiffly: 'There's really no need to come any further. I shall be quite all right now.'

In the dim illumination of wall-lights, his face was curiously shadowed, giving it an almost malevolent cast. His eyes seemed deeper set, heavy-lidded, the flaring hollows of his nostrils expelling the heat of his body upon her. She felt suddenly uneasy, apprehensive of the future and she could not dismiss her fears as fancies. She had the over-powering conviction that nothing was ever going to be the same again.

'Will your mother be up?' he asked now, and she shivered to dispel the chill that had wrapped itself about her.

'Perhaps,' she answered. 'Does it matter?'

'Will you explain?'

Miranda bent her head helplessly. 'I don't know.'

She heard his harsh intake of breath. 'You should,' he said. 'Then perhaps your mother can bring you to your senses!'

Her head jerked up. 'What do you mean?'

'I think you know.' His eyes were cold, glittering black diamonds in the muted light. 'You can't marry Mark now. Not after what's happened. Not considering what might be to come. I don't think even becoming mistress of the Hall is worth that, do you, Miranda?'

She gasped. 'You think I'm marrying him for his money?'

'Aren't you?'

'No!'

'Oh, come on. You're not telling me you love that little punk! After what's happened?'

Miranda's breasts rose and fell in her agitation, and her fingers holding his jacket in place trembled. She wanted to tear it off and throw it at his feet and trample on it, but the desire to retain her dignity was stronger.

'You're his cousin!' she declared. 'How can you speak of him like that?'

Jaime's mouth curled. 'Our relationship is remote, thank God! Do you think I want to be associated with someone who does this?'

Miranda's breathing was harsh. 'He—he didn't mean it.' If he did, she didn't want to admit it. 'He was drunk—en-raged! His mother saw to that.'

'You're making excuses for him,' exclaimed Jaime con-temptuously. 'My God! You're just like *her*, aren't you? His mother! She's made excuses for him all his life! Well, I wish you well of each other. You deserve everything you get!'

Miranda didn't know why, but she wanted to crumple up

and die. She despised Mark, she didn't love him. And she despised herself for defending him. But she hated Jaime for making her see herself for what she was.

He was turning away from her in disgust when a low groan reached them. It seemed to come from the kitchen, and with a cry Miranda whirled around and sped along the remaining length of the corridor to where a light was filtering through a crack in the kitchen door. She burst into the room with Jaime right behind her, and then stopped dead at the sight that greeted her stunned eyes.

Her mother was lying on the floor in front of the fire. Mercifully, she had not fallen into the flames, but the flags beneath the polythene tiles were hard and at first Miranda thought she had knocked herself unconscious. But then she saw how one side of her mother's face had twisted, and spittle was dribbling out of the corner of her mouth.

The sound Miranda made was a kind of choking gulp in her throat, and then Jaime cannoned into her, unable to prevent himself when she stopped so abruptly. The hard warmth of his body dispelled her momentary paralysis, and on shaking legs she moved across the room to kneel down beside Mrs Gresham. But Jaime was there before her, brushing past her and bending to his knees, taking her mother's wrist between his fingers, probing the rolling sockets of her eyes for any sign of life.

At first Miranda wanted to protest, but then she remembered that he had told her he was a doctor, and she sat back on her heels, staring at him mutely, beseeching him to tell her what was wrong.

'It looks like a stroke,' he was saying grimly, when the door behind them burst open again to admit Lady Sanders. But not the Lady Sanders they had left in the hall. This woman was wild-eyed and tearful, lips quivering, hands trembling, a shaking mass of desperation. Grief-stricken fingers tore her handkerchief to shreds, as she cried: 'Jaime! Jaime! Where are you? Oh, God, Jaime, it's Mark! *Mark*! A policeman's just been to the door. He's dead, Jaime, he's dead! Oh, God, what am I going to do?'

She held out her hands towards him, but Miranda who, like Jaime, had got to her feet as Lady Sanders entered the room, reached him first as she sank into a dead faint for the first time in her life.

CHAPTER THREE

It rained on the day of the funeral, exactly a week before Miranda had expected to become the new Lady Sanders. The guests who had been invited for the wedding all arrived for the funeral, as if not to be done out of a celebration of one kind or another, Miranda thought ghoulishly, numb with more than the realisation that her future which she had thought so secure was suddenly so uncertain again. Her mother was in hospital, unable to speak, paralysed by the stroke which had stricken her almost in the same moment that Mark's car had crashed through the tollbridge into the river. The dual tragedy had shaken them all in different ways, and Miranda was guiltily aware that her mother's illness had relieved her of the necessity to display a grief she could not feel. The mourners saw a pale shadow of the girl she had been on the night of the Rotary Club Ball, and made their own assessment of her feelings. They could not know that all her sorrow was for her mother, alone and lonely in her hour of need. Only Jaime, who thought he knew her so much better than anyone else, looked beneath the façade she was presenting and drew his own conclusions.

Lady Sanders had taken it badly, so badly that Miranda could not help but feel sorry for her. After all, she had lost her husband so early in her life, and now her only son. No one could fail to pity her. Strangely, during the past few days, Miranda had felt closer to her than at any other time in her life.

Miranda rode back to the hall in the black Rolls that had followed the hearse to its final resting place. Lady Sanders was with her as, too, was Jaime, the sombreness of his clothes accentuating the darkness of his skin. Miranda had worn black as well, unaware of how becoming the dark colours were to her, or of how the burnished glory of her hair stood out against the stark austerity of the graveyard.

A cold buffet had been laid in the dining room, and the guests who had accompanied them back to the house helped themselves to *canapés* and *vol-au-vents* and slices of home-cured ham. Miranda endeavoured to accept everyone's con-dolences with composure, but she was well aware that to most of these people present she had become somewhat of an embarrassment. She did not fit in here, and now she never would.

Sipping a glass of sherry, she tried to assimilate her situa-tion. What was she going to do now? Her mother's illness had curtailed her working life, and no doubt once she had recovered herself, Lady Sanders would require a new house-keeper. So where did that leave Miranda, or her mother? They had no home, nothing, and the salary she was paid by the council authorities would not stretch to buying a house. She thought of the cottage in the village. Perhaps Lady Sanders would allow them to rent that. It was of no use to her.

Miranda moved towards the buffet tables. Lady Sanders was there, talking to Canon Bridgenorth. Dared she take this opportunity to speak to her? If she didn't, when might she get the chance again?

A solid object stepped into her path, and about to apolo-gise and step aside, she looked up into Jaime's hard features. They had said little to one another since the night of the accident, but now he put out a hand to detain her when she would have passed by.

'I want to talk to you,' he said, in a low voice.

Miranda glanced apprehensively about her. 'Oh?'

'Yes.' He tucked his thumbs into the waistcoat pockets of his dark grey suede suit. 'Now we can do it here, or we can go into the library. As you wish.'

Miranda's cool eyes challenged him. 'I don't think we should leave the room again, do you?'

He returned her stare narrowly. 'I see. Perhaps you con-sider I was to blame for what happened with Mark.'

She gasped. 'I didn't say that!'

'You didn't have to.' He paused. 'But as a matter of fact, you're wrong. In one of her—how shall I put it?—more emotional moods, my aunt confessed to—er—encouraging Mark to think the worst, you understand?'

Miranda took an unsteady breath. 'I have only your word for that.'

'And I'm afraid that's all you're likely to get,' he remarked brusquely. 'I do not anticipate my aunt ever repeating such an allegation.'

Miranda looked away from the almost hypnotic bril-
liance of those dark eyes. 'So! I can't think what we have
to say to one another.'

'No?' Dark brows quirked. 'You have made arrangements
for your future?'

Miranda's eyes widened. 'What has that to do with
you?'

'Come into the library, and I'll tell you.'

Miranda sighed. 'I have to—circulate. Besides, I want to
speak to Lady Sanders.'

'Oh? Why?'

She gasped. 'Mind your own business!'

'Perhaps it is my business.'

She was amazed at his audacity. 'It couldn't possibly be,'
she declared shortly. 'Now, please—you must excuse me.'

'One thing more . . .' he added.

'What is it?'

'Whatever happens, will you promise to let me know
what your plans are?'

Miranda made an exasperated sound. 'I can't see why it
matters.' She pressed her lips together. 'I should have
thought you'd be cheering that everything's gone so sour on
me.'

His lashes shaded his eyes. 'Did you think I wasn't?' he
parried mockingly, and her cheeks flamed with colour.

'You—you beast!'

'Your vocabulary's sadly lacking,' he remarked dryly.
'There are far more suitable epithets than that.'

'And you know them all, I suppose?'

'A fair number,' he agreed, and with a tightening of her
facial muscles she left him.

Canon Bridgenorth attempted a sympathetic smile when
Miranda appeared. She wondered if she was being un-
charitable in supposing that of all of them there, he had had
the most experience at hiding his feelings, and perhaps that
was why he could look at her without either satisfaction or
envy.

'Dear Miss Gresham,' he said, patting her sleeve with

his plump white hand. 'So sad, so sad! I've just been telling
Lady Sanders you must both summon all your strength for
the week ahead. The week which should have been such a
happy one for both of you.'

Miranda's gaze flickered over the older woman's lined
face. 'I expect we'll find plenty to do,' she said quietly.

'Ah, yes.' Canon Bridgenorth shook his head. 'All the
presents to return.' He sighed. 'I'll do whatever I can, of
course.'

He moved away to speak to his wife, and for a moment
Miranda was alone with the woman who was to have been
her mother-in-law. It was the moment she had been waiting
for, and she could not let it pass.

'I saw the specialist at the hospital yesterday, Lady Sanders,' she said, and pale eyes were turned in her direction.

'Indeed? And what did he say?'

There was a chilling lack of feeling behind the question,
and Miranda guessed that it was a perfunctory inquiry and
no more. A tragic state of affairs considering her mother
had worked at the Hall for over twelve years. But she had
to go on, for her mother's sake.

'He said—it's doubtful that she will ever walk again.'

Lady Sanders' lips twitched. 'I see.'

Miranda licked her own lips that were suddenly dry. 'You
understand what I'm trying to say?'

'Perfectly.' Lady Sanders was in complete control of herself. 'Your mother will not be able to continue here as
housekeeper.'

'No.' Miranda inclined her head. 'Of course, she wasn't
going to anyway, after—after——'

'After the wedding, you mean?' Lady Sanders said it
without emotion. 'No. But now there is to be no wedding.'

Miranda wished she would make it easier for her. 'As a
matter of fact,' she murmured, 'that was what I wanted to
talk to you about.'

Lady Sanders frowned. 'Indeed? Why, pray?'

'The cottage ...' Miranda hated having to beg. 'The cottage at Blind Lane: I wondered whether we might—rent it
from you.'

'From me?' Lady Sanders' mouth tightened. 'From me!'
She gave a mirthless little laugh. 'My dear girl, you're wast-

ing your time speaking to me. I don't own the cottage at
Blind Lane. The estate is entailed, didn't you know? To the
eldest male heir.'

Miranda stared at her aghast. 'No! No, I didn't know.'

Lady Sanders sniffed, taking out her handkerchief and
blowing her nose. 'Why should you? I never thought—
no one ever expected—' She broke off as emotion threatened
once more. 'The home farm is mine, except that it's tenanted,
of course. But this house—and its contents—the estate, the
land, everything, belongs to my husband's family.'

'But what will you do?' For a moment, Miranda forgot
about her own troubles.

Lady Sanders shrugged. 'I don't know. I expect I'll be
given time—to decide.'

The appearance of Elias Bell, the Sanders' solicitor, curtailed their conversation, and Miranda moved politely away,
aware that in estate matters and death duties she had no
part.

So, she thought bleakly, she and her mother were not the
only ones to lose their home. The old order changeth, with
a vengeance.

She wandered out into the hall, looking up the carved
staircase to the balustered gallery that curved round the
well of the hall. To think she had been within an inch of
being mistress here! She might have occupied the master
suite, and descended those stairs every evening for dinner.
She might have had servants to fetch and carry for her, and
been invited to all the county functions. Countess Sanders—
the housekeeper's daughter. Of course, she would have had
to accept other responsibilities, too, not least the commit-
ment to let Mark into her bedroom every night. That was
not so easy to contemplate, and she determinedly thrust
away the memory of the last time she had seen him ...

'Reflecting on what might have been?' a lazy voice
drawled behind her, and she spun round resentfully to face
her tormenter.

'Would it do any good to deny it?' she demanded.

'It might. But I'd find it very hard to believe. The old
place has a lot to commend it.'

Miranda folded her hands round her handbag. 'I'm surprised you think so. It must be much different from what

you're used to.'

His smile was mocking. 'Now how am I supposed to take that? Am I to assume you think we live in squalor back home? Or have I simply not the taste to appreciate it?'

Miranda expelled her breath on a sigh. 'I was merely stating that rural England must be vastly different from—where is it you live? South America? Brazil?'

'South America will do,' he returned, his voice noticeably cooler. 'And yes, of course, it is—vastly different. Geographically at least.'

Miranda wanted to walk away from him, but something held her where she was. She didn't like the way he could disconcert her without any apparent effort on his part, and although she knew he was only six or seven years her senior, he seemed much older than that. Perhaps it was due to the differences in their ways of life. She guessed that conditions in South American countries were much less civilised than in her own, and the heat and the insects held no appeal for her.

Trying to take the conversation on to a lighter plane, she said: 'Will you be leaving now? Or will you stay with your aunt until after Christmas?'

'That rather depends.' Jaime folded his arms, standing feet apart facing her, his expression impossible to read.

'Depends?' Miranda was aware of the quiver in her own tones. 'On what?'

He pushed his lower lip forward. 'To quote an earlier conversation—what has that to do with you?'

She coloured deeply, half turning away. 'I'm sorry, I didn't mean to pry.'

Her voice was stiff with embarrassment, but when she would have left him, he stepped forward and caught her arm. 'Have you spoken to Lady Sanders?' he asked.

Miranda looked up at him. 'You know I have.'

'What did she tell you?'

Miranda pressed her lips together to suppress her indignation. Then she said tautly: 'She told me the estate is entailed, and that she, like my mother and me, is losing her home.'

'Is that what she said?' Jaime's lips twisted. 'Those were her very words?'

Miranda tried to pull her arm free, but it was a useless exercise. 'She might not have said that exactly, but that was what she meant. Why? What has any of this to do with you?'

He let her go then, and she rubbed her sleeve to stimulate the blood circulating through her numbed flesh. 'Perhaps I feel sorry for you,' he said provokingly. 'Or then again, perhaps I don't.'

Miranda uttered a word under her breath that she would never have voiced, but from his expression she suspected he had heard her. 'I think you're despicable! It may have slipped your notice, but I cared for Mark, and now he's dead! That's all that matters to me.'

'Really?' The scepticism in his voice was denigrating. 'How touching! Forgive me if I don't shed a tear!'

'You don't care about any of us, do you?' Miranda said accusingly. 'You just enjoy making fun of us.'

He ran a probing hand over the fine silk of his tie, and regarded her intently for a moment. Then he said, 'Would you think I was making fun of you if I asked you to marry me?'

Miranda groped weakly for the newel post at the foot of the staircase. Her fingers curved round the polished ball on its pedestal, and its coolness was like a lifeline in a broiling sea.

'I see the prospect had not occurred to you,' he said mildly. 'And there are certain advantages in the element of surprise.'

Miranda gathered herself and stared at him resentfully, half suspecting that this was yet another attempt to humiliate her. 'You're not serious, of course!'

'Why not?' His mouth thinned. 'Is it such a distasteful proposition?'

Now was her chance, and Miranda seized it with both hands. 'Frankly, yes,' she declared coldly. 'I think you must be quite mad to consider it!'

She had not really thought that she could arouse him, but she was wrong. Before her half fearful gaze, she saw the sudden tautening of the skin across his cheekbones, the aggressive tightening of his jaw, and the diamond-hard congealing of his eyes. The temperature in the hall lowered a terrifying number of degrees, and she knew she had been right to be apprehensive of this man.

'Very well,' he said now, and she was almost shocked at the lack of emotion in his voice. 'But you'll remember what I said.' And he walked away.

Miranda stood for several minutes in the hall after he had gone, desperately trying to regain her former composure. But composure would not come, only a devastating conviction that for all her small victory, the war was not yet over.

The guests began to drift away in the late afternoon, and by five o'clock only Miranda, Jaime and Lady Sanders, and the caterers she had hired for the occasion, were left in the echoing mansion. Avoiding Jaime's eyes was becoming increasingly more difficult, and Miranda excused herself on the pretext of checking that the hired staff knew where to put everything. The kitchen was her domain, she told herself bitterly, refusing to contemplate what her lot might have been had she accepted Jaime Knevett's offer. She had no idea why he should have made such an outrageous suggestion, but in any case, marrying him was out of the question. Apart from anything else, she could not consider leaving the country with her mother a helpless invalid in some National Health establishment. Besides, she had no desire to marry him, or anyone else for that matter. It was all rather unreal and insubstantial, part and parcel of the unreality of these last days.

She had seen Lady Sanders having a long conversation with her solicitor, and guessed she was making her own arrangements for the future. Perhaps she would offer Miranda a position in her household when she acquired one, and while the prospect was bleak, Miranda was practical enough to know that unless she could rent the cottage at Blind Lane, she might well have to give up her career as a librarian and take it. She could not contemplate leaving her mother in hospital for the rest of her life. Somehow she had to make a home for both of them.

The caterers washed up and left, and the kitchen was curiously empty after they had gone. Miranda made up the fire, and then looked thoughtfully into the refrigerator. In an hour she was leaving for the hospital to visit her mother,

and as she had partaken of little of the cold buffet, she supposed she ought to eat something before attempting to drive.
These past days she and Lady Sanders had eaten sparingly,
and fortunately the older woman had taken most of her meals
at the homes of friends. But Miranda had provided toast and
coffee at breakfast time, and once she had prepared an
omelette for Lady Sanders' lunch.

She was making a pot of tea when the kitchen door
opened to admit the woman she had once held in such awe,
and she added the boiling water to the tea-bags before carrying the teapot back to the table.

'Would you like some?' she asked politely, gesturing towards the cups, and although Lady Sanders looked as though
she was going to refuse, she eventually said:

'Yes, all right. Thank you.'

Miranda drew the tea-pot towards her and said: 'Won't
you sit down?' and after the other woman was seated she
poured the tea. She wondered what was the import of this
visitation, and silently decided that Lady Sanders was about
to give her notice to quit.

The tea poured, and a tin of biscuits refused, Miranda
herself sat down, stirring the cream round and round in her
cup. Perhaps she ought to have some sugar, she thought,
although it had always been abhorrent to her in hot drinks.
That was what was recommended in times of stress.

'Have you—decided what you're going to do, Miranda?'

Lady Sanders broke the uneasy silence which had fallen,
and Miranda looked up. 'Not yet.'

'You realise I can't help you.'

Miranda looked down again. 'Of course.'

'I can't even help myself,' went on the other woman
bitterly. 'A fine state of affairs!'

Miranda gave her a compassionate look. 'I'm sorry.'

'Are you?' Lady Sanders' mouth twitched. 'I wonder.'

'I beg your pardon!'

Miranda could feel her colour rising at the veiled insult,
but Lady Sanders quickly made amends:

'I didn't mean—that is—oh, it's so difficult to explain,' she
sighed, and Miranda, who had never known her at a loss for
words, felt unaccountably disturbed. Why should Lady Sanders feel compelled to explain herself to her?

'I'm sure your husband's family won't see you destitute,' she murmured awkwardly, feeling obliged to say something, and Lady Sanders caught her embarrassed eyes with her own.

'They might,' she said tautly. 'It all depends on you.'

'*On me?*' Miranda could not have been more shocked. 'What on earth do you mean? What has it to do with me?'

Lady Sanders' lips were thin. 'Jaime asked you to marry him, didn't he? But you refused!'

It was an accusation, and Miranda didn't know of what. She pushed back her chair and got to her feet, unable to sit still under such an indictment, and sought desperately for some sense in all of this.

'I don't understand what my private affairs have to do with your position here,' she protested tremorously, but Lady Sanders merely gave her a contemptuous stare.

'You're not a fool, Miranda,' she declared, but it was scarcely a compliment. 'You wanted to marry my son, and I'm not so blind as to imagine it was wholly because of his blue eyes! You saw yourself as mistress of the Hall, didn't you? As Lady Sanders, the Countess. Does it matter so much that you'd be Jaime's countess instead?'

'Wh-what are you talking about?'

Miranda's eyes were wide and troubled, and suddenly Lady Sanders seemed to realise what was wrong. With an exclamation of protest she got to her feet to gaze penetratingly at the girl facing her. Then she uttered a harsh laugh.

'Of course,' she exclaimed scornfully. 'Why didn't I guess? I should have known Jaime had something more up his sleeve. He didn't tell you, did he?'

Miranda put a bewildered hand to her head. 'Tell me? Tell me what?'

'That I'm the next heir,' remarked Jaime, letting himself through the kitchen door with lazy indolence. 'The estate is entailed to me!'

'What?' Miranda's legs gave way suddenly, and she sank down weakly into her chair, while Lady Sanders turned on her nephew.

'You brute!' she declared, but without the malice she had directed towards Miranda. 'You let me do your dirty work for you!'

'An occupation that is no novelty to you, I am sure, Aunt Lydia,' he replied dryly, ignoring her sudden intake of breath. 'And besides, I was interested to hear how you'd go about it.'

'You've been eavesdropping?' Miranda was scornful.

'Hardly that, as my aunt knew I was there,' retorted Jaime briefly. 'But yes, I have heard most of what has been said.'

Miranda's eyes dropped to her tea-cup, unable to withstand the abrasion of his. Of course, he had known this when he asked her to marry him earlier; but she hadn't, and he knew that. It was a kind of back-handed revenge he had accomplished, believing as he did that she had only been marrying Mark for his money. But now Jaime was the master of the Hall, and—horror of horrors—the new owner of the cottage at Blind Lane! But that still didn't explain why he had done it, or why Lady Sanders should believe her refusal had any bearing on her own situation.

Now Lady Sanders dropped into her chair again and pushed her cup towards Miranda. 'I think I'll have another cup of tea, if I may,' she said, somewhat unsteadily, and Miranda swiftly complied.

Jaime, tall and disturbingly masculine in that most feminine of departments, came to stand with his back to the fire, directly behind Miranda's chair. It made her overwhelmingly conscious of him, of the feeling of his eyes boring into the small of her back, the nerve-racking awareness of the vulnerable position she was in, both physically and mentally.

'So,' he said softly, and she sensed the malicious mockery in his tone. 'Isn't this cosy?'

'You're not being very amusing, Jaime,' stated his aunt coldly, but all she aroused was a snort of amusement, and the look she exchanged with Miranda was pure venom.

'I'm sorry,' he said, but the two women knew better than to take that on its face value. 'I just meant—afternoon tea round the fire, that's all. We don't do much of this back home.'

'Oh, for heaven's sake, Jaime, get to the point!' declared Lady Sanders frustratedly. 'Stop playing games with us. It's mean and small-minded; and not at all suitable on this day of all days.'

She drew out a handkerchief and blew her nose delicately after speaking, and covertly Miranda waited for Jaime's reaction. She did not have to wait long. There was a moment's silence, and then he left the fire to walk round the table to face them, his hands folded behind his back. The attitude he struck strained the buttons of his waistcoat across his chest, and drew Miranda's unwilling attention to the line of grey silk visible between the hem of the waistcoat and the low belt of his pants. She found herself wondering if the skin beneath was as deeply tanned as that exposed to the elements, and then coloured deeply when he intercepted her thoughtful gaze.

'So,' he said again. 'You have not yet explained the whole situation, Aunt Lydia. Would you like to continue?'

Lady Sanders looked up at him coldly, but her anger had little obvious effect. 'I see you'd rather not,' he observed mildly. 'Very well then, I'll explain, shall I?'

Miranda summoned all her courage and got to her feet. 'I don't see what any of this has to do with me,' she declared, 'so if it's all the same to you, I have to go to the hospit——'

'Sit down!'

Both Jaime and his aunt spoke in unison, and too surprised to do anything else, Miranda subsided. But she glared at Jaime, and this time she refused to allow him to intimidate her.

'I myself will escort you to the hospital to visit with your mother in fifteen minutes,' stated Jaime flatly. 'But for the moment you will remain where you are.'

Miranda's lips pursed sulkily, but she made no argument and Jaime and his aunt exchanged a glance. Then he said quietly: 'What my aunt was trying so unsuccessfully to tell you was that had you agreed to become my wife, she would have been allowed to remain here at the Hall as its tenant, indefinitely.'

'But that's not fair!' The words were out before Miranda could prevent them, and she turned indignantly to Lady Sanders. 'You can't do this to me! You can't make me the scapegoat for your disappointments!'

'I haven't!' retorted the older woman coldly, and Miranda shivered uncontrollably.

'Well?' Jaime regarded her with derision. 'I told you you'd remember what I said.'

'You're crazy,' she told him fiercely. 'And don't think this has changed my mind, because it hasn't.'

'No?' He sounded sceptical. 'We'll see.'

'We won't see,' she stormed at him, getting to her feet again. 'Don't imagine because you own the Hall now that I feel any differently towards you!'

'Did I ask you to reconsider?' he inquired dryly, and her face burned as she realised she had anticipated him. He paused, allowing his words to sink in. 'Just out of interest, what do you plan to do about your mother when she comes out of hospital? Where do you plan to live?'

Miranda drew a deep breath. 'Don't worry about it. I'll manage.'

'Will you?' His lips twisted. 'On a librarian's salary? My aunt tells me you asked her about renting some cottage. Well, I'm sorry, but I'm not renting any cottages to you.'

Miranda's mouth trembled, and she bit hard on her lower lip to hide it. 'I didn't expect anything else,' she declared, and then bent her head because frustrated tears persisted in filling her eyes.

'All right.' It was amazing how mild his voice could be when he was saying the most destructive things. 'Get your coat. I'll take you to the hospital.'

Miranda clenched her fists. 'There's no need. I have a car——'

'Get your coat!' he repeated, and when he said it like that, she had to obey.

She had not been in the Daimler since the night of the accident and she could not help the memories from flooding back. They did not help the emotional way she was feeling, and she stared blindly through the frosted windows, trying not to give in to the despair which was slowly engulfing her.

Halfway to the hospital, Jaime pulled the car off the road on to a lay-by, and all her fears and anxieties manifested themselves in her expression. Jaime, who had switched on the interior light to help himself to a cheroot from a pack in the glove compartment, regarded her with scarcely-veiled antagonism, and said harshly:

'In the name of heaven, what do you think I'm going to do to you?'

'I don't know, do I?' she asked unsteadily, shrinking into her corner. 'Why have you stopped the car?'

'Because I want to talk to you, and spacious though the Hall may be, there never seems to be enough room there for us.'

Miranda bent her head. 'Well?'

He lit his cheroot and exhaled the aromatic vapours into the atmosphere. Then he gave her a sidelong glance. 'You're going to marry me, Miranda,' he told her, and when she began to hotly protest, he added without emphasis: 'You're going to marry me so that when your mother comes out of hospital, she will have somewhere to live and expert help to take care of her.'

'You really think I would marry you to get a home for my mother!' Miranda exclaimed scornfully. 'You underestimate me, Mr Knevett!'

'I don't think so.' He inhaled deeply, studying the glowing tip of the cheroot. 'You haven't heard the whole of my proposition yet.'

'I suppose it has something to do with Lady Sanders,' muttered Miranda, huddling into her coat. 'Well, you can't make me responsible for her, too.'

'No? Not even if I tell you that unless you agree to my arrangements she will be as destitute as yourself?'

Miranda shifted restlessly. 'Then we'll help one another.' She stared at him with resentful eyes. 'You see, Mr Knevett, you can't intimidate me. Nothing would persuade me to go and live in—in South America. Nothing! And I shouldn't dream of forcing my mother into such a position either.'

'You will persist in anticipating me,' he drawled sardonically. 'I do not recall mentioning my home in Santa Madalena. I would not take you there, believe me!'

Miranda's aggression shrivelled. 'What do you mean?'

'What I say.' He was infuriatingly cool. 'I do not intend that you should meet my family. That was not what I had in mind.'

Miranda swallowed convulsively. 'I'm not good enough for them, I suppose.'

'You could say that,' he agreed, arousing all her hatred against him. 'But again, you are anticipating me.' He paused, and she was aware of her nails digging painfully into the palms of her hands. 'What I had in mind was this—you marry me, become mistress of the Hall, which was what you wanted all along, and I will undertake to support your mother for the rest of her life.'

'Where would we live?' The involuntary question was irresistible.

'Why, at the Hall, of course. With my aunt. With the—er—positions somewhat reversed.'

Miranda gasped. 'Of course, that would appeal to you, wouldn't it? To your distorted sense of humour!'

His indolence disappeared, to be replaced by something much more disturbing. 'Have a care, Miranda,' he snapped coldly. 'I am a vengeful man. Don't make me do something we might both regret!'

Miranda held up her head. 'You're just playing with us!' she accused him tremulously. 'Manipulating us to your own ends!'

'And you were not playing with Mark? Manipulating him for the same purpose?'

'No!'

'I think you were. I think you are a mercenary little bitch, Miranda, and worthy to assume my aunt's mantle!'

'You don't like her either, do you?' Miranda choked.

'Let us say, I don't like the feeling of being manipulated also. You and my aunt deserve one another. And I intend that you shall have one another!'

Miranda pulled her coat about her throat. 'If that's all you have to say, I'd like to go on now.'

'Very well.' He pressed out the stub of his cheroot in the ashtray. 'But you will think about what I have said.'

'It doesn't need thinking about,' retorted Miranda angrily. 'I do not intend to marry you, Mr Knevett. Mercenary or otherwise.'

He shrugged and switched out the light, setting the car in motion without another word. The remainder of the journey to the hospital was completed in silence, and when they got there Miranda climbed out with a trembling sense of relief. But it was short-lived. Jaime got out, too, and locked the car, obviously ready to accompany her inside.

'Please go away,' she said fiercely. 'I don't need you.'

Jaime ignored her, and walked away towards the lighted entrance of the hospital, and clenching her teeth, Miranda followed him. Of course, she thought bitterly, he was a doctor. He would know better than she did what her mother's condition would be.

Mrs Gresham lay motionless, as usual, no flicker of recognition darkening her eyes. Miranda felt a rising sense of helplessness just looking at her. And a feeling of isolation that refused to be displaced.

Jaime disappeared to speak to the doctor in charge of the case, and Miranda sat beside her mother's bed, wondering whether Mrs Gresham was really aware of her presence. How long would she remain like this? How long would the authorities permit her to stay in hospital?

She had been sitting there for perhaps fifteen minutes when the doctor appeared and requested Miranda to accompany him into his office. She half expected Jaime to be there, too, and she looked round resentfully, but the office was empty. The doctor closed the door, and then he said carefully:

'No change, I'm afraid.'

'No.' Miranda pressed her palms together.

'A tragic situation.' The doctor was middle-aged and sympathetic, but he had seen other cases like this and he knew the futility of it all. 'You realise, of course, that it could be weeks, months, before there is any change? If ever. I'm sorry, but I must be frank.'

'Of course.' Miranda nodded, apprehensively anticipating what was coming next. Had Jaime Knevett put him up to this? Would a doctor permit himself to be so influenced by another?

But it wasn't what she had expected, and she hunched her shoulders defensively. Perhaps Jaime was right. Perhaps she should stop jumping to conclusions.

'The thing is,' the doctor was explaining, 'we can't keep your mother here much longer. There's very little anyone can do for her, and we are so short of beds. You understand? Unless you can see your way clear to looking after her at home, I'm afraid she will have to be moved to Mount Carson.'

Mount Carson! Miranda's spirits plummeted. She had heard about Mount Carson. It was a kind of old people's home, where they sent terminal cases. The staff did what they could, but with so many old people, many of them incontinent, they had little time to spare for the niceties. To imagine her mother an inmate of Mount Carson, just another body to wash and feed, filled her with dismay.

'I—is there no alternative?' she ventured.

The doctor shook his head regretfully. 'Hospitals nowadays are never large enough to accommodate patients. Only emergency cases ever get inside the doors, and once they're there, we're working to get them out again. I'm sorry, but there's nothing I can do.'

'No.' Miranda sighed.

'Look, I know how you feel,' he said compassionately, 'but Mount Carson's not so bad. And you couldn't possibly take on the responsibility yourself. Your mother needs full-time nursing, and that costs money, I know.'

Miranda bent her head. 'So do I,' she murmured chokingly, and then rose abruptly to her feet. 'Thank you, anyway. You've been very kind.'

'I only wish there was more I could do,' the doctor apologised, and she felt he really meant it.

Jaime was sitting in the reception hall when she came downstairs again, and when she would have walked past him he got to his feet. Their subsequent encounter was viewed with great interest by the nurse on duty in the reception office who had been wondering for the past ten minutes who the attractive man was sitting so patiently in the waiting room.

'Well?'

Jaime's inquiry was polite, but Miranda was too distraught to notice.

'You knew what was going to happen!' she accused him bitterly. 'What have I ever done to you that you should want to do this to me?'

Jaime's lean face was expressionless. 'I think we should go to the car,' he said quietly. 'Unless you enjoy making scenes in public.'

'Am I embarrassing you?' she demanded childishly, but he merely shook his head.

'You're embarrassing yourself,' he replied. 'Shall we go?'

It would have been satisfying to walk off and leave him there in the car-park, but the buses to the village were casual at best, and at this time of night she might have to wait for an hour or more. She was too cold, both inside and out, to contemplate such an action.

The Daimler still retained the heat of the outward journey, and before starting the car, Jaime looked at her. 'There's no change?'

'You knew there wouldn't be.'

He acknowledged this silently. Then he said: 'What will you do?'

Miranda cast a contemptuous look in his direction. 'What can I do?'

'You know.'

She sighed. 'Marry you!'

'That's right.'

'And what do you get out of it?' She shivered. 'I don't love you.'

His mouth curled. 'Love! I doubt you could love anybody.' Miranda let that go, and he went on: 'I don't want to make love to you. At least, not yet.'

'What do you mean?'

'You're a child, Miranda, a selfish greedy child! I'm not interested in children!'

'You're only six years older——'

'Seven, actually. But in fact, it feels like twenty!'

'So what do you want?'

'I want to go back to Santa Madalena.'

'You don't intend to stay in England!' She was flabbergasted.

'No.' His half smile was not pleasant. 'I do not intend to stay in England. Unlike you, I do not care for this country. I prefer my own—where the people are warm and feeling, not cold and calculating.'

'*You* can say *that*!'

'Oh, I can be as calculating as the next man, if I have to.'

'Why are you doing all this?' she cried, and he shrugged his broad shoulders.

'You wanted to marry Mark, the heir to the estate. I am merely giving you the same option. I want you to know what it was you were prepared to give up your freedom for.'

Miranda wished she felt more competent to cope. 'There is such a thing as divorce!' she declared helplessly, but he shook his head.

'Not for me.'

'What do you mean?'

'Didn't I tell you? I am a Catholic, Miranda. If you marry me, it's for life.'

'Is that what *you* want?' She was confused and aghast.

He leaned forward to start the engine. 'Let us say, women do not worry me greatly,' he said. 'Like Mark—only not like Mark, if you see what I mean.' He gave a harsh mirthless laugh.

'But why? Why me?'

'I've told you—it pleases me to do so.' He glanced her way. 'Do I take it you are considering my proposal more seriously?'

She shook her head. 'I don't know ...'

'You would be mistress of the Hall,' he tormented her. 'My aunt would live there, too, but she would be only the dowager Lady Sanders, while you ...'

'Oh, stop it, stop it!' Miranda put her hands over her ears. 'I *can't* do it! I won't!'

'Not even for your mother? She would be more comfortable at the Hall, with a full-time nurse to look after her —good food, servants! I'd undertake to see you were very comfortable ...'

Miranda put a confused hand to her head. 'What about death duties? Lady Sanders said something about that ...'

'I am not a poor man, Miranda. My father was quite a successful man in his own right, and when he died I succeeded to his estates without crippling death duties. You would never have to worry about money again.'

Miranda stared blankly through the windows. 'You— are—a—bastard,' she said, through her teeth, and he laughed.

'You're learning,' he told her mockingly, and she had the overpowering desire to break down and cry. He knew her. This man knew her so well! He knew what he was offering she would never find the strength to resist.

CHAPTER FOUR

'But, darling, aren't you being just a little ridiculous? Why shouldn't I come with you? I want to. I want to be there to support you. Miranda, you're not making sense.'

'Aren't I?' Miranda fingered the broad gold band on her third finger with curious reluctance. 'You don't know my husband, Paul. I do. And I just know this is something I have to do on my own.'

'You haven't seen him for four years, Miranda. How well do you think you know him now?'

'I don't know. I shall have to find out, shan't I?'

On high heels, Miranda crossed the soft drawing room carpet to stand staring out of the window on to croquet-smooth lawns. But she scarcely noticed the ordered gardens, so much better cared for now than they had been in old Croxley's day, or the stand of elm trees in the distance. Was it only four years since she had undertaken that almost morganatic marriage with Jaime? she was thinking, aghast. It seemed so much longer than that. But perhaps that was because of all that had come after, not least her own mother's death two days before her twentieth birthday. She had cabled Jaime the news, but if he had received her message, he had not replied, and she had been left with the crippling realisation that so far as he was concerned she did not exist.

Certainly the years had wrought great changes in her, if not physically then at least mentally. Living with Lady Sanders had changed her, and she was no longer the gullible teenager she had once been. Perhaps Jaime had been right, she thought in her more scrupulous moments. Maybe she was more like the Dowager Lady Sanders than she cared to believe. After all, she had quickly learned the art of dissembling, and no one of her acquaintance ever really knew what she was thinking.

Only alone with her mother had she shed the cloak of indifference she unvaryingly wore, and talked to her with a freedom of expression she might never have employed had

57

she been able to answer back. In time, Miranda convinced herself that her mother could hear and understand everything she was saying, and every flicker of an eyelid or spasmodic jerk of muscle became a reaction to what she had heard. The nurse whom Jaime had employed to live at the Hall and take care of the patient considered it was not entirely healthy for Miranda to spend as much time as she did in the sickroom, and both she and Lady Sanders were relieved when Mrs Gresham's tenuous hold on life was extinguished.

For a time, Miranda was distrait, but gradually she took up the threads of living again, and with Lady Sanders' tacit approval, she began to live as Jaime would have expected. While her mother had been alive, she had consoled herself with the thought that without her marriage, Mrs Gresham's last months would have been much less comfortable. But now she was dead, and the full weight of the responsibility she had undertaken fell upon her.

After a time though, her conscience was appeased. An unwilling pupil to Lady Sanders' guidance, Miranda allowed herself to be taught the many duties that went with her position, as well as behaviour and etiquette, and good dress sense. Unresponsive at first, she was soon at ease in the salons of Mayfair, making her own opinions felt as she learned what suited her and what didn't.

Her new-found sophistication did not go long unnoticed. Gradually, excuses were made for the unusual circumstances of her marriage, and she began being invited to dinner and house parties. She learned how to ride, and play tennis, and parry all questions about her background with a ready wit that attracted attention, and sometimes she could even forget she was married, or that her life had ever been any different. But only sometimes ...

'Miranda ...'

She turned to face the man who had spoken her name, a rueful smile lifting the corners of her mouth. Poor Paul, she thought compassionately. He didn't understand at all. He didn't realise that great tact had to be used in this matter. Of course, it was four years since Jaime had made that statement about not giving her a divorce, but a marriage had to be consummated. He had said nothing about an annulment. Even so, she had the feeling he would not take kindly to her bringing her new fiancé out to meet him.

'Paul, I'm sorry, but I have to go alone.'

'To Brazil!' Paul Courtenay shook his head in exasperation. 'Why can't you get your solicitors to write to him—explain the situation?'

'Do you think that's what I should do?'

'Yes.'

'And what if he doesn't reply? What if he refuses?'

'He could anyway.'

'Do you think I don't know that?' Miranda's smile disappeared. 'Believe me, Paul, this is the best way. When he sees me again—when he sees what I've—become——'

'Become?' Paul's brows descended. 'What do you mean?'

'Oh, nothing.' Miranda forced her smile to return. 'Stop looking so grim, darling. I can reach Brazil in a matter of hours. I should be there and back within a week.'

'A week!'

'All right, two weeks then,' remarked Miranda mischievously, and he came forward to take her forcefully by the shoulders and bend his head to hers. But when he held her closer and attempted to run his fingers beneath the tied waistband of her blouse her hands on his arms held him away.

'Oh, God, Miranda,' he muttered thickly. 'What's the matter with you? As soon as I get near to you, you're backing off!'

Miranda felt the familiar sense of anxiety rising inside her. She wished Paul had not said that. It wasn't true. He had held her and kissed her, and pressed his body close to hers and she had let him, lots of times. It was only when he tried to touch her flesh that she felt that awful feeling of revulsion. But it would pass, she told herself fiercely. It had to. When they were married—once it was legal . . .

Paul raked back his hair with an unsteady hand, and then gave her a sheepish look. 'All right,' he said, reading her expression. 'I'm sorry, I shouldn't have said that. But, hell, Miranda, we are engaged!'

'Not yet,' she retorted lightly. 'But soon . . .'

The drawing room door behind them opened suddenly to admit Lady Sanders. She had changed little over the years, and Miranda could find it in her heart to admire this grey-haired elegant woman who had given in so gracefully.

Now, however, she exchanged a knowing glance with Paul, silently teasing him with the knowledge of how embarrassing the situation might have been, and he pulled a face at her before turning to greet the dowager lady of the house. Miranda knew Lady Sanders liked him. And why not? His father was Sir Cecil Courtenay, owner of Courtenay Towers, and incidentally one of the richest men in the county. Recently returned from South Africa, where he had been staying with his cousin, who bred racehorses, Paul was a wealthy man in his own right, having inherited a Scottish estate from his grandmother. He was twenty-five, young and attractive, and exactly the sort of husband Lady Sanders would have chosen for a daughter of her own.

'Paul!' she said now, permitting him to kiss her cheek. 'I didn't know you were here. Chadwick's just told me. You're staying for dinner, of course.'

Paul glanced awkwardly at Miranda. 'I—we're dining out this evening, Lady Sanders,' he murmured apologetically. 'That is—aren't we?'

He looked at Miranda, and she knew he was hoping she would agree. She had just broken the news to him about her proposed trip to South America, and she guessed he wanted to talk to her more about it. It would have been easier to dine here, the threesome preventing any intimate conversation, but his words earlier had made her uneasy, and before confronting Jaime again she wanted to reassure herself that Mark had not irreparably damaged her for some other man.

'Yes, we are,' she said now, smiling blandly at the woman who might have been her mother-in-law. 'You don't mind, do you, Aunt Lydia?'

Lady Sanders seated herself in one of the striped Regency armchairs. 'Of course not, my dear,' she replied, and they both knew the game they were playing. 'Perhaps another evening . . .'

'Another evening,' Paul agreed, with some relief. 'And now I'd better go.' He looked across at Miranda. 'I'll pick you up about eight, right?'

'Right,' she agreed amicably, and accompanied him to the door. 'Drive carefully.'

Paul looked at his Lamborghini, and then back at her. 'I will,' he said. 'I have too much to live for.'

Back in the drawing room, Lady Sanders had rung for tea. As well as Mrs Savage, who had taken over the housekeeping duties of the Hall, they had a maid, Chadwick, and a daily woman who came in to do the rough work. Croxley, who had retired soon after Miranda's mother died, had been replaced by a 'horticultural expert', and the younger man was infinitely more efficient. If efficiency replaced character, too, Miranda had schooled herself not to care, and Lady Sanders never seemed to notice.

'Where are you going this evening?' Lady Sanders asked, her eyes showing faint dissatisfaction at Miranda's choice of dress, as she walked rather thoughtfully back into the room.

Miranda looked at her rather blankly for a moment, and then she gathered herself. 'Oh, I don't know,' she shrugged, subsiding into an armchair herself and draping one denim-clad leg rather inelegantly over the arm. 'Maybe we'll try the Swan. I believe they do a decent steak.'

Lady Sanders' face mirrored her reluctant admiration. 'How you've changed, Miranda,' she observed, bidding Chadwick enter with the tea trolley. 'Not long ago, you wouldn't have known the difference.'

Miranda leaned forward to help herself to a sandwich as the elderly maid departed. 'Funnily enough, I was thinking the same thing myself,' she remarked without rancour, realising how little satisfaction the knowledge gave her. 'Thanks to your expert tuition, of course, dear aunt.'

Lady Sanders pulled a wry face. 'Did you tell Paul?'

Miranda didn't pretend not to understand. 'About going to Brazil? Yes. You really think I should go, don't you?'

'Of course. What did Paul say?'

'He wants to come with me.'

'You're not going to let him, are you?'

'Would you?'

Lady Sanders frowned. 'Definitely not.'

Miranda reached for a second sandwich, not quite knowing why she should suddenly feel so hungry, but she was.

'Anyway, I can't,' she declared, the ham in her mouth losing its taste. 'It's going to be difficult enough as it is.'

'You think so?'

'Don't you?'

'Perhaps. Jaime always was an unpredictable boy.'

'Well, he's not a boy now, he's a man! And he's been so for some years, and you know it.' Miranda put the uneaten remains of the sandwich on her plate. 'I just wish I knew more about him, that's all.'

Lady Sanders raised her eyebrows. 'What do you want to know? He told you about his family, didn't he?'

Miranda shook her head. 'Only that his father was dead, and his mother had remarried, that's all. I have his address, but I have no idea where Santa Madalena is.'

'Well, I'm afraid I can't help you there,' remarked the other woman, pouring tea into delicately patterned porcelain. 'I scarcely knew Patrick—his father, you know. I believe his mother's name is Teresa or Terese or something, but I wouldn't know her if I saw her.'

Miranda sighed. 'I wonder why he——' She broke off abruptly, aware that Lady Sanders knew exactly what she meant. 'I mean—I wonder if he has a girl-friend.'

'Jaime?' Lady Sanders sipped her tea. 'I shouldn't think so. I know that once he spoke of entering the Church ...'

'The *Church*!' echoed Miranda disbelievingly. 'Jaime! A priest?'

'Well, I do know Patrick was a highly religious man,' murmured Lady Sanders thoughtfully. 'And I believe Jaime is very like him.'

Miranda stared at her incredulously. 'But—but he's such a—a physical person!'

'What has that to do with anything? Good lord, Cesare Borgia was a cardinal, and you couldn't find anyone more physical than he was!'

'But that was different.'

'How was it different?'

'Well, you're talking about the fifteenth or sixteenth century, for a start. This is the twentieth century, Aunt Lydia. Things have changed.'

'Perhaps they have, perhaps they haven't. In any case, I've told you, it would be foolish to take Paul with you. After all, you can hardly stay in Jaime's home with the man you are intending should take his place!'

Miranda gasped. 'Jaime never had a place, Aunt Lydia, and you know it! Apart from the ceremony and immediately afterwards, I've never spent any time with him as my husband. Besides, I shan't be staying in Jaime's home. I shall stay at an hotel.'

'Where? In Santa Madalena? How do you know there is one?'

'Don't be silly.' Miranda was getting irritable. 'There are hotels everywhere. And if I can't stay in Santa Madalena, I shall stay in Rio. I rather fancy the Copacabana Palace.'

'Do you? And do you know how far it is from Rio to Santa Madalena?'

'No.' Miranda frowned. 'Do you?'

'No,' conceded the other woman dryly, 'but I get the distinct feeling that it's further than you imagine it to be.'

Miranda reflected on Lady Sanders' words as she changed for dinner with Paul that evening. It was true, she had not really considered the size of the country when she agreed to go there, and her estimates tended to be based on British standards. Now, satisfied with the casual elegance of her simple ankle-length chemise, she made her way down to the library to flick through the pages of the Encyclopaedia Britannica. Brazil, she saw with dismay, was more than two and a half thousand miles in each direction, north to south and east to west, and the possibility of Santa Madalena being within a day's journey of Rio seemed very slight indeed. In addition to which, the roads around the cultural capital were apparently barely adequate, and for the first time she doubted her ability to cope alone. Perhaps she should take Paul along, if only because he was a man.

But she couldn't do that, she told herself impatiently, so she might as well make the best of it. Who knows, perhaps the railway provided a service between Santa Madalena and Rio, and if not, she would face the problems when she came to them. She didn't intend informing Jaime of her advent until the day before she left England. That way, she would ensure that he could not forbid her to come.

Later that evening, dining with Paul in the comfortable grill-room of the Swan Hotel, Miranda attempted to put all thoughts of the trip out of her mind. Instead, she concentrated on Paul, trying to imagine how it would be once they were married. They would probably live at the Towers, as Sir Cecil and Paul's mother were considering retiring to Ireland, and Paul would take over his father's business interests. She didn't exactly know what they were—something to do with horses and horse-breeding, she thought—but that wasn't particularly important. She did wonder what Lady Sanders would do, and then decided that Jaime was not so unscrupulous as to threaten to turn her out of her home a second time. Besides, she was an asset in many ways, and she could continue to run the estate for as long as she desired.

Being married to Paul was less easy to contemplate. But in truth, she had never been married before. She refused to consider her relationship with Jaime as anything more than an expedient arrangement, and her greatest hope there was an annulment. Surely even the Catholic church could not object to that, *but would Jaime?* It didn't matter if he did, she decided firmly. How could he stop her?

Paul reached across the table to take her hand, and she gave him a warm, enveloping smile. He was so sweet, she thought with satisfaction, so handsome! Not unlike Mark in some ways, with his soft fair hair and blue eyes, but with more strength of character in his face. *Oh, why did she have to think of Mark now?* she asked herself restlessly. He was dead. Paul was alive—and he loved her.

It wasn't late when they arrived back at the Hall, and reluctantly Miranda asked him in for a nightcap. She knew Lady Sanders would be in bed, watching television, so she invited him into the library, curling into a chair while he poured two glasses of brandy.

'To us,' Paul said, raising his glass to her, and silently she echoed the toast.

Then he pulled her up out of the chair into his arms, causing her to protest that she was spilling the brandy. Firmly, he took the glass from her and set it beside his own on the desk, before gathering her closely to him.

'Now,' he said huskily, 'there's no one to interrupt us ...'

'Paul ...' Almost of their own volition, her hands were against his chest, pressing him away from her. 'Paul, please, you're crushing my dress ...'

She steeled herself to suffer his kiss in silence as she had done before, and wondered if she would ever find love-making enjoyable. Perhaps she was frigid. Perhaps Mark had not been entirely to blame for that awful scene between them. Perhaps that was why Jaime had married her—because he had sensed the kind of woman she was ...

Paul's lips nuzzled her neck, and then he drew back, pulling a wry face. 'It's Jaime, isn't it?' he asked, getting it all wrong. 'You still feel you're married to him.'

'I *am* married to him,' she said, and for once she was glad to mean it.

'I'd better go.' He bestowed a caress on the corner of her mouth. 'Will I see you tomorrow?'

Miranda hesitated. 'If you like. I—I have to go into town, to arrange about air tickets and so on. Ring me when I get back.'

'All right.' Paul nodded and smiled, and she thought how lucky she was that he was so gentle with her. Gentleness was what she needed, and once they were married ...

Judith Masters worked for the travel agent, and in recent years Miranda had seen quite a lot of her old school friend. There had been several trips to Paris with Lady Sanders, for instance, and two holidays in the South of France, and occasionally the two girls had lunch together.

Today, Judith was busy when Miranda entered the office, but she refused the help of the manager and waited until Judith was free.

'Another holiday?' Judith teased her, as she asked about flights to Rio de Janeiro, but Miranda shook her head.

'I'm going to ask Jaime for a divorce,' she said, in a low voice. And then, on impulse, 'Could we have lunch together?'

Judith glanced round at the young manager, tactfully ensconced in his cubicle at the back of the office. 'As a matter of fact, *he's* asked me to lunch,' she volunteered with a shy grin. 'Mr Stanley. I'm sorry, Miranda.'

Miranda made an indifferent gesture. 'It's okay——'

'I could meet you after work.'

'No, I can't.' Miranda tapped the timetable on the desk in front of them. 'I want to leave on Friday, if possible. How long does the flight take?'

Judith looked at her anxiously. 'Miranda! I'd like to talk to you, honestly.' She paused, glancing round at the manager once more. 'What about now? We could have coffee together. I sometimes go out for twenty minutes during my morning break. Shopping, and that sort of thing.'

Miranda chewed her lower lip. She needed to talk to Judith, too, and with a rueful nod she agreed. Judith went into the manager's small office for a moment, and then emerged carrying her handbag and jacket.

'All set,' she said cheerfully, and the two girls went out into the main street together.

It was a chilly autumn day, and the wind that tunnelled down between the tall buildings was icy. Miranda led the way into the local department store, and they took the lift up to the Mezzanine Restaurant, glad of the benefits of central heating.

A waitress served them coffee and scones, and then Judith looked quizzically at her friend. 'Well?' she said. 'So you want a divorce. To marry Paul, I suppose.'

'Yes.' Miranda eschewed the scones in favour of the coffee. 'Do you think I'm right?'

'Do *I* think you're right?' Judith stared at her blankly. 'Miranda, surely *you* know, and that's all that matters!'

'Oh, yes, yes.' Miranda looked restlessly about her. 'Of course I do. I just wanted to know what you thought.'

'About Paul?'

Miranda lowered her lids. 'Well—yes.'

'I didn't like Mark, you know that,' said Judith slowly. 'And Paul—well, Paul's not so different.'

'Oh, he is, he is! He's much steadier,' exclaimed Miranda.

'Steadier!' Judith pulled a face. 'What a way to describe him.'

'Judith, you know what I mean.' Miranda plucked nervously at the cloth. 'Mark used to drink, that's common knowledge.'

'Do you love Paul?' Judith was direct.

'I think so . . .'

'You only *think* so?'

'That's what I wanted to talk to you about,' said Miranda uncomfortably. 'Judith—Judith, do you think I'm frigid?'

Judith stared at her. 'Frigid? Is that what Paul says?'

'Oh, no, no!' Miranda sighed frustratedly. 'It's my idea. Well? Do you?'

'How should I know?' Judith regarded her compassionately. 'Love, that's something you can only find out for yourself.'

Miranda bent her head. 'Jaime and I—we never—well, you know what I'm trying to say.'

Judith nodded. 'I know. The village talked about nothing else for months.' She shook her head reminiscently. Then: 'And Paul?'

Miranda made a negative gesture. 'No. No one.'

Judith uttered a sound of amazement. 'You mean you're twenty-three and still a virgin!'

Miranda flushed. 'Don't talk so loudly! People will hear.'

Judith smothered a laugh. 'I'm sorry. But I never dreamed —I mean—I thought Mark——'

'No.' Miranda concentrated on her coffee cup. 'I gather you have.'

Judith sighed, 'I was engaged once myself, remember?' Miranda nodded, recalling the relief schoolmaster who had taken over Judith's father's position when he fell ill two years ago, and Judith went on: 'Most people do, you know. I admire Paul's self-restraint.' She paused thoughtfully. 'Or is that why you're talking to me now?'

'Sort of.' Miranda was honest. 'When he comes near me, I just—freeze up.'

Judith looked concerned. 'And have you always? Even before Mark?'

'I—can't remember.' Miranda frowned. 'Mark was my first steady boy-friend.'

'And he really loused things up for you, didn't he?' exclaimed Judith bitterly.

'I don't know. Did he?' Miranda made a helpless gesture. 'Or was I always like this?'

Judith studied her friend's worried face, and then said quietly: 'Perhaps we're not looking back far enough. A psychologist would insist that there had to be something in your past, some incident to account for the way you feel. Some other man, perhaps ...'

'There was no other man!' declared Miranda vehemently, and then, aware that Judith was watching her strangely, she added: 'Anyway, that's enough about me. Tell me about you —about Mr Stanley! How long has this been going on?'

Judith allowed herself to be diverted, but later that night, lying between the cool silk sheets of the four-poster she slept in, Miranda's thoughts returned unwillingly to the problem. As had happened a hundred times before, she relived the night Mark died in all its sordid detail. But before she recalled the events leading up to Mark's violent departure from the cottage, she let her mind drift back over the earlier part of the evening. And she remembered what it was that had driven her to take sanctuary in the ante-room behind the dais . . .

CHAPTER FIVE

AHEAD, a heat haze shimmered on the road, distorting the tortuous mountain track and making Miranda's stomach heave as she was given terrifying glimpses of the precipice that fell away beside them. Inside the limousine it was chilly, cooled by air-conditioning, but the rigours of the journey kept her body clothed in perspiration. For the umpteenth time she wondered whether she would have felt any better had she been driving, instead of putting herself in the hands of a professional chauffeur, but it was too late to do anything about it. Besides, she doubted she would have come this far, given the choice, and returning to Rio without even reaching her destination would have depressed her even more. So far the trip had been a disaster, and although she was not normally a superstitious girl, she was rapidly coming to the conclusion that her journey was fated.

She had flown to Georgetown without incident, but the plane bringing her from Georgetown to Rio had been forced back with engine trouble, and she had spent eight hours at Atkinson Field, kicking her heels in humid temperatures that did not improve her temper. By the time she reached Galeao, she was tired and distrait, and in no mood to appreciate the beauty of Guanabara Bay, or the twin peaks of Sugarloaf and Corcovado, rising behind the five-mile stretch of promenade.

A night's sleep had helped to improve her temper, and an early morning swim from that most famous of beaches, Copacabana, had put her in a good mood to face the quelling news that Santa Madalena was more than seven hundred miles from Rio. A quick review of the transportation available vouchsafed the information that there was no rail or air link between Santa Madalena and Rio, and unless she was prepared to take the week-long trip by sea and river steamer, the road was her only means of access.

The courier at the hotel had been sympathetic, but he had insisted that she should not attempt to drive herself over the rough and mountainous terrain to her destination.

'Permit me to obtain for you a car and driver, *senhora*,' he exclaimed, and Miranda had allowed herself to be persuaded. Only now did she ponder the shrewdness of her decision, as the vehicle swung dangerously near the edge of a ravine, and her wet palms slid heedlessly across the raw leather of her seat.

She tried to concentrate on the majestic beauty of the mountains rising ahead of them, but their mist-shrouded peaks seemed as insubstantial as her belief that she would eventually reach Santa Madalena. Though not as impressive as the Andes they were awe-inspiring; but savage too, like the rivers that poured down from their plateaus to form the huge network of waterways that helped to fill the Amazon basin. The gorge beside them in no way compared to that vast crater, which even from an aeroplane was only half visible.

Miranda sat back in her seat and closed her eyes as her stomach heaved once more. She was still far from fit, and the food-poisoning which had resulted from a night's stay at a roadside *estancia* had left her feeling curiously weak. But that had been only another disaster to add to the others, and after two nights at a mission hospital she was at last within fifty miles of her destination.

The driver turned round to grin encouragingly, and she couldn't help but admire his nonchalance. In the face of such hazards he had time to share his happiness with her, while she was a trembling mass of jelly.

'*Nem tempo, senhora,*' he said cheerfully. 'Not long now, no? We will be there in one hour.'

'An hour!' Miranda hid her consternation. She didn't know if she could control her stomach muscles that long. 'Thank you.'

'*De nada!*' His grin deepened, and she realised her irony had gone over his head. He really didn't appreciate that it was his fault the journey had taken five days instead of three and she felt the urgency of her mission slipping out of her grasp. Was that what this place did to you? she wondered confusedly, groaning as another pot-hole in the road jarred the tender base of her spine. Had she really told Paul she would be here and back within the week? It was a week now since she had left England, and she still hadn't seen Jaime.

The plateau when they reached it was like something out of another time and another world. Miranda had decided that Brazil was composed of rushing rivers and rocky canyons, where moist foliage steamed in the noonday heat of the sun. She looked for pine forests, and the tall cliffs of the escarpment, with nothing of charm or gentleness about it. What she found was an upland plain, where the long grasses of the savanna stretched as far as the eye could see, a lonely primitive grazing land interspersed here and there with stands of low broadleaf trees and deeply cut river valleys.

But if anything the roads were worse here. It had been raining and the car's wheels skidded sickeningly on the muddy surface. They left the highway at the head of the escarpment and joined a track that ran between a narrow watercourse and the open prairie, and Miranda had her first glimpse of the cattle that brought prosperity to this area of the country. Solid red beasts they were, heavy and compact, ideal beef-breeding animals, and somehow more aggressive in this semi-wild state than comfortably penned in fields back home. She saw some men, too, riding in the distance, and when she said: 'Cowboys!' almost wonderingly, her driver corrected her with a smile.

'*Gauchos!*' he said. 'You must learn our language, *senhora.*'

Miranda forced a smile in return and refrained from pointing out that she did not expect to be here long enough to learn anything.

Santa Madalena was just a village, and Lady Sanders had been more right than she knew when she had suggested there might not be an hotel. Had there been one, Miranda doubted she would have had the courage to stay there after her recent experience, and in spite of herself she was learning the difference between the urban and rural communities.

The people of the village appeared to be a cross-section of the ethnic races of the country. Miranda saw children whose features were predominantly African in origin and others who were just as obviously of white Portuguese extraction. But the housing was primitive in sections, and while some of the Indian women stood around, wide-eyed at their intrusion, the old men of the village squatted at the doorways of adobe dwellings, puffing their pipes and showing no interest whatsoever in what must be an unusual incursion.

The driver stopped the car outside a store where sacks of rice and cassava flour were stacked on a verandah that stood on wooden supports, shaded by leathery palm leaves, woven skilfully together. There was a kind of hitching rail, where someone had tied a skinny donkey, and Miranda's heart went out to the sad-faced beast.

'You are staying here?' the driver asked in amazement, and quickly Miranda shook her head.

'I—do you think we could find out where—where a Senhor Knevett lives?' For she knew that in his own home Jaime never used his title.

'Nee-veet?' said the driver carefully. 'Senhor Nee-veet?'

Miranda sighed. 'Do you think we could?'

'I ask.'

He climbed out of the car, and ignoring the curious stares of the women and children watching her, Miranda got out, too. She had some peppermints in her handbag, and she was approaching the donkey with one extended on her palm, when it was suddenly dashed to the ground. She swung round indignantly, prepared to make some angry protest, and then caught her breath in surprise. Standing behind her was one of the most beautiful women she had ever seen in her life: small, and exquisitely proportioned, with long dark hair tied back with a bandanna and secured beneath a broad sombrero, she was dressed in riding gear, knee-length boots completing the ensemble. Before Miranda could say anything, she began to speak, and as she did so, Miranda wondered where she had heard that particular intonation before.

'Forgive me,' she was saying, in an attractively husky voice. 'But the *burro* is infested with fleas, and I would not like that to be your introduction to our country—Miranda.'

Miranda! The girl stared at her blankly. 'You know my name?'

The woman smiled. 'Who else could it be? Who else would make the journey here by car! Oh, Miranda, my son will be so glad that you are safe at last!'

'Your *son*!' Miranda felt totally incapable of coherent thinking. 'You mean ... you ...'

'... are Teresa Monteiro Carvalho! Jaime's mother, *no*?'

Miranda made a helpless movement of her hands, immediately conscious of the dust smudges on her cream blouse, the creases in her brown slacks. Beside such diminutive elegance she felt clumsy and awkward, the peppermint still clinging damply to her hot fingers.

'I—I can hardly believe it,' she got out at last. 'You! Here! Were you waiting for me?'

Teresa Carvalho seemed equally charmed at meeting her daughter-in-law, but she shook her head apologetically, and said: 'Alas, no. My presence in Santa Madalena is purely coincidental. We knew you were coming, of course. Jaime got your cable. But he has been driven almost frantic at your disappearance.'

'Disappearance?' Miranda glanced about her confusedly. 'I—oh, you must mean our delay in getting here.'

'That is correct.' Teresa frowned. 'You say—*our*? You are not alone?'

Miranda gave a rueful smile. 'I mean my driver,' she explained, and her mother-in-law's face cleared miraculously. 'We—that is, *I*—have been slightly unwell——'

'No!' Teresa sounded concerned. 'What was wrong?'

'Oh, it was nothing really.' Miranda made a deprecating gesture. 'Just a stomach upset, that's all. Too much rich food, I suppose.'

Teresa still looked anxious. 'Such upsets can be serious,' she said gravely. 'You must have Jaime give you a thorough checkover when he gets back.'

'Really, that's not necessary ...' Miranda was beginning in alarm, when something else the woman had said registered. 'Jaime—is *away*!' *This was the last straw!* 'When will he be back?'

Teresa put reassuring hands on her arm. 'Do not sound so dismayed, *pequena*. I told you, he was concerned about you. He has flown to Rio to make inquiries as to your whereabouts.'

'Flown?' Miranda looked astonished. 'You mean there's an airport here!' And she had suffered this awful journey!

But Teresa shook her head. 'No airport, no. But the

estado has its own airplane. Communications are not good around here, as I am sure you have noticed. We need better roads. But until we have them, we invariably use the river steamers—or the airplane.'

'I see.'

Miranda was beginning to feel rather faint. It was hours since she had consumed the two rolls and the apple the sisters at the mission had packed for her lunch, and standing there in the cool, moist atmosphere, redolent with the scents of pigs and cattle, and what might have been open sewers, was beginning to tell on her. Not to mention the flies ...

Just as she was trying to think of some excuse to get back in the car again, the driver emerged from the store, munching one of the flat pancakes Miranda remembered with loathing from her night at the *estancia*, and seemingly unperturbed that she had been waiting so long. He cast a long look at Teresa, and then said rather incoherently, on account of his full mouth, 'No Nee-veet here, *senhora*.'

Miranda turned to Teresa to try and explain, but her mother-in-law seemed to have understood. 'My husband's name is Carvalho,' she said. 'My son is known by that name, also.'

Miranda pushed back the weight of her hair with a slightly unsteady hand. 'Then thank heavens I met you,' she exclaimed. 'I don't know what I'd have done otherwise.'

'You should have given Jaime more notice that you were coming,' replied her mother-in-law, with the first note of reproof in her voice. 'But had you asked for the *medico*, they would have known who you meant.'

The driver was looking blankly from one to the other of them, and Teresa, noticing Miranda's perspiration-glazed features, spoke swiftly to him in his own language. The exchange was brief and to the point, and then, with a casual salute, the driver made to get back into his car. That brought Miranda alert again, and she said weakly: 'What's going on?'

Teresa took her arm. 'Come with me. I have dismissed your chauffeur.'

'But I haven't paid him——'

Teresa shook her head as the car drove on down the narrow village street. 'I have told him to charge his account to the Carvalho Estate, *cara*. Do not worry. He will be paid, I assure you.'

Miranda felt too sick to worry about anything, but she suddenly remembered something else. 'My cases!' she exclaimed in dismay, and Teresa's fingers squeezed her flesh.

'They are being put into my car,' she reassured her gently, and Miranda wondered how long her legs would continue to support her.

She was inordinately relieved when they turned a corner and she saw the dust-smeared station wagon parked in the shade of a group of gum trees. The driver who had brought her from Rio was presently offloading her cases, and a husky, black-skinned individual was putting them into the back of the station wagon. The man was easily six feet tall with massive shoulders, clad in faded blue jeans and a collarless sweat shirt. He dwarfed the other man, but Teresa approached him confidently.

'This is Joachim,' she confided to Miranda. 'He is employed by my husband. He came with me today.'

Miranda just wanted to sit down, and as if understanding and sympathising, Teresa helped her into the passenger seat. Then she went to speak to Joachim before seating herself behind the wheel. Miranda roused herself to ask why Joachim didn't appear to be returning with them, and Teresa looked at her gently.

'You are still far from fit, I think,' she said, stretching forward to turn the ignition key. 'Joachim will buy the supplies we need before coming home, and I will send one of the other boys back for him.'

'But I'm upsetting your schedule,' Miranda protested weakly, only to receive an understanding smile from her mother-in-law.

'It is little enough to do for the wife of my only son,' she declared firmly. 'We have so much wanted to meet you, Miranda. It is good that now you feel able to come to us. It has been a long time.' Which made Miranda feel even worse!

'But I——' She broke off abruptly, at a loss for words. 'You —you're very kind.'

Teresa's smile deepened, and looking at her Miranda could see the network of tiny lines that fanned out from her eyes and mouth, belying her otherwise youthful appearance. She scarcely looked old enough to be Jaime's mother, however, and thinking of her husband brought a wave of apprehension to drench Miranda in perspiration once more.

'Your introduction to our country has not been of the best,' Teresa was saying now, as they left the village behind to plunge into a forest that in places hid the sun completely. It was late afternoon, and the sun was sinking, but the moisture from the trees still rose in tiny spirals of mist. This was the highlands, Miranda had read, hoping for coolness, and instead finding a kind of damp humidity. 'You will find it has many faces, not all of them unpleasant.'

'I—Rio was very civilised,' murmured Miranda awkwardly, and Teresa laughed.

'You think so? I think it is one of the most uncivilised places in the world! But I hope you will like Monte Paraiso. Jaime's home is yours!'

'Thank you.'

Miranda could think of nothing else to say, and she turned to stare blankly out of the windows. It was obvious her cable to Jaime had told them nothing, as indeed she had intended at the time, but how could she have known she would so soon find herself in such an ambiguous position?

The forest gave way to scrubland, and ricefields and wheat, and what might have been maize, although Miranda's knowledge of such things was limited. There were people working in the fields, and here and there were oxen competing with tractors doing the work they had done for hundreds of years. Beyond this, was open pasture land, where more of the stocky cattle grazed, raising their heads to gaze broodingly after the station wagon bumping recklessly over the packed-earth road.

'The land is fair,' remarked Teresa, noticing Miranda's interest. 'When I was a child, this area was covered with trees, but gradually they have all been burned to make way for cultivation. We have to rotate our land here, not our crops. The soil will only produce a good harvest for a couple of years, and then we must leave it to pasture and move elsewhere.'

Miranda was amazed. 'But won't you soon run out of land that way?' she exclaimed, forgetting her own problems for a moment, and Teresa shrugged.

'That is what my father used to say. We lived in the forest

when I was a child, and he never got used to any other life. He died when I was seven, and I was taken in by the Portuguese Sisters of Mercy at Voltas.'

'I'm sorry.'

Miranda didn't know how else to answer her, but Teresa shook her head. 'Don't be. I was very happy with the Sisters of Mercy. It was through them that I met Jaime's father.'

Miranda looked her way. 'But he's dead now, isn't he?'

'Patrick? Yes.' Teresa nodded and raised her hand in greeting to a group of *gauchos*, herding some cattle into a pen, and looking ahead Miranda saw a collection of buildings, flanked by broadleafed trees. From this distance, it looked like a small settlement, and as they got nearer she could see the corrals and stockyards, the barns and sheds and outbuildings, all enclosed within the home paddock, as vast and impressive in their way as the huge plateau that was their heritage. It was a settlement, a living community, that relied almost entirely upon itself. 'Monte Paraiso,' added Teresa unnecessarily. 'We are home.'

A boy of about fourteen came running to open the gate for them, and then they were driving along a paved track between white-painted fencing. The track was lined with the gnarled trunks of pepper trees, and the house beyond showed whitely between the thick leaves. Two-storied and rambling, with shutters at all the windows, it reminded Miranda of a picture she had seen of a Spanish hacienda, the low eaves drooping over a wide verandah. White-painted pillars were overhung with the trailing beauty of a passion-flower vine, and tubs of bougainvillaea and oleander spilt their pink and white flowers across the slatted woodwork. In all her imaginings, she had dreamt of nothing like this, and the subtropical beauty of it all made anything she might say inadequate.

'We are fortunate,' said Teresa, as if sensing Miranda's amazement. 'Anything will grow here, providing one takes the time and the trouble to care for it.'

Miranda shook her head, unable to grasp it all in a few moments. She had expected—*what*? Some kind of primitive dwelling, a wood-built ranchhouse, with saddles on the step and pigs snorting about the yard. Not this gracious house, built of adobe brick, and as freshly painted as if the brushes were not yet dry. Not the grilled ironwork at the balconies, or the vines that clung to them, or the arched porchway, where the blood-red coronas of the passion-flower, whose resemblance to Christ's crown of thorns had given them their name, dripped velvety petals to the earth. This was Jaime's home, this was the place he had denied to her—and she had come here, as an interloper ...

Teresa stopped the station wagon, and the boy who had opened the gate for them came running to meet them. Obviously, the mistress of Monte Paraiso was a popular person, and Miranda envied her her casual acceptance of this homage. And yet once Teresa had been no different from herself. If what Lady Sanders had said was true, Teresa's father had been an Indian, and she must have had to learn, as Miranda had, the lessons of command.

'Ola, Pedro,' Teresa greeted the boy affectionately. 'Onde e o patrao?'

The boy said something in reply, his eyes going irresistibly to Miranda as she got out of the car, shyly appraising her before returning his attention to his mistress.

Teresa turned to Miranda. 'Carlos, my husband, is at home. Come—we will find him in his study, no doubt.'

With a backward glance for Pedro and the enchanting sight of a mare with two foals in a small paddock, Miranda followed her mother-in-law up the shallow verandah steps. Basket-work chairs, bright with many coloured cushions, and a table which had been topped by a pane of fluted glass looked inviting as shadows swept the courtyard. It would be delightful to sit there on warm afternoons, she thought in passing, and then gazed with admiration at the cool panelled hall of the house.

A wrought iron staircase curved to the upper floor, but the decor of this lower hall was predominantly wood. The polished blocks of the floor echoed to the sound of their feet, and long narrow windows gave a tapestry-like effect to panelled walls. A split-level area was created beyond the staircase, where two steps led down to a kind of sun lounge, with long windows that gave a magnificent view of the setting sun. It was sinking steadily behind the mountains, their ragged peaks etched in sharp relief against the purpling sky.

Between the house and the mountains, beyond a stretch of grassland, stretched a smooth expanse of water, perhaps half a mile away and probably twice that distance across.

'The Negresco,' remarked Teresa, matter-of-factly. 'Our main highway of communication.'

'And the mountains?' Miranda's nausea had disappeared, dispelled by her wonder in her surroundings.

'They are known by the ancient name of the Brazilian highlands,' Teresa told her thoughtfully. 'But in fact they are the Serra do Espirito.' She smiled. 'The Brazilian highlands is easier, no?'

'Yes,' agreed Miranda fervently, and her mother-in-law laughed.

They turned aside to enter another room as a black-clad Indian woman came from the back of the house to greet them. She was not very tall, and enormously fat, several chins wobbling above a vast expanse of bosom. Long hair was plaited into a coil at the nape of her neck, and she had one of the most cheerful countenances Miranda had ever seen. She greeted Teresa warmly, and then looked with interest at her companion.

'This is Sancha,' Teresa told Miranda, by way of an introduction. 'She is what you would call a housekeeper, yes? She has been with me since Jaime was a baby.' She turned back to the old woman. 'Sancha, *esta* Senhora Jaime, *sim?*'

To Miranda's surprise and embarrassment, Sancha gave a little cry of welcome before enfolding her in her arms, bestowing warm kisses on her cheeks, and gazing at her wonderingly.

'Senhora Jaime!' she declared, with evident emotion. *'Muito bela!'*

Miranda knew what that meant, although she doubted she looked very beautiful at the moment, pale and tired from the journey. But she managed to return the salute without too much awkwardness, and although Sancha let her go, she continued to gaze at her with unconcealed admiration.

'We were all so sad when Jaime chose to get married in England,' added his mother quietly, unknowingly increasing Miranda's unease. 'And when he told us his wife did not wish to come to South America ...'

She let the words trail away and Miranda's pale face

burned. So that was what Jaime had told them. What else had he told them? she pondered, wondering at Teresa's friendliness towards her if she believed her son's wife to have married him for mercenary reasons. How had he explained his departure so soon after their wedding? These were questions she had never hoped to have to answer.

Leaving the ample form of Sancha crooning away to herself in the hall, Miranda followed her mother-in-law into a book-lined study. It reminded her of the library back home, except that the view beyond the long windows was so incredibly different. And the man who rose from behind the square, leather-topped desk was obviously not of her nationality. He was not especially tall, but he was stockily built, which added to his stature. A receding hairline was supplemented by long sideburns, and a luxuriant moustache which curled down to his jawline.

'Carlos! See what I have found!' Teresa explained charmingly, leading the way into the room. 'Can you guess?'

'Miranda!' The way Carlos Carvalho said her name was rather attractive, almost disposing of the *r* and replacing it by an *h*, in the Portuguese idiom. 'You are here at last! Did Jaime find you?'

'No. *I* did!' Teresa interposed, as her husband came round his desk to take Miranda's hand, and he glanced at her curiously.

'You did?'

'Miranda was driven up—by automobile!' his wife explained. 'We met in Santa Madalena.'

'*Quel*' Carlos looked amazed for a moment, and then he bent to raise Miranda's hand to his lips. '*Bem-vindo!* You are welcome to our house, Miranda.'

'Thank you.' Miranda was touched by his sincerity. They were all being so nice to her, and she half wished they weren't. It was easier to hurt people who had hurt you. 'I'm sorry I have to impose on you like this, but there was no hotel ...'

'Hotel?' Carlos cast a puzzled look at his wife before returning his attention to Miranda. 'Why should you need an hotel? You are my son's wife, *cara*. And Jaime is as much my son as Teresa's, believe me. Naturally you must stay here. With him!'

With him! Miranda felt a gulp of hysteria rising inside her. She wondered what Jaime's reactions to that statement would be. She had the feeling he would not see it quite like that. And she didn't want him to, after all. She was here for one reason, and one reason only—to get out of this impossible situation.

'Miranda has been ill,' Teresa added now, and her husband took up the inquiry.

'Ill?'

'It was nothing really,' Miranda said hastily. 'I—something I ate upset me. We stayed at an *estancia*, and——'

'You have been staying at an *estancia*!' interrupted Teresa, in dismay, but Miranda went on to explain how she had only spent one night at the inn, but two nights at the mission hospital.

'*Valha-me Deus!*' Teresa exclaimed. 'You were fortunate there was a hospital nearby. They are not plentiful in this area, as no doubt Jaime will convince you.'

'Well, I'm perfectly all right now,' Miranda assured her quickly, unwilling to open that topic of conversation again, and only wishing for a quiet place to lie down and rest her aching body and head.

As if sensing her weariness, Carlos snapped his fingers, and as if she had been waiting for the summons, Sancha appeared in the open doorway.

'Sancha will show you to your room,' he said, after issuing the old servant with incomprehensible instructions in her own language. 'As soon as Jaime returns, I will send him to you.'

'Thank you.'

Miranda trembled at that eventuality, but she was glad to make her escape.

As she left the room, however, in the wake of Sancha's ambling gait, Teresa added: 'We will eat later—much later. But I will have one of the servants fetch you some tea. You would like that?'

'Very much,' agreed Miranda fervently, and then closed the door on their sympathy. It was useless trying to pretend. In a matter of hours they would know why she had come here, and then their sympathy would disappear.

With many admiring backward glances, Sancha waddled

up the stairs ahead of the girl. Miranda assumed her cases
were still in the car, but they could be dealt with later. Right
now, she longed to soak her face in cold water, and prepare
herself for the ordeal that was to come.

Even so, she couldn't fail to admire her surroundings. The
stairs wound round in a graceful arc to the upper floor, and
above a grilled screen framed the long gallery that overlooked the hall below. Here there were portraits—of long-
dead Carvalhos?—set between the windows as was common
in European houses, and in the window embrasures, small
statuettes of Christ and His saints, signifying more eloquently
than words that this was a Catholic household.

But Miranda's room when she was shown into it momentarily dispelled her depression. Wide and high-ceilinged,
with long windows that opened on to a balcony, it was
scented with the perfume from a bowl of lilies which occupied a prominent place on the dark wood dressing table.
The walls were white and unadorned, except for a small
prie-dieu in one corner which could be illuminated by candles.
All the woodwork was dark, matching the dressing table,
while the curtains and bedspreads were tan-coloured wild
silk.

'*E bom, senhora?*' Sancha was regarding her anxiously,
and recognising the word for good, Miranda nodded.

'It's beautiful!' she said, smiling for the old woman's
benefit. Then: 'Do you speak any English?'

'*Ingles, senhora?*' Sancha frowned. '*Nao e facil*—is not
easy, no?'

Miranda heaved a sigh of relief. At least Sancha understood
something. Now she said: 'Thank you, anyway. *Obrigada!*'

'*Obrigada, senhora.*' Sancha's face beamed at her attempt
to use what little Portuguese she had. 'Is—anything else?'

Miranda shook her head then, her momentary elation
leaving her. 'Nothing else, thank you, Sancha.'

Sancha left her with obvious reluctance, but as soon as the
door had closed behind her wobbling form, Miranda sank
down weakly on to the side of the bed and surveyed her surroundings once more. She was here; she was actually *here*,
in Jaime's home. It was hardly believable.

After a few moments, the discomfort of her clothes made
itself evident, and she got to her feet and looked round for

the bathroom. There were two further doors—one which she discovered led into a kind of dressing room, with more heavy wardrobes and a single divan bed, and the other which opened into the biggest bathroom she had ever seen anywhere.

In the centre of the floor was a circular tub, big enough for her to float in, and all around was veined marble tiling in a delicious shade of copper bronze. Chrome-faced mirrors lined the walls, but leaved against one another so that it was possible to avoid one's reflection if one chose to do so. A shower cubicle, a pair of washbasins, a bidet; Miranda looked about her in astonishment, remembering her anticipation of this place with self-derision. She ought to have known that anyone who could reject the charm and beauty of the Hall had to have something better.

On impulse, she turned on the four chrome-plated taps that filled the bath, and quickly shed her clothes. There was no lock on the bathroom door, but that didn't trouble her. No one was likely to disturb her, except perhaps one of the servants, and they would not enter without permission.

She had made the water tepid, but warm enough to melt the oily perspiration from her skin. There were various kinds of fragrances to choose to scent the bath water, and she lay in its depths with the perfume of attar of roses seducing her tired mind into a state of numbed inertia.

She must have fallen asleep, because she awakened with a start to the sound of the outer door being slammed, and a harsh voice calling: *'Miranda!* Miranda, where are you?'

It was quite dark, and the water in the bath was cold, but there was no mistaking her husband's voice. She gasped in dismay, trying to reach for the towel and scramble out of the bath all at the same time. Her feet slipped on the marble tiles, but she managed to save herself, and was draping a huge green bathsheet about her like a sarong when the door opened and a light blinded her.

CHAPTER SIX

BLINKING helplessly, Miranda realised what a traumatic moment this was. Facing him after all this time was bad enough, but holding a far from secure towel about her damp body was worse. This was not how she had planned it would be. She had intended to be completely in control of herself when she met her husband again; cool, composed and elegant, the kind of woman he would be expecting to see. Instead, as was usual with him, he had put her at a disadvantage, and she was supremely conscious of her damp tousled hair and her bare feet visible below the folds of her improvised robe.

For his part, Jaime looked very little different from the way she remembered him. He was older, of course, and perhaps a little leaner, dressed in the kind of clothes she had never before seen him wearing. A dark blue shirt was open almost to his waist, exposing the brown expanse of flesh she had once speculated upon. His breeches were tight and black, moulding the powerful muscles of his thighs, and thrust into knee-length black boots which gave him a vaguely Cossack appearance. But it was to his face that her eyes were drawn, and she caught her breath at the bitterness she found there. Gone was the slightly mocking expression, she had once grown used to seeing; in its place was an angry scorn that was mirrored in the coldly smouldering depths of his eyes. His attitude towards her was one of arrogance and aggression, but she knew she must not be intimidated by it.

She opened her mouth to protest at his invasion of her privacy, but his words forestalled her:

'What the hell are you doing in here in the dark? Trying to drown yourself?'

Miranda gasped. 'No!'

He indicated the switch on the wall beside him. 'This is electricity, you know. Not a doorbell!'

'I know that,' she declared hotly. 'But is this any way to behave? If you must know, I fell asleep in the bath! What's so terrible about that?' She gathered the folds of the towel closer about her, and held up her head. 'What a way to greet anyone!'

His eyes narrowed, moving over her with a kind of ruthless appraisal. 'To greet anyone? To greet *you*, you mean? My wife!' His eyes moved to hers. 'What would you have me do? *Kiss* you?'

Miranda thought she could feel firmer ground beneath her feet. 'Oh, no!' she taunted coldly. 'No, I wouldn't expect that. Not from you!'

She realised her mistake as soon as the words were uttered, but there was no retracting them.

'Why not from me?' he demanded, his voice low and menacing. 'Yes, why not from me? I've waited long enough to try you out, God knows. Perhaps this is the moment.'

'Don't touch me——' she began, taking a step backward, only to be baulked by the open expanse of water behind her, and smiling almost maliciously, Jaime reached for her.

His hands dug into the soft skin of her upper arms, squeezing and moulding the flesh with almost sadistic pleasure. Miranda struggled manfully, but her feet were bare and she had no weapons against him. A picture of Mark came into her mind, increasing the panic inside her, increasing the realisation of how, by coming here, she had placed herself at this man's mercy. Who would help her here? Who could help her anywhere?

Letting go of the towel with one hand, she fought to reach his face, longing to rake her nails down his cheek, to draw blood as he was drawing blood of a different kind. But it was useless, and he just pulled her closer to him so that she was made unavoidably aware of the hardness of his body confined within the tautness of his clothing. Were all men like this, she thought bitterly, only intent on satisfying their own beastly appetites, uncaring that a woman did not feel as they did, did not know the demands of the flesh that governed their actions? Mark's distorted features appeared before her again, his arms tight bands about her, forcing her down on to the planks, his wet lips seeking to soil her cringing flesh ...

Yet it was Jaime's hand that was at her nape now, turning her face up to his, she realised dazedly, and she closed her eyes against the lustful gaze she was sure she would see

there. Oh God, she prayed desperately, make him stop ...
But then his mouth was covering hers, and she waited despairingly for the revulsion which was sure to follow.

Perhaps if his kiss had been as aggressive as his words
had been, she might have reacted differently, she thought
afterwards, but it wasn't. His mouth against hers was caressing, persuasive, parting her trembling lips without effort,
arousing an answering response deep within her. Almost
without volition, her fists stopped pressing against his chest,
relaxed, uncurled, spread across the smoothness of bone and
muscle, only lightly covered with fine dark hair. The towel
was forgotten as his lips continued to play with hers, softly,
tantalisingly, until with an abandon she afterwards con-
demned herself for revealing, she wound her arms around
his neck, and with her hand behind his head, compelled a
hardening of his mouth.

She heard the mocking laugh that started deep in his throat;
heard it, and hated him for it. He was just playing with her,
she thought bitterly, as his lips were playing with her mouth
he was using her, amusing himself with her, finding out how
far she was prepared to go. *And she had let him!* She
who, until this moment, had never welcomed any man's
touch. Why was it that she must always subjugate herself to
this man's will, make herself look small, lose what little self-
respect she had in his presence? Was she a complete fool?
She had made this journey to ask him for an annulment
of their marriage, and instead she was behaving as if she
wanted it consummating! She must be mad to imagine he
could ever change from the sardonic brute he had always
been.

She struggled to free herself, and because he wasn't entirely expecting it, Jaime let her put some space between
them, although the recklessness of her action caused the
remaining shreds of towelling to slide ignominiously to the
marble tiles. Miranda was horrified and embarrassed, her arms
automatically reaching to cover herself, while he watched her
with the mocking expression which had partially replaced his
earlier coldness.

'Do not be ashamed,' he drawled lazily. 'You have a
beautiful body—and a man may look at his wife, may he
not? I give you permission to look at me any time you

choose.'

Her cheeks flamed. 'You're disgusting!' she declared furiously, arousing his derisive laughter. 'And I'm not your wife!'

His look narrowed. 'But you are, little one,' he contradicted her succinctly. 'Make no mistake about that. I once told you—our marriage is for life. I meant what I said.'

Miranda clenched her fists as a feeling of impotence spread over her, and with sardonic gallantry Jaime bent to retrieve the towel she had dropped. She looked down at his bent head and something irresistible came over her. Without really stopping to think of the consequences, she brought her hands down hard upon his shoulders, pushing him sideways and jerking him off balance. There was a moment when he tried to save himself and the eyes he turned up to her mirrored his astonishment. And then, with a splash which sent a wave of water sweeping over her toes, he was submerged in her cold bath water.

It was a horrifying moment. As soon as he hit the water, Miranda realised the enormity of her crime, but a kind of hypnotic paralysis kept her glued to the side of the bath.

He surfaced, almost in slow motion she felt, shaking back the hair from his eyes, water streaming from his head and shoulders. His eyes sought and found hers, blazing with a fury she had never seen before. It was sufficient to bring her to her senses and life to her immobile limbs. Grasping the towel which, although it was damp, still maintained a semblance of absorption, she ran for the bedroom, stopping short at the sight of a dark-skinned maid busily unpacking her suitcases into the drawers of the dressing table and wardrobe.

'Oh!' Miranda sucked in her breath and hastily wound the towel about her, moving slowly into the room as the sounds of Jaime's emergence from the bath came clearly to her ears. What would he do now? she wondered apprehensively, and looked almost appealingly towards the maidservant, wishing she understood and could speak her language.

'*Boa noite, senhora!*' The girl was smiling, and casting an anxious look over her shoulder, Miranda managed to return the smile.

'*Boa noite,*' she responded awkwardly, and the girl went

on to indicate what she was doing, chattering away all the
while. Miranda didn't understand a word of what she was
saying, she spoke much too fast, but she knew the moment
Jaime appeared in the doorway behind her, because the girl's
mouth curved into a silent *O*, and she stared in amazement.

Miranda couldn't resist a glance towards the door, catching her tongue between her teeth when she saw her husband.
He had stripped off his wet shirt, but his pants clung to him
like a second skin, exposing his undoubted maleness. The
sight of him did things to her she did not and *would not*
acknowledge, and she forced away the primitive emotions
that flooded her whole being with unwelcome warmth.

'*Senhor!*'

The maid's involuntary exclamation caused him to look her
way, and controlling his features, he dismissed her anxiety in
a few words. '*Nao importa*, Elena,' he reassured her curtly.
'*Pode ir. Quero mudar.*'

'*Esta certo, senhor?*' she protested, and he nodded, half
impatiently, so that with an apologetic look towards Miranda,
Elena left them.

The silence after the door had closed was almost stifling,
broken only by the occasional sound of water dripping from
her husband's saturated clothes on to the polished blocks of
the floor. Miranda turned nervous eyes in his direction, sure
that her chastisement, whatever form it might take, was
no longer to be avoided, but he ignored her. Half to her
dismay, he squelched his way in the water-filled boots across
the rug-strewn floor and disappeared into the dressing room.
She was left with the oppressive awareness of retribution
to come, and her shoulders sagged with nervous exhaustion.

If it had not been so terrifying, it might have been funny,
and a wave of hysteria rose inside her, to be as quickly
doused. Punishment had been postponed for the moment,
but it was up to her to ensure that it was never realised. The
most disturbing thing was to discover that Jaime appeared
to use these rooms as his own. If only she had thought
to look inside the wardrobes in the dressing room, what
might she have found? His possessions? His *clothes*? Could
this possibly be his room as well as hers?

With this horrifying thought she turned to look at the bed.
It was certainly big enough to accommodate half a dozen

adults, and like the bath was bigger than any bed she had ever slept in.

But *no*! She gathered the folds of the towel closer about her. It couldn't be true, could it? And if it was, how could she explain to his mother that she wanted to sleep alone? Unless she told her the truth, of course ...

She started violently as a huge moth, attracted by the lamps which had been illuminated in the room, propelled itself suicidally against the glass. Was everything larger than life here? Miranda wondered, realising she was near to tears. Oh God, perhaps she should have let Paul come with her, after all. At least it would have destroyed once and for all the ambiguity of the situation.

She was still standing there, shivering a little, when Jaime emerged from the dressing room. He had taken off his wet clothes and put on a navy blue towelling bathrobe, and for a moment all her previous anxieties returned to torment her. But then she saw the garments folded over his arm and realised he intended to use the bathroom himself.

'Don't look so terrified,' he told her coldly. 'I'm only going to take a shower. I'm not addicted to bathing in someone else's water.'

Miranda licked her dry lips. 'You—you deserved it,' she got out tremulously.

'And what do you deserve, I wonder?' he parried harshly. 'Coming here, without an invitation?'

'Your mother said I was welcome!' she broke in defensively, but he had gone past her into the bathroom, and seconds later she heard the sound of the shower.

He had not closed the bathroom door, and pressing her lips together resentfully, Miranda made her way towards it, and reaching in, slammed it shut. Then she went across to her almost empty cases before pulling open the dressing table drawers to see where Elena had put her underclothes.

The maid had left several garments lying on the bed, dresses that were creased from being so long in the suitcases, and Miranda guessed she had been going to take them and press them. But hanging in the wardrobe were halter-necked culottes, in a becoming shade of pearl grey, that complemented the golden colouring of her skin and was a foil for the burnished glory of her hair. Made of polyester, they had not been crushed, and Miranda decided they were sufficiently sophisticated to accomplish the image she wanted to achieve.

Collecting a scanty pair of briefs, she cast a doubtful look at the bathroom door. She would change in the dressing room, she decided, and pray that Jaime didn't finish before she did.

It took little time to complete drying her body. She had no talc to hasten the process, but a brisk rub with the towel toned up her skin and dispelled the shivering. Dressed again, she felt more capable of facing him, and pushing back the weight of her hair with a critical hand, she emerged into the bedroom again.

She was considering her appearance before the long mirrors of the wardrobe when she suddenly became aware of eyes watching her, and turning, she saw that Jaime had opened the bathroom door and was waiting for her to notice his presence. She flushed, but did not move away from the mirrors as she guessed he expected her to do, and he walked lazily towards her.

'Don't let me interrupt,' he remarked sardonically, and she faced him with as much confidence as she could muster.

'I won't,' she retorted coldly. 'But perhaps you could tell me whether your parents dress for dinner.'

'Do you call this dressing?' he inquired, sliding an inquisitive finger along the low neckline of the halter, and she jerked back from him angrily.

'I've worn culottes for more formal occasions than family dinners,' she exclaimed angrily, becoming increasingly aware of how easily he could destroy her confidence. 'Are you going down like that?'

Jaime looked down at his maroon shirt, unbuttoned at the neckline and wrists, the cuffs folded to reveal the dark hairs on his arms, and the leather strap of his wristwatch; and close-fitting corded pants in a darker shade of maroon that flared slightly at his ankles. His feet were bare, she saw now, and there was something disturbingly initimate about that realisation.

'You do not think I am dressed suitably?' he suggested evenly, and Miranda felt the situation slipping away from her once more.

'I really don't care how you dress,' she replied tersely, and deliberately seated herself on the stool at the dressing table, reaching for her vanity case and extracting her eyeliner.

Jaime stood watching her for several disruptive moments, showing no regret when she smudged the mascara on to her cheek and had to remove it with a tissue. Her hands were shaking so much she was amazed she could draw a line at all, and she thought with fury that he knew exactly what he was doing.

'Interesting,' he said at last, when she fumbled blindly for eye-shadow. 'I've often wondered how women achieve that result.'

Miranda did not answer him, and with a sigh he leant over her, resting one hand on the dressing table, and hooking the other into the low belt of his pants. It brought his face unnervingly close to her, and she had to steel herself not to move away.

'There is just one thing . . .' he murmured, and his tone was deceptively mild. 'How much longer are you going to take to tell me why you've come here?'

Miranda dropped the tiny brush she was holding, and a cloud of eye-shadow rose from its bristles. 'I—I've hardly had the chance, have I?'

'Perhaps not,' he conceded levelly. 'But you have now. I'm interested to know why—after making the journey here— you should tell me that you're *not* my wife.'

Miranda heaved an unsteady breath. 'Don't you—don't you think we should—should wait? Until later?'

'Why?' He didn't move, and she could feel the shallowness of her breathing beginning to make her breathless.

'I—well, this isn't—there isn't time, right now.'

'What you really mean is, what you have to say is going to cause one hell of a row, and you'd rather we didn't have it just before going down to eat dinner with my parents, right?' he told her grimly, and Miranda stared at him uncertainly.

'You—you don't know that!'

'What if I tell you I do?'

'I—you—you can't. I—I haven't spoken to anyone.'

'No one?' His lips twisted. 'Not even—Aunt Lydia?'

'Aunt Lydia!' Miranda stared at him aghast. 'What—

what about Aunt Lydia?'

'Did you or did you not tell Aunt Lydia?' he demanded.

'I—why, yes. Yes, of course. But you haven't—that is——'
she broke off as an awful thought struck her. 'Did Aunt
Lydia write to you?'

'No.'

He shook his head and she breathed again, but not for
long.

'Ask me if I've spoken to Aunt Lydia,' he taunted her
coldly, and she gasped.

'You—*haven't*!'

'Oh, yes, I have.'

'But—but how——'

'You had disappeared, remember? I wanted to know where
you were. I wanted to know what your plans were. Who
better to ask than Aunt Lydia?'

'Oh, my God!'

Miranda felt sick, and all the colour drained out of her
face. But for once Jaime was indifferent to her feelings.

'My God, indeed!' he muttered harshly. 'But let's get one
thing straight, here and now. There will be no annulment of
this marriage, do you understand? None whatsoever!'

The evening meal was served in a long gallery that adjoined
a kind of indoor garden. Luscious velvety leaves preened
themselves beside exotically coloured blossoms that opened
their petals beneath the artificial lights that floodlit the area.
Musky perfume mingled with the incense from candles
that lit the length of the table, blood-red candles that rivalled
the passion-flowers for prominence.

Jaime had left Miranda to make her own way downstairs
after delivering his ultimatum, and it was on shaking legs
that she finally joined the other members of his family in
the conservatory for drinks before the meal. Teresa Carvalho
was there, and Carlos, her husband, but as well as Jaime,
there was another young couple present.

'Allow me to present to you our youngest daughter, Julia,
and her *novio*, Miguel Santana,' exclaimed Carlos when
Miranda appeared, going to meet her with admiring eyes.
'Julia, Miguel, this is Miranda!'

Jaime's sister was like him, Miranda thought. Dark-haired,

dark-eyed, with the same straight nose and uncompromising mouth. She guessed the Portuguese girl to be in her early twenties, as she was, but she looked older.

Julia regarded her sister-in-law without enthusiasm, and then, inspired no doubt by her stepfather's expectant smile, she kissed her briefly on both cheeks.

'Good evening, Miranda,' she said politely. 'You are not at all as I expected you to be.'

Not sure whether or not this was a compliment, Miranda managed an equally polite rejoinder, and then shook hands with Miguel. He, unlike his fiancée, lingered longer than was necessary over the greeting, making Miranda aware of the hardening cast of Jaime's features as he watched them.

Then Carlos offered her a drink, and she accepted the champagne he suggested. 'It is not every day that we can greet such an attractive new member of our family,' he said as he handed her the tall glass, and she cast a discomfited look in Jaime's direction as she accepted the pretty compliment.

'Jaime tells us you drove up from Rio,' Julia commented, coming to stand beside her, her dark eyes roving critically over Miranda's bare shoulders. She herself was wearing a dress similar to the one her mother was wearing, all black, with only touches of white at the neckline and wrists. Their attire reminded Miranda of something she had read once about Spanish and Portuguese women preferring black to any other colour, and she wondered if that was why Jaime had mocked her appearance.

Now she nodded, and said: 'Yes. I hired a chauffeur. I didn't trust myself to drive so far, and—and over—such roads.'

Her voice trailed away towards the end, as she realised that Julia might not appreciate the criticism of her country's transportation facilities, and as if to confirm this belief, the other girl said: 'We do not expect miracles overnight, Miranda. We have a big country here. Naturally it will take time to create the kind of urban civilisation you are used to, if indeed we ever want it to happen.'

Miranda considered herself reproved, and was surprised when Jaime, who had been standing indolently to one side, regarding the proceedings with a certain air of detachment, suddenly said: 'You would not have wanted my wife to

plunge to her death over a precipice, would you, Julia? You
have to admit the road from Rio leaves a lot to be desired.'

Julia's magnolia complexion became tinged with pink.
'Of course not, Jaime,' she retorted crossly. 'I was merely
pointing out that Brazil cannot be compared to a little
country like England.'

'I'm sure Miranda has been made painfully aware of that,'
put in Teresa lightly, and Jaime's brows drew together.

'Painfully?' he echoed. 'How so?'

'Oh, *caro*, I didn't have time to tell you, did I?' his mother
exclaimed regretfully. She gave Miranda a confiding smile.
'When he learned that you were here, he didn't give me time
for explanations.'

Guessing to what Teresa was referring, Miranda quickly
tried to evade the issue by turning to Carlos and saying:
'This is a beautiful garden. Tell me, what are these white
flowers? They look so fragile somehow.'

'They are called *Inocencia*,' Carlos told her smilingly, but
Jaime was beside her, and judging from his expression he
was not about to be diverted.

'In what way was your introduction painful?' he repeated,
and she sighed impatiently.

'It's not important,' she protested. 'I—if you must know,
I had a—tummy upset.'

'What kind of tummy upset?' he insisted, and to her
dismay Carlos turned away to attend to his wife's request
for another glass of champagne, leaving her to answer
Jaime's questions alone.

Speaking in an undertone, Miranda tried to make light of
it. 'We—the chauffeur, that is—suggested we spent the night
at a roadside *estancia*. I—I must have eaten something that
didn't agree with me.'

'*Meu Deus!*' He shook his head in exasperation. 'Why did
you not stay in one of the small towns you passed? At least
you would have found an hotel there. What did you eat?'

'Oh, please ...' She glanced round in embarrassment. 'I
can't remember now——'

'*Tortillas?*'

Miranda swallowed sickly, remembering. 'Perhaps.'

He nodded. 'What happened?'

She gasped. 'Do you want all the sordid details?'

'Did any doctor treat you?'

'Yes. I was taken to the local mission hospital.'

'Where?'

'I don't know.' She frowned. 'Some place—Marmora—Marmara—something like that.'

'Marmoreo?'

'That sounds like it.'

'You would see a Doctor Gonzales, yes?'

'Honestly, is all this important?'

'Food poisoning is always important.'

'I'm perfectly all right now.'

'Like these flowers you so admire?'

'If you like,' she sighed.

'But not so innocent, mmm?'

Miranda's colour defeated her. 'Will you please stop this! You know nothing about me. You never have.'

His dark brows lifted. 'No? I think I do, *Lady* Sanders.'

'If you must know, I don't use that title!' she declared fiercely. 'I never have.'

Jaime's lips thinned. 'Perhaps it's time you did.'

'I don't intend to be entitled to it much longer,' she retorted in a low angry voice, and then was relieved of whatever reply Jaime might have made by Carlos taking her arm.

'Come,' he said. 'Supper is served. Permit me to escort my daughter-in-law to the table.'

Miranda could not have felt more discomfited by his choice of words, particularly as she was aware of Jaime's eyes following their progress. Tomorrow, she told herself firmly, tomorrow she would speak to Carlos—and Teresa. She would tell them exactly why she had made this journey to Monte Paraiso.

CHAPTER SEVEN

THE sound of men's voices woke her; men's voices shouting to one another, and the less aggressive sounds of cattle protesting at their handling. There was the vibration, too, from hooves striking the hard surface of the courtyard, and the occasional whinny from an excited horse.

Unable to resist her curiosity, Miranda pushed back the bedcovers and went barefoot across the floor to the long windows, drawing aside the curtains tentatively, peering through the rails of the balcony down to the yard below.

A group of *gauchos* such as she had seen in the distance the day before were milling around, talking and laughing together, and in a small corral she could see the handful of steers they had brought in. Another man she had not seen before was talking to the men, and she guessed from his attire that he was some kind of estates manager. He was dressed much as Jaime had been dressed when he burst in upon her the day before, boots and breeches, and rough cotton shirt, but without the leather leggings the *gauchos* were wearing to protect their legs.

Thinking of Jaime brought Miranda round to rest against the wall beside the windows, her lips parting as her tongue sought her upper lip. It brought back the memory of the previous evening, and its nerve-racking finale.

Supper had been over too soon and Miranda, who had partaken little of the spicy mixture of meat and vegetables and swallowed only a few mouthfuls of the light lemon soufflé that followed, had dreaded the moment when she and Jaime would be alone together once more.

When the meal was over, they had all adjourned to the *sala*, a kind of drawing room, where Julia seated herself at a magnificent grand piano and played while her mother served coffee. She was quite an accomplished pianist, and Miranda tried to relax in a deep velvet armchair, sipping her coffee and surveying her surroundings with objective admiration.

As in most of the rooms she had seen, the walls of the *sala* were white, but here the ceiling was intricately moulded, and there were some attractive miniatures hanging over the marble-framed fireplace. It was a large room and in tall cupboards beside the windows Miranda could see an exquisite collection of porcelain. She would have liked to have walked across and examined the pieces more closely, but shyness, and the sense of being here under false pretences, kept her in her seat. Luckily, Miguel Santana's attentions kept Jaime at bay, and he stood squarely before the screened fireplace swallowing a succession of brandies. His very stillness was unnerving, however, and Miranda waited apprehensively for the axe to fall.

Conversation played over a variety of subjects, including the impressions Miranda had formed since her arrival in Brazil. She was quite willing to speak impersonally about Rio, and the problems of communicating over such a large area, but when her own experiences were brought up once more she made a determined effort, to evade further discussions of her health by insinuating that she was tired, which indeed she was.

Teresa excused her at once. Unfortunately, she excused Jaime too, her manner proclaiming an intimacy between them which Miranda had hoped to avoid. There was nothing for it but to allow him to accompany her upstairs, but when she reached the door of *the* room—she could hardly consider it *hers*—she halted uncertainly and turned to confront him.

Jaime reached past her, however, and opening the door pushed her unceremoniously inside. Protesting silently, Miranda stumbled across to the bed and Jaime closed the door before saying harshly:

'Have the sense to keep your arguments behind closed doors. This is not England; this is not the Hall!'

'Believe it or not, but I had noticed,' she retorted, anger momentarily overriding her nervousness. 'Will you please get out of here?'

Jaime regarded her coldly. 'Why should I? This is my room.'

'It can't be——'

'I assure you it is.' He flung open the door into the dressing room. 'My clothes are here, should you doubt me.'

'But—but how——'

'Naturally when my mother learned you were coming she made arrangements for you to share my apartments. What is so unusual about that? We are married, as I keep reminding you.'

'But—but we've never lived together——'

'She doesn't know that.'

'We haven't seen one another for four years!'

'She doesn't know that either.'

'What do you mean?' Miranda was confused.

'Do you imagine I've spent the whole of the last four years in Brazil?' His lips twisted. 'I have visited England several times, as a matter of fact. I've even seen you—if only from a distance.'

'What?' Miranda stared at him. 'You mean—you—you——'

'I mean my mother thinks our marriage has been strained. That your refusal to come and live in Brazil——'

'*My* refusal!'

'—is responsible for our estrangement. She sees your arrival here now as a confirmation that you have decided you can't live without me any longer.'

Miranda's face blanched. It had all been too much. First the rigours of the journey, then that first encounter with her husband, and now this! She felt physically sick, and she leaned against the carved bedpost, striving for calm.

'You—you'll have to tell her the truth,' she gulped, haunted eyes gazing despairingly at him.

'I don't think so,' he replied inflexibly. 'And now I can see you really are tired. I was going to examine you, but I don't think that is necessary tonight. Several hours' sleep should prove invaluable, and you'll have plenty of time to recover.'

'I—I won't stay here!' she declared unsteadily. 'You can't make me.'

'Don't be childish,' he retorted brusquely, walking back to the outer door, and Miranda stared at him helplessly.

'Where are you going?'

'I shall sleep elsewhere tonight,' he informed her, with a cold smile. 'I am not so inhuman as to force myself upon an exhausted woman.'

'Aren't you?' she demanded tremulously, and earned a distinct hardening of his jawline.

'Don't try me too far, Miranda,' he advised her quietly. 'Or I may change my mind.'

She remained silent then, remembering uneasily the emotions he had aroused in her earlier. She didn't want to recall the wanton way she had responded, or speculate upon the outcome of that encounter if he had not found her behaviour amusing.

But surely he couldn't mean what he was saying now. Could his mother really not know the circumstances of their so-called marriage? Did she not regard her son's wife as the mercenary social climber Jaime considered her to be? Was that why, although he had forbidden her to come here, he was determined that she should stay?

'I'll say goodnight, then,' he said now, reaching for the handle of the door, and her eyes were irresistibly drawn to the way the maroon material of his jacket was stretched tautly across his broad shoulders. Then, aware that his eyes missed little, she dropped her gaze, studying the toes of her sandals until she heard the door close behind him. But when she went hastily to it afterwards, there was no key with which to lock it against him, and she undressed for bed with a distinct feeling of vulnerability.

But now it was morning, and the sun was filtering through the curtains, warming the tiles beneath her feet, and making her aware of her state of undress. She would take a shower this morning, she thought firmly, moving away from the wall. At least that way she could close the door of the cubicle and avoid another fiasco such as she had experienced the previous day.

She had showered and dressed in purple jeans and a sleeveless vest before she thought to look at her watch, and when she did so she gasped. It was six-thirty. *Six-thirty!* She couldn't ever remember being up so early, except perhaps on that long-ago tenth birthday ... But she wouldn't think of that now.

She brushed her hair until it shone, and realised with relief that she felt completely well this morning. Even the lingering aftermath of nausea had gone, and she felt ready to face anything. *Anything?* She shrugged the thought aside.

Anything, she decided firmly.

Unable to sit still with the sun shining and a whole new world waiting to be explored, she paced restlessly about the bedroom. She had no idea of the arrangements for breakfast, but if it was anything like the Hall, the meal was invariably served in the guest's bedroom, and she dreaded to think how long it might be before anyone got around to rousing her. Jaime would no doubt expect her to sleep late after her journey, but her mind was too active. Right now, she was putting all thoughts of her relationship with Jaime out of her mind and concentrating instead on the undoubtedly exciting prospect of what lay beyond the cool walls of the hacienda.

On impulse she pulled open the door to the dressing room, intending to confirm Jaime's statement about the whereabouts of his clothes, and then stopped dead at the sight that confronted her. Jaime was sleeping in the dressing room, his long length reclining beneath the thin sheet covering the divan, one brown arm trailing lazily to the cream rug beside the bed.

Miranda's hands went involuntarily to her face. This was an aspect of her husband she had never seen before. In sleep, he seemed younger, more approachable, vulnerable even. The silk sheets barely covered his lower limbs, and the bones of his rib-cage stood out whitely beneath the brown skin. The strong column of his throat was relaxed in sleep, his mouth without the thin line of scorn or derision it wore often when he looked at her. His hair, which normally followed the line of his collar, was tousled, revealing an unexpected tendency to curl, and that added to an air of unconscious sensuality. It made her wonder what it must be like to sleep with a man. Not this man, she mentally hastened, but any man: Paul, for instance. Until this moment, she had seen more of Paul's body than her husband's. They had swum together many times, and the brief shorts he had worn had left little to the imagination. But it was different with Jaime somehow. With him she always felt this intense awareness of suppressed sexuality, and even looking at him like now she could feel a curious stirring deep inside her.

With an unsteadily indrawn breath, she turned more silently than she had come, and quickly put herself outside the dressing room door. Jaime need never know she had entered the room, and it was certain she did not want to draw attention to the fact.

Even as these thoughts passed through her brain, they were superseded by other, more disturbing speculations. How had Jaime got into the dressing room? Was there another door? Or had he walked through her bedroom while she lay sleeping? It was an unsettling notion, and she wished she had paid more attention to the dressing room while she had the chance. As it was, all she could remember were the wardrobe doors and the bed, and practically nothing after that ...

She resumed her pacing about her own room and then, with a silent curse, she opened the door and stepped out into the hallway outside.

It was cooler in the hall, and the draught moved the pale chiffon curtains in a window embrasure. Further along was the grilled screen of the balcony which overlooked the hall below, and feeling too restless to stay in her room, Miranda moved towards it.

Even at this hour of the morning a maid was busily dusting the intricate ironwork of the balustrade, kneeling on the stairs as she descended, humming softly to herself. She looked up in surprise when she became aware of Miranda at the head of the stairs, and getting to her feet made a sort of bob.

'Bom dia, senhora,' she greeted her shyly. 'Posso ajuda-la?'

As this sounded totally incomprehensible, Miranda took two steps down the stairs, and said rather hopefully: 'Er—fala ingles?'

'Ah, ingles.' The girl nodded knowingly. 'A little, senhora.'

She said little as if it was spelt with a double e instead of double t, and Miranda, who was not yet used to their soft accent, was enchanted.

'What is your name?' she asked, and the girl bobbed again.

'Chiquita, senhora. Er—you wish—pequeno almoco?'

'Pequeno almoco,' echoed Miranda cautiously. 'What is that?'

Chiquita frowned. 'Pequeno almoco, senhora.' She bit her lip, and then, her eyes brightening, she mimed eating and drinking and Miranda realised what she was saying.

'You mean breakfast,' she said, and Chiquita giggled, looking much relieved.

'*Sim, senhora*. Breadfas'.'

Miranda expelled her breath on a sigh. It was going to be harder than she had thought. Choosing her words carefully, she said: 'Where does Senhora Carvalho take breakfast?'

'You, *senhora*?' Chiquita looked confused again, and Miranda suppressed a moment's impatience.

'No,' she shook her head. 'Not me. Senhora Carvalho.'

'You are Senhora Carvalho, *senhora*,' protested Chiquita anxiously, and Miranda remembered suddenly what Teresa had said the day before.

Clasping her hands together, she tried again. 'I mean Senhora *Teresa*,' she explained precisely, and Chiquita at last understood.

'Senhora Teresa, *senhora*? Senhora Teresa does not eat—er—breakfast, no? She has the *cafe, senhora*.'

'*Cafe*? Oh, you mean coffee.' Miranda understood this. 'Well, perhaps I could have some coffee—*cafe*—too?'

'You like some *cafe, senhora*?'

'That's what I said.'

'*Imediatamente, senhora.*'

'Thank you.'

Chiquita clattered away down the stairs, upsetting a can of polishing fluid at the bottom, and leaving Miranda feeling as exhausted as if she had just climbed the stairs at top speed. It was obvious that a knowledge of the language was going to be essential for a prolonged stay here, but, she consoled herself determinedly, a prolonged stay was not what she had in mind.

Once downstairs, she stepped down into the split-level lounge which gave such a splendid view of the mountains. At this hour of the morning with the sun barely touching the higher slopes with a creamy opalescence and the valleys hiding themselves beneath thick foliage, only the vivid stretch of the river had reality. As she watched, a flight of wild geese rose from their nesting place in the reed-edged shallows and ascended skyward, the shadow of their wing-span moving swiftly over the land. Someone had opened the windows and through them she could smell the water, dark and deep, and as mysterious in its own right as the mountains it moated. At this height above sea-level, the air was fresh and clear, and cool enough to warrant a sweater.

Miranda was rubbing her elbows with her palms when she heard footsteps behind her, and turning apprehensively she was relieved to find it was only Carlos who had come to join her.

'*Madre*, you are an early riser, Miranda,' he greeted her warmly. Then his eyes showed concern. 'You did not sleep well?'

'I slept very well, thank you,' she reassured him swiftly, 'and I feel wonderful this morning. But—well, I heard some voices outside, and I couldn't wait to find out what was going on.'

'The *gauchos*!' Carlos exclaimed at once. 'I forgot Jaime's apartments are directly above the courtyard. I am sorry. He is, of course, used to it.'

Miranda managed not to show her disconcertment. Until he mentioned it, she had forgotten that these people would expect her and Jaime to have shared the same bed.

'I—we—Jaime is still asleep,' she managed at last, and Carlos gave her an old-fashioned look.

'He is? He must be tired, eh? He does not usually sleep so late.'

Miranda was really embarrassed now, and to hide her feelings, she turned once again to the mountains, asking Carlos to point out the different peaks to her, showing an interest in the *serras* she would never normally have shown. If he thought her curiosity was misplaced, no doubt he put it down to a natural reticence, she thought, and was inordinately relieved when Chiquita appeared with her coffee.

'Is good, *senhora*?' she asked, obviously showing off her English in front of her master, and Carlos bestowed an affectionate slap on her rump as she ran giggling from the room.

There were two cups and a pot of steaming coffee, as well as cream and sugar. Perhaps Chiquita had expected her to take the tray back to the bedroom, but Miranda had no intention of returning there until Jaime had put on some clothes.

'Will—will you join me?' she asked Carlos instead, and after a moment's hesitation, he agreed. They sat on the low

window seat, which was covered with a long brown cushion
striped in an attractive bamboo pattern, and Miranda took
charge of the coffee pot. It was quite strange, serving Carlos
coffee in his own house only the day after her arrival. But as
Carlos spoke, she began to understand that the situation was
not as straightforward as she had thought.

She said: 'I think your house is beautiful!' but Carlos
quickly explained that the house was not, in fact, his.

'You know that Jaime's father, Patrick Knevett, owned
this estate, do you not?' he asked, and she volunteered that
in fact she knew very little.

'Aunt Lydia—that is, Patrick's cousin's wife—only told me
that Jaime's father had had estates in Brazil, and that after
he died, Jaime's mother married again,' she said awkwardly,
wishing she could explain that this past history did not
concern her, but Carlos obviously wanted her to understand
the situation.

'You are correct, of course. Patrick did own estates in
Brazil, but he died when Jaime was just a boy, and it was
obvious that Teresa could not continue to run the place alone.
That was when I stepped in. My own land bounded the
Knevett land on two sides, and I agreed to buy the land from
Teresa on the understanding that when Jaime was older,
should he wish to take over, he could buy it back again at
what you would say was a—nominal fee.'

'I see.'

'Of course, as you know, Jaime was more interested in
people than cattle, and as by then Teresa and I were married,
instead of uprooting the children to go and live at Valmonte,
which was my house, I moved in here. But this house and
the land immediately around it belongs to your husband.'

Miranda was disturbed to find that this news affected her.
It had no bearing on her circumstances, and yet she felt a
sense of pride in the knowledge that as Jaime's wife she had
as much right here as Carlos himself. But not for long, she
told herself soberly, forcing an image of Paul into her mind.
She wondered what he was doing now, what he was thinking. It was over a week since her departure, and she had sent
him no word. But what could she tell him, after all? Until
she had made her position clear ...

'Tell me about yourself,' Carlos was saying now. 'Jaime

has told us so little about you, but I know he is delighted that you have seen your way clear to come and join him at last.'

Now was her opportunity, but she faltered. 'You're very kind,' she murmured, and inwardly scorned her cowardice for what it was when he went on:

'Teresa—Jaime's mother—so much wanted to see her son married. He has three sisters, as you know, two of whom are already married themselves, but he is her only son. I hoped—we both hoped—when we married that there might be other sons. But ...' he spread his hands expressively, 'it was not to be.' He smiled. 'Our greatest hope now is for a grandchild, no? Neither Juana nor Jaquetta have any children, and I know Teresa would be overjoyed if her firstborn produced the first grandchild.'

The situation got worse! Miranda had not thought it could, but it did. Now not only did they think she was Jaime's wife, in every sense of the word, but they expected her to bear his son. How could she say to this man that she was here because their marriage had never been a marriage? That her intention was to obtain an annulment, as soon as possible, to marry someone else? She should never have come, that realisation was being borne in on her, but what could she have done when Jaime never wrote to her, had not even replied when she told him her mother was dead?

Realising that Carlos was watching her reactions closely, Miranda managed to lift her coffee cup to her lips and sip gratefully at the contents. It gave her something to do, and silenced any reply he might be expecting her to make.

'This Aunt Lydia you mention,' Carlos said consideringly, 'she was some relation to Jaime's father, no? You and Jaime are distantly related, yes?'

'No!' Miranda put down her cup with a clatter. 'I mean —well, of course, we—we're married now. But Aunt Lydia— well, she's only my Aunt Lydia because of Jaime.'

'Ah!' Carlos looked throughtful. 'How long did you know Jaime before you realised you wanted to marry one another?'

That was more difficult. 'I—we—knew one another for years,' admitted Miranda uncomfortably. 'He—we met when I was ten, actually.'

'Ten years old!' Carlos slapped his knee and laughed

delightedly. 'A schoolboy passion, no?'

'Well, no,' said Miranda slowly, aware of the ludicrous aspects of the situation, and suppressing an hysterical desire to laugh also. 'Anything but.'

'Ah!' Carlos seemed to accept this, and raising his cup to his lips, finished his coffee with one gulp. 'And now, regrettably, I must leave you. There is work to be done.' He rose to his feet, and looked down at her. 'Do you ride, Miranda?'

'Why, yes,' she nodded.

'Good. Good. You must get Jaime to take you riding. This land can best be seen from the back of a horse.'

'Thank you.' Miranda wished she could take him up on that. She could not deny a fascination for her surroundings, but she must not let them seduce her from her purpose.

After Carlos had left her, Miranda finished her coffee, feeling considerably warmer. Whether the import of his words had had anything to do with it, or whether it was simply the warming influence of the hot liquid, she could not be sure, but she sat on in the window-seat, kicking off her shoes and drawing up her knees, and staring blindly out towards the river.

Eventually her flesh cooled again, and she looked reluctantly at her watch. It was after eight, so surely Jaime must be awake by now. Stretching her stiff legs, she got up, pushed her feet back into her canvas shoes, and climbed the steps into the hall again.

The smell of beeswax scented the air, and she guessed the polished blocks of the floor received regular attention. There was no sign of any of the servants, however, although the heavy doors to the building stood wide, and only a meshed screen divided her from the sounds of the stockyard beyond. She was tempted to open the screen and step outside, but somehow her ambiguous situation curtailed the kind of freedom she would have welcomed.

With a shrug of indecision, she climbed the stairs to the gallery once more, but as she passed along it, there were sounds of activity from outside, and even as she hesitated, a girl came striding into the house. She was of medium height and slim, with curling dark hair that formed an aureole around her head where the sunlight streaming in behind her projected her in bright relief. Dressed in a silk shirt and riding breeches, a crop gripped in her hand, she reminded Miranda of the society girls she had met in England—full of confidence.

Miranda wondered who she could be to walk into the house unannounced, and felt herself shrinking behind the iron grille, unwilling to be the one to greet their unknown visitor. She hoped no one would see her hovering uncertainly, and then her hand covered her mouth to suppress the gasp that rose inside her.

A man was entering the house behind the girl, dressed in the same kind of dark gear he had been wearing the day before, different only from the girl in that he was not carrying a riding crop. She turned as he came in and held out an eager hand towards him, and he took her hand and carried it warmly to his lips.

Jaime! Miranda turned away, sickened by what she had just seen. But she had left Jaime in bed! How could he be out with this girl, whoever she was? Unless it wasn't him? She took another fleeting look, and her cheeks burned. Oh, it had to be Jaime! Or his double!

On legs that were undeniably shaky, she walked quickly across the gallery and along the hall to her bedroom. And as she went, she inwardly seethed. This was the man who only last night had told her she would get no annulment of their marriage, the man Aunt Lydia had insinuated was more interested in spiritual things than physical ones. She turned her door handle with trembling fingers. Of course, last night should have shown her how wrong Aunt Lydia's assumption was. The way he had held her and kissed her, the way his body had responded to hers ... She ought to have realised he was no novice when it came to women. No man came by such expertise without experience.

Clenching her fists, she crossed the bedroom and flung open the dressing room door. As she had known it would be, the bed was empty. Jaime had gone!

She turned back into the room where she had slept with a feeling of frustration such as she had seldom felt before. My God, she thought furiously, that he should come downstairs and ignore her! And then make his reappearance with that—that female!

Pacing angrily about the room, she caught a glimpse of

her reflection in the vanity mirror and came to an abrupt halt. Was that really how she looked? So tight-lipped and sulky? In heaven's name, what was the matter with her? What had he done after all, if not play into her hands? Hadn't she wanted just such a lever as this? Wasn't it going to be easier to fight him with a few weapons of her own? The way she was behaving, anyone would think she was jealous! *Jealous!* She forced her features to relax and expelled the breath she had unknowingly been holding on a long sigh. She wasn't jealous, she was just angry, that was all. Angry, and irritated at the way he apparently thought he could deceive her!

She looked again in the mirror and her lips tightened once more at the casualness of her appearance. Was this the image she wanted to create? Jean-clad, easy-going, *unsophisticated*? Of course it wasn't. Even that girl downstairs in her well-cut riding breeches looked more sophisticated than she did, and with a grimace she tore off the offending cotton vest and rummaged in the wardrobe for something more suitable. Her fingers found a pleated cotton smock with wide sleeves and a square neckline, hand-embroidered in multi-coloured threads. She slipped it over her head, and was wriggling out of her jeans when her door opened and Jaime appeared.

'Don't you ever knock?' she demanded hotly, smoothing the smock down over her hips, and his lips twitched in faint amusement.

'As you seemed perfectly adequately covered five minutes ago when you were skulking on the landing——'

'I was not skulking!' she exclaimed, and then realised what he was saying. 'How did you know I was there?'

'How could I not be aware of the waves of antagonism sweeping down upon me?' he asked, in hollow tones, and she turned frustratedly away, reaching for her hairbrush.

'You're imagining things,' she told him coldly, wincing as the brush, rashly wielded, tangled itself, almost jerking the hair from her scalp, but Jaime's reflection in the mirror revealed his disbelief. Stepping forward, he lifted the brush out of her hand and before she could move away, commenced to brush the heavy curtain of silk with strong even strokes.

'I'd hazard a guess that your imagination is working overtime right now,' he remarked dryly, his free hand smoothing the hair as he brushed it, sliding down to her nape and lingering longer than was necessary against the acutely sensitised skin.

Miranda could only stand it for so long before she broke away from him, upper lip caught between her teeth, holding out her hand for the instrument of her torment.

'Thank you,' she said tautly, almost snatching the brush from him. 'I could have managed.'

'A husband should do things for his wife,' he drawled, hooking his thumbs into the belt of his pants, and she dropped the brush on to the dressing table, bitterly frustrated.

Swinging round again, she used the unit behind her for support as she faced him. 'How long are you intending to prolong this charade?' she demanded. 'When do you intend to tell your parents that my visit here is not a social one?'

'Isn't it?' He was infuriatingly cool. 'What else could it be?'

'Jaime, you know why I'm here——'

'I know why you made the trip.'

'Stop playing with words! You know what I mean.'

'And you've heard my opinion on it,' he responded, his voice perceptibly hardening. 'Don't remind me that some other man has pre-empted my rights with you, or I might be tempted to stake my claim!'

'Wh-what do you mean?'

'Oh, come on, Miranda. You're not some innocent school-girl, facing up to the headmaster. You're a woman—*my* woman!'

Miranda clenched her teeth to silence the retort that sprang to her lips. So what if he thought she and Paul were lovers? All the better for her. Another lever, perhaps.

Now she said provokingly: 'I'd have thought you'd be glad of your freedom!' but his reactions were less than gratifying.

'Why?' he taunted. 'Because of what you saw a few minutes ago? I wondered what had triggered this little scene.'

'You couldn't be more wrong,' she answered shortly, angrily aware that he had turned the tables once more. 'If you imagine I care what you do with your time——'

'You don't?'

'Of course not.'

'I'll remember that.'

Miranda heaved a sigh. 'Oh, why do you persist in behaving like an ostrich? I intend to have my divorce—annulment—call it what you will. And you can't stop me!'

'Can't I?'

Miranda put a nervous hand to her hair, vaguely disturbed by his inflexibility. 'Jaime, for heaven's sake! We're two adult people ...'

'I go along with that.'

'... so why can't you accept that it does no good pretending things are normal between us?'

'Did I do that?'

The muscles of Miranda's face seemed to seize up, and with a helpless shake of her head she turned her back on him, unable to withstand any more of this double-talk. Tears filled her eyes, but they were tears of anger and impotency, and it was all she could do not to stamp her feet in frustration.

When she felt his hands close round her arms, just above the elbow, her head jerked back to see his reflection behind her in the mirror. Their eyes met and held, and when he pulled her back against him she had no will to resist him. But he bent his head to stroke her neck with his tongue, and at once the realisation of what she was doing brought her to her senses.

'Don't touch me!' she panted, twisting away from his lips, and with a shrug he let her go, thrusting his hands into his pockets.

'Very well,' he said flatly, and turned towards the door.

At once, other emotions assailed her, and clasping her hands tightly together, she exclaimed: 'What am I supposed to do now?'

'Now?' His dark brows lifted. 'Do you mean now—this minute? Or now that you've realised that I'm not about to let you go?'

'Oh, Jaime ...' It was not in her nature to maintain this kind of feuding, and her head was beginning to ache.

His mouth tightened as he watched her and then, almost offhandedly, he said: 'If you'd like to resume the clothes you were wearing earlier, I'll take you riding. But not in that—

that thing!'

Miranda was feminine enough to feel affronted at any-one's censure of her clothes. 'This just happens to be the latest style,' she protested, but Jaime was obviously unimpressed.

'I liked the jeans better,' he replied. 'Do you want to go riding or don't you?'

She would have loved to have been able to refuse, but the prospect of the morning spent in the confines of the house, faced with the unpleasant facts of her failure to make any progress with him, made her long for the freedom of the outdoors.

'I—will your—your *friend* be coming with us?' she asked peevishly, and his expression lightened.

'Juana? I shouldn't think so. She probably has much too much to say to her mother.'

'Her—*mother?*' Miranda was staggered. 'You mean—you mean she——'

'——is my sister, yes. Didn't you notice the resemblance?'

Miranda felt confused. 'But I saw you—that is——'

'You're wondering why I kissed her as I did?' he suggested lazily, and her expression answered for her. 'Why, to make you jealous, of course. And I succeeded, didn't I?'

'No!'

Miranda denied him, but the faint smile touching the corners of his mouth assured her that she would be wasting her time by arguing further.

'Cool it,' he advised, his expression hardening again. 'You may be older now, and infinitely more experienced, I've no doubt, but you still haven't learnt to hide your feelings, Miranda. They're a dead giveaway.'

'Oh, you—you——'

'I'll see you downstairs,' he said, opening the door, and she eventually showed her agreement by a sulky nod of her head. 'By the way,' he added, pausing in the doorway, and she tensed, 'next time you come into my bedroom early in the morning, make a little less noise, would you?'

Her sandal hit the closed panels of the door, and she heard him whistling as he walked away along the landing.

CHAPTER EIGHT

WHEN Miranda came downstairs, dressed in her jeans but in place of the cotton shirt a roll-necked purple sweater, she found her husband and his mother waiting for her in the hall. And with them was the girl she had seen earlier.

'Good morning, Miranda,' Teresa greeted her warmly, surprisingly bestowing a kiss upon her cheek. 'I hope you slept well.'

'Very well, thank you.' Miranda avoided Jaime's mocking stare, and looked instead at Juana. 'Hello. You're Jaime's sister, aren't you?'

Juana looked surprised at the frankness of the introduction, but she responded politely enough, casting a not unspeculative glance at her brother as she shook Miranda's hand.

'I should have told you, Miranda prefers the casual approach,' Jaime inserted lazily. 'She's not yet used to our somewhat—old-fashioned values.'

Juana fingered the pearls that encircled her slender throat. 'That sounds ominous, Jaime. Do I take that to mean that introductions are not the only bone of contention between you?'

'Did I say it was a bone of contention?' Jaime countered dryly, and disliking the feeling of being spoken about as if she wasn't there, Miranda turned to Teresa and said:

'I had coffee with Senhor Carvalho this morning. I hope I wasn't wasting his time.'

Teresa patted her arm reassuringly. 'My dear, Carlos would not consider having coffee with a beautiful girl to be a waste of time!'

'You're very kind ...'

'Yes, aren't we?' Jaime's hand in the small of her back was suddenly compelling her towards the door. 'Come! We'll see you both later. *Adeus*!'

Miranda had no choice but to go with him, and forcing a faint smile of farewell, she walked ahead of him out of the door. But once outside she turned on him impatiently.

'Will you stop treating me like a child?'

'Will you stop behaving like one?' he countered with deceptive mildness, and her lower lip jutted.

'I didn't.'

He shrugged, beginning to walk with loose easy strides across the courtyard, and she had perforce to fall into step beside him. But she couldn't leave it like that.

'What did I do?' she demanded, and he cast a sideways glance at her.

'This petty squabbling you go in for. This desire you have to score points ...'

'You do that, too,' she retaliated, and he raised his eyebrows as if by saying what she had she had proved his point. 'Well ...' she protested feebly, 'you don't make it easy for me.'

'Do you think you make it easy for me?' he asked steadily, and she bent her head and scuffed her toe against the rough pebbles that crunched beneath their feet.

They had reached the stables, and Miranda looked about her curiously, unable to prevent the latent feeling of excitement that was gradually overtaking all other emotions. There was so much to see and absorb, so many sights and sounds and smells; she wanted to imprint them all on her memory to store up for the days ahead when she would be back among the gentler things of home.

The air was gradually getting warmer and the sun on the top of her head was pleasant. But the wind still blew down coolly from the *serras*, and she wondered how Jaime could walk around without a jacket or a sweater.

Inside the stables they came on the old man who looked after the horses. His dark features were seamed with wrinkles, pale streaks appearing when he spoke, revealing the crevices where the sun's rays never penetrated. Dark eyes roved over Miranda with undisguised approval, and she wondered what Jaime was saying to bring the light of laughter to the old man's eyes. She was sure it had to do with her, but Jaime chose not to include her in their amusement, and she turned away feeling ridiculously hurt.

The stables were bigger than she had expected, long and low-ceilinged, a series of stalls, many of which were empty. They were spotlessly clean, but nothing could dispel the

odour of horseflesh and hay, and the musky scent of sad-
dlery.

Jaime indicated which mount he wanted for Miranda, and
the old man began to saddle her mare while Jaime handled
his own choice, a chestnut stallion. The mare was smaller,
less aggressive, with fine grey lines and a white star in the
centre of her forehead, but the stallion was all male, strong
and powerful, its coat gleaming with the shine of good health
and grooming.

Miranda approached the old man as he was fastening the
girth straps on the mare, and said tentatively: *'Muito
obrigado!'* smiling to excuse the inadequacy of her accent.
He seemed surprised and pleased at her gratitude, but she
saw Jaime watching them with a much more guarded expression. She returned his look challengingly, as if to say:
'Well!' and then realised he would think she was trying to
score points again.

They led the horses outside for mounting, but Miranda
jarred her spine on the cantle as she swung herself into the
saddle. She was trying to show her independence, but the
sudden impact with her spine brought an involuntary gasp
of pain from her.

Jaime, who had not yet mounted, came towards her at
once, but she managed to look down into his lean face without flinching. 'I was going to warn you about the height of
the back of the saddle,' he said, one brown hand smoothing
the mare's neck as he spoke, but Miranda was in no mood to
appreciate the gesture.

'You mean cantle, don't you?' she inquired coolly. 'You
don't have to talk down to me, Jaime. I do know about such
things.'

His head moved in an indifferent gesture, and then she
saw he was holding two wide-brimmed hats in his free hand.
He offered one to her silently, and although she could see no
reason for needing it, she took it without speaking and he
walked away to swing himself expertly on to the stallion's
back. Of course, he wouldn't jar himself, thought Miranda
childishly, looping the strap of the hat under her chin, and
then dug her knees into the mare's sides to encourage her to
follow the other animal.

The mare needed little encouragement, and cantered

obediently after Jaime's mount. They came out of the stable yard and then Jaime swung about to wait for Miranda to come abreast of him.

'I thought we'd ride to the river,' he said, his face showing no emotion. 'It's quite a distance. Are you up to it?'

'The river!' she exclaimed. 'But that's not far!'

'As you say,' he conceded, and digging in his heels he urged the stallion forward.

They skirted the house at a comfortable pace, crossing a stretch of cultivated turf which bounded a walled vegetable garden. There was a belt of trees which all but hid the back of the house, and Miranda was intrigued to glimpse the meshed fencing of a squash or tennis court.

Beyond the immediate environs of the house, the country opened out quite alarmingly. The expanse of open grassland which stretched towards the river was wider than she had thought, and when Jaime gave the stallion its head, it was all Miranda could do to keep them within calling distance. Like the mountains which had seemed so imminent when viewed from the house, the river was at least five miles away, and she was hot and breathless by the time Jaime reined in his mount and decided to wait for her.

She came up to him panting, regretting the impulse to wear a high-necked sweater, her hat at her nape, giving her head no protection whatsoever. She turned her eyes resentfully up towards the sun, now gaining in strength also, and felt Jaime's knee against her before his hand came out, roughly compelling her hat on to her head once more. She winced as his heavy-handedness pulled her hair, and fixed him with a watery green gaze. But she could not sustain his unwavering stare, and turning her head she looked towards the river, still glinting some distance away.

'How much further do we have to go?' she asked, sniffing, and he drew his mount alongside her and matched her appraisal.

'About half a mile, I guess,' he replied, looking at her more closely now. 'Why? Is it too much for you?'

She pursed her lips mutinously, refusing to rise to his bait, and as if relenting, he said: 'Didn't anyone ever tell you about how deceptive distances can be in prairie country like this?'

'You must know they haven't,' she replied shortly, soothing the mare as it shifted skittishly when brought into such close contact with the stallion. 'You might have told me yourself!'

'What! And be accused of talking down to you again?' he taunted, and she pressed her lips tightly together.

'You love tormenting me, don't you?' she accused him emotionally, aware of how the strenuous ride had sapped her strength. She should have had some breakfast, she thought uneasily, as a wave of remembered nausea swept over her, but it was too late to think of that now.

'I think we should take a break when we get to the river,' he told her quietly, putting out a hand to hold the mare's bridle, preventing her from dancing out of reach. 'You look as though you need it.'

It was hardly flattering to be told she looked sick, Miranda thought resentfully, but she was glad when he kept to a much less arduous pace for the rest of the way.

Jaime climbed down from his mount about half a dozen feet from the edge of a sharp ravine, and Miranda realised that like everything else around here, the river was equally deceptive. From a distance, its width gave the impression of a smooth, flat expanse of water, flowing freely between two tracts of land. In fact, it lay at the foot of quite a rugged ravine, but because of its width it was impossible to judge that from the house. Now she dismounted too, to stand looking down at the swift-moving torrent, realising that without the protective banks on either side it might easily flood.

'The Negresco,' remarked Jaime unnecessarily. 'Life-blood of this part of the country.'

Miranda quelled the breathlessness of nervousness. 'It's very—big!'

'Like everything else around here,' he added dryly, echoing her thoughts of a few moments before.

Miranda looked at him, but bit her tongue on the retort that trembled on her lips. 'Your—your mother said there are river steamers . . .'

'There are. If you look to your right you can see the landing.'

She gasped. 'But how do you get down to it?'

'If you're interested, I'll show you.' Jaime looked thoughtfully at her. 'You're looking a little less strained, but are you sure you feel like it?'

She moved her shoulders in a defensive gesture. 'I'm not an invalid.'

'No,' he agreed, 'but sooner or later you're going to learn that you can't neglect your health out here.'

'I don't expect to be here that long,' she returned, keeping her voice as mild as his, and saw the familiar hardening of his mouth.

'To vary an old cliché, what you expect and what you get may be two different things,' he told her evenly, and she pulled a face at his broad shoulders as he turned away to attend to the horses.

'What exactly did Aunt Lydia tell you?' she demanded. 'And what did you tell her?'

Jaime tethered the horses to an outcrop of rock, and came back to her. 'I think you ought to save your breath,' he said, tightening the strap of her hat beneath her chin, his fingers briefly coming into contact with her skin.

She forced herself not to flinch away from his touch. Somehow she had to convince him she meant what she said, and reacting to any physical contact she made with him was not going to achieve it.

'I—I don't believe Aunt Lydia told you anything,' she declared rather breathlessly, and he pushed his own hat to the back of his head to regard her through narrowed lids.

'No?'

'No.'

'Such faith you have in people,' he mocked.

'Why should Aunt Lydia try to cause trouble between us? She tried to manipulate our marriage!'

Jaime half smiled, a curiously knowing little smile that infuriated Miranda. But he said nothing, and she was obliged to put her own interpretation on his expression. He was not about to tell her anything, and perhaps it was just as well. It wouldn't do for them to have an argument out here. She would hate for him to ride off and leave her to make her own way back. Out of the corner of her eye she could see a plume of dust, in the distance it was true, but definitely moving, and remembering the cruel horns she had seen from the comparative safety of the station wagon, she moved automatically nearer her husband.

Whether Jaime guessed the direction her thoughts were taking she had no way of knowing, but he gestured towards the ravine and said: 'We can climb down this way, or ride to the landing. It's up to you.'

Miranda cast another revealing glance over her shoulder. 'We—we'll climb down,' she determined quickly. 'I suppose there is a way.'

'Oh, yes, there's a way,' he agreed lazily, and putting her life into his hands she accompanied him to the edge of the ravine.

From above, it was frightening. It seemed nothing more than a rocky cliff face, in places thickly covered with vegetation and in others granite-hard and rugged. An overhang fortunately prevented her from seeing all the way down, but another terrifying thought struck her.

'Are there snakes?'

Jaime regarded her with resignation. 'Are you sure you want to do this? We can easily ride round the bluff. There's a mud-baked track that the cattle use!'

Standing there, Miranda became aware of other sensations. Her spine ached from the base of her skull to her coccyx, and the idea of getting back into a hard saddle just yet was anathema to her. Her legs, too, felt distinctly like jelly, and she wondered what Jaime would say if she suggested sitting down right here and now and resting for a while.

Aware of him looking at her troubled face, she forced her weariness away. 'I'm sure,' she said, and with a shrug, he went ahead of her down a steep incline that led to the first overhang.

To begin with, it wasn't as difficult as she had expected. There was plenty of vegetation to hang on to, and her delight in finding clumps of amaryllis growing wild between the roots of stunted trees and the profusive liana creepers kept her thoughts away from the less attractive inhabitants of the ravine. Once a brown body appeared ahead of them, half concealed beneath a curtain of greenery, and her heart leapt into her mouth. But it bounded away harmlessly, and Jaime laconically explained that it was nothing more than a tapir, more startled than they were by the intrusion.

As they neared the bottom, Miranda found it harder to keep her balance. The ankle-length suede boots she had worn for riding were not meant for rock-climbing, and she cannoned into Jaime time and again, as her feet slid away from her. They were disturbing encounters, compelling as they did an awareness of the muscular hardness of his body, the latent strength which she was rapidly coming to depend on.

She was admiring a peony-red blossom when Jaime sprang down the final few feet that brought him to the base of the ravine. It left her with perhaps six feet still to negotiate and she looked down at him in alarm, missing his supporting shoulder.

'Jump,' he told her, bracing himself to catch her, but Miranda hesitated.

'I—I can't ...'

'Of course you can. What are you afraid of? You're yards away from the river.'

'Har-hardly yards ...'

'Feet, then. Come on!'

'I—can't——'

'You'll have to. Unless you want me to leave you there.'

'You wouldn't!'

Her eyes mirrored her distress, and he relented. 'No, I wouldn't. But you've got to jump down. I can't reach you from here.'

'Come back up.'

'No.'

Miranda licked her lips, and as she did so there was a sudden, curious noise behind her, like the sound of a crinkly body unwinding itself from its resting place. A *snake*!

With a terrified cry, she leapt over the edge of the drop, catapulting into Jaime and felling him like a stone. He went down on the gravel-hard ground with her on top of him, winding him and briefly stunning his consciousness.

Miranda was horrified, more concerned now with what she had done to him than with any thought of the possible whereabouts of the reptile. His eyes were closed, and she tried not to panic. What ought she to do? Had she knocked him out? What if he had fractured his skull?

His arms came around her as she tried to scramble off him, and she saw to her relief that his eyes were open now. It made her aware of his hips beneath her, of the fact that she was lying half between his legs.

'You—you're all right?' she asked tremorously, feeling obliged to say something, and his lips twisted.

'You had reason to suppose that I might not be,' he remarked with asperity. 'In God's name, what possessed you to do a thing like that?'

Miranda found a relieved laugh rising uncontrollably. 'I—I always do the unexpected, didn't you know?' she choked, and saw the anger she had mistaken for tolerance.

'Do you?' he snapped. 'Well, that was a bloody stupid thing to do!'

Miranda's amusement disappeared. 'I'm sorry!' she said, sulkily. 'I should have realised you wouldn't see the funny side of it.'

'What funny side?' he demanded, shifting his shoulders experimentally. 'I could have broken my back!'

'Well, you haven't,' she retorted, making another effort to get up and being baulked by his hands at her waist. 'Can I get up now?'

Jaime's mouth took on a thoughtful curve, and as she strained away from him his eyes dropped to where the impact of her fall had separated her sweater from the waistband of her pants revealing a welt of creamy skin. Immediately, she endeavoured to cover herself, but it was difficult when his hands moved up to her shoulders, jerking her down to him. Their eyes were perhaps six inches apart now, their lips that much closer, but still she held herself back from him.

'You asked me what Aunt Lydia told me,' he said softly, his breath fanning her cheek. 'Shall I tell you?'

Miranda twisted uselessly against him, and as she did so she realised her movements were in no way cooling his emotions. The warmth of his body spread to hers, and with it the disturbing realisation that his closeness was not unpleasant to her. On the contrary, almost against her will, her legs sought the nearness of his and a weakening lethargy was destroying the barriers she wanted to raise against him.

'I—I think you ought to let me go,' she got out breathily, but he took no notice of her.

'Aunt Lydia informed me that you had a friend—of the masculine gender,' he continued, almost as if she had not spoken. 'Someone called—Paul? Is that right?'

'She had no right to——'

'And did you?' he demanded harshly. 'You are my wife, remember? And adultery is a cardinal sin.'

'Committed by cardinals, you mean,' she tried to taunt him, failing abysmally. Then: 'You don't know anything about me!'

'I know it's time I put in my claim,' he insisted, one hand finding the curve of her nape and compelling her face down to his. 'Why should I show you consideration when you don't grant me the same privilege?'

'You told me you didn't want me!' she protested, trembling as she felt his lips moving along the curve of her cheek, but he moved his head in a negative gesture.

'Correction, I believe I said I didn't want to make love to you. At least, not then. Now—I do!' and with a lithe movement he rolled over, imprisoning her beneath him.

His hand holding her jaw prevented her from evading his kiss even had she wanted to, which in all honesty she doubted right then. His mouth was so firm and demanding, and deep inside her some wanton impulse urged her to give in to him. His lips explored hers with increasing urgency, opening her mouth to the sexuality of his, and when the pressure became a bruising hardness she felt every inch of her yielding to his touch.

Her arms slid round his waist, her fingers finding the belt of his pants and clinging to it like a lifeline. The strength of the emotions he was arousing in her was frightening, but she learned the true meaning of frustration when he drew back a little to smooth the sweat-moistened hair back from her forehead, sliding his fingers over her ear and on to her scalp.

'Well, well,' he murmured, and although his tones were mocking she heard the note in his voice that forswore the derision. 'We have grown up, haven't we? I wonder who taught you.'

'No one taught me . . .' she was beginning, when she saw that he patently didn't believe her. And the only way to convince him she was telling the truth was to let him find out for himself . . .

Afterwards, when the practicalities of common sense had reasserted themselves, and she was back in the fleeting privacy of her room, Miranda wondered if she would really have let him make love to her, there on the riverbank, had he chosen to do so. It would have been so humiliating, she thought, the coolness of reason grating on the veneer of self-respect she was struggling to hold about her. To have known her first experience of a man in a public place—even if the only *voyeurs* were not likely to have been capable of talking about it. But at that moment the greater humiliation came when Jaime thrust her aside to get to his feet, and she knew that he had rejected her.

He turned away, thrusting his shirt back into his pants, and gathering up his hat which he had worn without the strap and which had been thrown aside in his fall. He was giving her time to get to her feet, she knew, but she felt so weak, she doubted her legs would support her.

However, she had to get up, and she did so clumsily, using the method she had used as a toddler, pushing her tail-end up first, and straightening with an obvious effort. Jaime turned back as she was almost upright, and with evident reluctance said:

'Are you all right?'

Miranda's voice sounded rather croaky to her ears, but she managed to answer him positively, looking round with deliberate determination for her own hat.

'It's up there,' observed Jaime dryly, pointing towards the ledge, and she shivered when she saw the wide brim projecting a little way over the edge.

'Will you get it for me?' she requested politely, and he regarded her broodingly.

'I suppose I'd better. Otherwise you might take it into your head to make another dive at me,' he derided, and she tensed with indignation.

'I didn't do it deliberately,' she retorted. 'And I certainly shouldn't repeat it.'

Jaime's mouth sketched his scepticism. 'You—er—fell before,' he drawled, and she felt the angry tears smarting at the backs of her eyes.

'If you must know, there was a snake!' she told him haughtily, and suffered his gasp of disbelief. 'There was!' she insisted angrily. 'You don't imagine I wanted to fall into your arms, do you?'

'Well, you didn't exactly turn me off a few minutes ago,' he remarked, with abrasive candour, but a frown of consideration had formed between his brows. 'Where was it, then? This dangerous specimen!'

'Up there. On the ledge,' she declared resentfully. Then, in alarm as he dropped his hat on to the ground again and moved towards the rugged outcrop: 'What are you going to do?'

He turned resigned features towards her. 'Now what do you think?'

'Well, be—be careful, won't you? It—it might still be there.'

'Your concern would be more touching if I could just reassure myself that it's not because you're afraid of being stranded out here,' he commented dryly, swinging a leg up on to the stump of some long-dead parasitic growth. 'If I should happen to die of rattlesnake poisoning, you'll find the track up from the landing along there much less gruelling than climbing over my dead body!'

'Oh, stop it!' she cried, putting her hands over her ears. 'You're so sarcastic! It never occurs to you that I might have been telling the truth, does it?'

'Of course.' He cast a derisive grin over his shoulder. 'At least you won't have to worry about rattlesnakes, anyway.'

'Wh-why not?'

'Well, if I'm half as bad as you make out I am, the poor thing will likely die of food-poisoning ...'

Miranda's hands balled into fists as he climbed the rest of the way up to the ledge. She wanted to look away, but she was hypnotised by the realisation that if it was a rattler up there, Jaime had nothing to defend himself with.

He swung himself over the ledge, and her breathing felt as if it was suspended. Her hat came floating down almost immediately, but Jaime had stepped back from the edge and she could only see his head. She wanted to call up to him, to ask if it was all right, to assure herself that he was not about to put himself in some terrible danger, but a fear of precipitating the very thing she was afraid of kept her silent.

Then, just when she was beginning to relax, there was a sudden surfeit of noise. So many sounds erupted all at once, the startled squawk of a bird, the cracking of a brittle branch, a startled oath, and a muffled sound like dried corn rattling round in a dish ... *Rattling!*

'*Jaime!*' His head had disappeared and his name broke involuntarily from her lips. Hardly thinking of what she was doing, what danger she might be running herself into, she reached for the rotted stump, and swung herself up the first couple of feet from the ground just as he appeared above her.

'What are you doing?' he asked, but there was an edge to his voice which she couldn't quite identify. Then she saw the twitching rope-like thing hanging from his left hand, and the squat, thick-bladed knife in the other, and stepped back aghast on to the riverbank.

'It—it *was* a snake!' she said faintly, and passed out.

CHAPTER NINE

WHEN she came to she couldn't understand where she was, or what was going on. She seemed to be suspended in mid-air, and her swimming eyes registered the sickening depth of the ravine below her. Then she realised Jaime had draped her over his shoulder, like a sack of potatoes, she thought dully, unable to summon up any protest right at that moment. He was climbing the side of the ravine with sure, steady strides, and a sense of shame and inadequacy gripped her when she considered how much harder it must be with her weight to carry as well as his own. Why was he carrying her? She tried to remember, and the recollection of the snake performing its death throes in his hand turned her stomach. Fortunately, she wasn't sick. She had nothing inside her, but that didn't stop her from retching or despising herself for doing so.

If Jaime heard her, he made no comment until he reached the top of the ravine and deposited her without ceremony on the rough tussocky grass. Then he flung himself beside her, flat on his back, pushing hands that were not quite steady through his hair.

'I—I'm sorry,' she said, panting a little as her rib-cage protested against the pressure he had put on it. 'I—I'm not usually so—so——'

'Squeamish?' he supplied flatly, turning his head to one side to look at her. 'Don't fret. It's taught me a lesson, too.'

Miranda plucked delicately at a blade of grass. 'It—it was a rattlesnake, wasn't it?' He nodded, and she hid her grimace of distaste. 'Did—did you kill it?'

'Well, I didn't put it in my pocket,' he teased, and she realised with a sense of amazement that he was trying to dispel the images she had implanted in her brain.

'It—it didn't bite you?'

He shook his head, and pushed himself up to sit cross-legged. 'No.' He grinned. 'Not for want of trying. They're

125

not very sociable animals.'

'Oh, Jaime!' Weakness made her chin tremble, and with
a lithe movement he got to his feet and pulled her up too,
supporting her with his hands until the world had stopped
spinning dizzily about her.

Then he frowned. 'Say, did you have any breakfast this
morning?'

Miranda moved her head slowly from side to side, and
with a muffled expletive he stared at her impatiently.

'You're mad, do you know that?' he told her roughly, and
then, as if unable to maintain his anger against such obvious
exhaustion, he swung her up into his arms again. He strode
across to where the horses were tethered, and deposited her
on the chestnut stallion's back, holding the reins while he
released both horses and attached the mare's leading rein to
the metal horn on the pommel of his saddle. Then he swung
himself up behind her, his arms around her holding the reins
and supporting her against his chest.

The journey back was much slower than the journey out,
and yet, amazingly, it was over all too soon for Miranda.
There was something immensely satisfying about riding with
Jaime, her back against his body, the muscles of his thighs
alongside hers. The cattle the plume of dust had heralded
earlier had moved within sight of them, but she had no fear,
secure in Jaime's arms. She felt completely content.

If he was aware of the way her body yielded to his, he
made no move to show it. It would have been so easy for him
to let the fingers that spread across her stomach move intim-
ately in either direction, but he didn't. Instead, she tormented herself with thoughts of what might have been,
uncaring of what interpretation he might put upon the
sensuous movements of her body.

The chestnut cantered into the stable yard soon after
twelve, to be met by Carlos Carvalho, and the man Miranda
had seen earlier from her windows and who she had
decided was his foreman.

'*Que?*' Carlos looked anxiously at Miranda and then at the
mare. 'What is wrong? You have fallen? Ah, but Marinka
is the gentlest of animals! Jaime, tell me quickly—has there
been an accident?'

Jaime swung down from the horse's back but made no

immediate effort to help Miranda. 'Calm down, Carlos!' he said, patting the stallion's muzzle. 'There's been no accident. Miranda was—unwell, that's all.'

'Unwell?' Carlos looked up at her anxiously. 'Unwell? Miranda *pequena*, what is wrong?'

'It's nothing really,' Miranda protested weakly. 'There— there was a snake——'

'A snake?' Carlos turned to his stepson, and with a sigh Jaime explained that they had encountered a rattler in the ravine. He made light of the incident, but Carlos was disturbed.

'I told you, you should always carry a rifle!' he scolded, but Jaime dismissed his fears.

'I've used a knife since I was in diapers,' he assured the older man with a return of mockery. 'Now, do you mind if I take my wife indoors? Like you, she doesn't appreciate the finer points of decapitation.'

Miranda shuddered and pressed her lips together as Jaime helped her down from the mare, but she moved a few steps away from him as he called for the old man to come and take charge of the animals. It demonstrated her ability to walk the few steps to the house, and with a wry glance in her direction, Jaime granted her small bid for independence.

'I'd rather you didn't tell my mother what happened,' he remarked casually, falling into step beside her.

'All right.' Miranda was intent on achieving the verandah, which was the goal she had set herself, but his tone commanded her attention. 'Why not?'

'That was how my grandfather died,' he replied flatly, and without giving her chance to express the horrified exclamation that sprang to her lips, he vaulted on to the verandah and waited for her to precede him into the house.

Miranda had lunch served in her room. On Jaime's instructions, she had taken off her clothes and got into bed, and what a wonderful relief it was to relax behind closed curtains and drawn blinds. When Chiquita brought her tray, she was almost asleep, but she stayed awake long enough to sample the iced consommé and a little of the fluffy omelette that accompanied it. The luscious black grapes defeated her, however, and she drifted off to sleep without thinking of anything but sweet oblivion ...

She was swimming, she thought happily, swimming in the river. The cool waters washed softly past her ears, and her arms moved lethargically, describing a rhythm that was just enough to keep her afloat. The water was warm, green-tinted and inviting, overhung by swaying reeds that stroked her legs as she passed. She had never known such a feeling of freedom, and she couldn't understand why no one else was coming to join her. Jaime was standing on the riverbank, watching her, and he seemed to be cheering her on. But on to what? He had a rattle in his hand, the kind used at football matches, and he was swinging it loudly, grating on her nerves. She tried to escape the sound, but there was no getting away from it, and when she looked again terror struck her because it wasn't the wooden toy she had thought but long and black and venomous, the horny rings in its tail shaking convulsively ...

'Miranda! Miranda! Come on, wake up!'

The fingers that lightly struck first one side of her face and then the other were hard and masculine. Miranda pressed her head back into the pillows, trying to get away from them, but it was no use, they stayed with her.

'Miranda! Come on, snap out of it!'

She threshed about desperately, and then opened her eyes to see who was abusing her so. Her aching brain registered Jaime's dark form bending over her, illuminated by the light from a bedside lamp. Her head jerked to the window, but beyond the drawn curtains it was night. Blinking, she sought for coherence, and he said gently:

'Relax! You've been dreaming. Scaring yourself silly, by the sound of it. You're safe now.'

Miranda became aware that her limbs were moist with sweat, and that the cotton nightdress she had put on earlier was wet and clinging to her. 'Wh—what time is it?' she stammered, trying to prop herself up on her elbows and falling back again as dizziness hit her.

'About half after eleven,' he told her quietly, and as the room steadied she saw that he was still dressed.

'Half past eleven!' she echoed. 'But it can't be!'

'I assure you it is,' he said, putting a hand on her forehead and bringing it away damp with her perspiration. 'You were exhausted.' He took her wrist between his thumb and forefinger and studied his watch for a few moments, before allowing her hand to fall limply against the covers once more. 'How do you feel?'

Miranda's breathing was shallow, but she forced a panicky feeling away, and said: 'Fine.' Then: 'Did I disturb you?'

Jaime shook his head. 'I was reading—in there.' He gestured towards the dressing room. 'What was it? The rattler?'

Miranda nodded silently, drawing in her breath with choking gulps, and he looked down at her with evident concern.

'Did you eat any of your lunch?'

The thought of food was nauseating, but she managed to nod. 'A little.'

'What?'

'Must I tell you now?'

'Like that, is it?' He frowned. 'You're running a temperature, *cara*. I'm going to have to change your bed.'

Miranda stared at him uncomprehendingly. 'What do you mean?'

'Sheets, bedding! And most particularly—that!' His fingers flicked at the offending nightgown.

Miranda felt too weary to contemplate a move. 'Couldn't it wait until morning?' she protested, but he was already drawing back the sheets, and she quickly pushed her nightdress down over her thighs.

'I'm a doctor,' he said mildly, swinging her up into his arms. 'I do know what's under there.'

Miranda didn't answer him, and he carried her across the bedroom and into the dressing room, setting her down gently on the divan. He left her for a few moments and then returned, having rummaged about among her belongings, with a clean nightdress.

'Put this on,' he advised. 'Unless you want me to do it. Then get into my bed while I change yours.'

Miranda pushed back her tumbled hair with an unsteady hand, glad at least that the room had stopped revolving. 'I'll help you ...'

Jaime gave her a wry look. 'I think not. Just get into bed. It won't take long.'

Miranda hesitated only a moment after he had gone before tugging the damp nightdress over her head. He had left the door between the two rooms open, and she was half afraid he might come back, but he didn't. It was an effort to struggle into the clean garment, though, and when it was done, she was only too glad to slide her legs between the sheets and relax against the pillows.

This was where Jaime slept, she thought drowsily, putting up a hand to the pillows, her fingers lingering against their silky texture. It was a very comfortable bed, not as wide as the bed she slept in, of course, but wide enough. She could stretch her toes for quite a distance in either direction, and its length quite defeated her. Her eyes felt so heavy, which was surprising considering she had slept for so long, but perhaps the journey had tired her more than she had thought. She could hear few sounds from the room next door, and only the wind whistling down from the *serras* and finding its way through the joints in the eaves disturbed the almost total stillness.

Her eyes closed almost without her being aware of it, and at once she could see the darting tongue of the rattlesnake as it uncoiled its length for the kill. It seemed to be there, in the room beside her, and although she knew it couldn't be, she couldn't stop the sounds of protest from spilling uncontrollably from her lips.

Jaime's hands on either side of her face, determinedly shaking her, brought her back to full consciousness, and she looked up at him through sticky lashes.

'I'm sorry, I'm sorry,' she faltered unsteadily, but he merely shook his head compassionately.

Then she saw the hypodermic needle on the table beside the bed, and her eyes widened as she turned back to him. 'You—you're not going to drug me!' she cried.

His expression softened. 'It's not a sedative, if that's what you mean,' he told her quietly. 'Just an antibiotic.'

'I don't want to go to sleep again!'

'Why not?' His thumbs brushed the circles beneath her eyes. 'You're worn out.'

Even in her state of reduced awareness, she could feel her senses' instant response to those inadvertent caresses. She wanted to lift her hand and hold his fingers against her cheek. Only when he was touching her did she feel truly safe.

'Don't make me go back to my own room!' she suddenly

burst out. 'Let me stay here.'

Jaime's brows descended as he reached for the needle, holding it up to the light and spraying a minute proportion of its contents into the air. He reached for her arm without speaking, straightening her elbow and exposing the vein on the inner side to the hypodermic's plunge. Miranda hardly felt the penetration, but when it was withdrawn, she looked at him desperately.

'Jaime ...'

'You can stay here, if you like,' he agreed flatly. 'I'll sleep in the other room.'

'No!' That was not what she wanted at all. 'Jaime, stay with me.'

'I can't do that, Miranda,' he muttered harshly, pushing the hypodermic needle back into its case. 'You're welcome to stay here if you want to. I can understand the associations——'

'I need *you*!' she implored, tears filling her eyes, and his mouth turned down at the corners.

'You're distraught. You'll feel better in a while. The antibiotic I've given you will lower your temperature and then you'll feel a lot better——'

'I won't stay on my own,' she told him mutinously. '*Please*, Jaime! I'll never ask you for anything ever again.'

He straightened, raking his hand through his hair. 'You don't understand,' he muttered, but she was not listening to him. 'All right,' he said at last, when it became obvious that she was going to become hysterical if he didn't agree. 'All right. But we'll sleep in the other bed.'

'I want to stay here,' she insisted, and although his mouth tightened, he did not argue with her. Instead, he walked slowly back into the other room and turned out the light.

When he came back, he was peeling off his shirt, and she turned her eyes away from the supple beauty of his physique, trying not to think of how she might feel tomorrow. She heard sounds of his shoes being removed, and the unzipping of his pants, and then the side of the bed gave as it accepted his weight as well as her own.

She moved across the bed as he got in, and was startled to feel his arm brushing hers. Immediately, the full import of what she was doing descended upon her, and when he turned out the light, panic of a different kind filled her.

Her body trembled as he turned on to his back, and as if sensing her anxiety, he said dryly: 'I should have warned you, I don't wear pyjamas.' She breathed only slightly more freely, and he added: 'You want to change your mind?'

She drew a deep breath and then said: 'No!' without much conviction, and heard his impatient oath.

'Go to sleep, Miranda!' he told her wearily, turning on to his side away from her. 'I'm not going to touch you. Believe it or not, but making love to an hysterical woman does not turn me on!'

Miranda couldn't entirely stifle the gasp of hurt humiliation this aroused. The beast! she thought resentfully, forgetting entirely how her withdrawal must have reacted on him. She had a good mind to climb over his prone body and go back to her own bed. But then she thought about the rattlesnake and changed her mind ...

In all, Miranda was in bed four days.

When she awakened the next morning she found herself back in her own bed, and without the minute puncture on her arm she might have been inclined to believe she had dreamed everything. But the sheets were yellow now, not tan-coloured as they had been before, and her changed nightdress convinced her it had been no figment of her imagination.

But when she tried to get up, she discovered exactly how weak she was, and Chiquita's appearance with her breakfast confirmed that Jaime had informed the other members of the household of her indisposition.

The tray of freshly-squeezed orange juice and warm rolls was not appealing, however, and the scent of the coffee reminded her of the weakness of her stomach.

By the time Jaime came to see her, she was feeling very sorry for herself, and his appearance, big and aggressively masculine in a bronze shirt and brown moleskin pants, was denigrating. However, there were lines of tiredness around his eyes which she had not noticed before, and she wondered with a pang whether she had been responsible for his disturbed night.

He checked her pulse and then produced a thermometer from its metal container.

'You've got all the equipment,' she remarked bitterly, as he put it beneath her tongue, and his eyes grew reflective.

'I would have, wouldn't I?' he parried, removing the thermometer a few moments later. 'How do you feel?'

'Weak as water,' she replied resentfully. 'What did you give me last night?'

He half smiled. 'Not what you expected, obviously,' and she blushed scarlet. 'You're still suffering the after-effects of the virus you picked up.'

'What virus?' she demanded, her lips trembling.

'A little thing called salmonella.'

'That—that's food poisoning, isn't it?'

'Well, poisoning anyway,' he agreed mildly, and she stared anxiously at him.

'Are you fooling me?'

He shook his head. 'Why would I do that?'

'To try and keep me here!' she declared tremulously, and then felt contrite as his expression scorned her foolish accusation.

'You think I'd do that?' he demanded. 'Infect you with some lousy poison to keep you here? My God! What an opinion you have of me!'

'I didn't mean it,' she mumbled, shamefaced, but his features barely registered her feeble attempt at apology.

'You want it in words of four syllables?' he commanded, but she pursed her lips and didn't answer him. 'Paratyphoid,' he went on, enunciating succinctly. 'Satisfied?'

'*Paratyphoid,*' she whispered. 'But—how——?'

'I don't have time to go into the history of the bacillus,' he retorted grimly. 'Think yourself fortunate I recognised it when I did.'

'But—it's infectious, isn't it? I mean—you shouldn't have slept with me last night, should you?'

His eyes showed his contempt. 'You're not concerned for me, are you? After all, in your eyes it would be a minor retribution, wouldn't it?'

'Don't say that!' She chewed unhappily at her upper lip. 'I'm sorry. I shouldn't have said what I did, but I feel pretty awful.'

'You'll probably feel worse before you feel better,' he told her callously. 'But to reassure you on one point, it's not infectious. Not in its present form, anyway.' He paused, and she continued to look at him appealingly. 'Now, I'm going to have to ask you some rather personal questions.'

They were personal questions, too, and Miranda's whole body felt as if it was suffused in colour by the time he had finished. But he seemed satisfied with her answers, and she let her limp body relax.

'What—what do I do now?' she asked tentatively, and he sighed.

'Not a lot. Stay in bed. Eat if you can.'

Miranda made a sound of protest. 'But I can't stay here . . .'

'Why not?'

She couldn't meet his gaze. 'I—I told Aunt Lydia I'd be away a week, two weeks at the most. Ten days have gone already.'

Jaime shrugged his broad shoulders. 'Send her a cable. Tell her you've been—delayed.'

Miranda lifted her eyes to his. 'She'll worry . . .'

'You mean *Paul* will worry,' he corrected her gratingly. 'All right, tell him to come out here.'

Miranda swallowed convulsively. 'You—you'd let him do that !'

'Why not?'

'But—you——'

'It can do no harm to meet the opposition,' he retorted. 'You want me to send the cable?'

Miranda moved her head helplessly from side to side. She didn't know what she wanted. All she did know was that since coming here her whole outlook was changing

'But where would he stay?' she objected.

'Why not here?'

'What would your mother say? She thinks . . .'

'I know exactly what she thinks,' Jaime told her harshly. 'To begin with I'll say he's a friend of mine. Until the situation resolves itself.'

'How will it do that?'

He shrugged. 'Let's wait and see, shall we? Now, I'm going to give you another injection, and then I want you to try and get some sleep.'

'Sleep?' She stared wretchedly up at him. 'I've just been to sleep !'

He ignored her protests, and she flinched as the needle made its second incision in her arm. Then he straightened the covers and looked down at her with a strangely brooding expression.

'You'll make it,' he told her ironically. And then, more enigmatically: 'I'm not so sure about me.'

Miranda felt discomfited by his words, by the sudden realisation that she didn't want him to go. 'I—I am really sorry for what I said,' she ventured in a low tone. 'Will—will you come back and see me later?'

He moved away from the bed. 'When I've attended to my other patients,' he agreed shortly, and she levered herself up on her elbows.

'What other patients?'

'Those in Santa Madalena,' he told her dryly. 'You didn't imagine my practice was confined to the *quinta*, did you?'

Miranda supposed she had. Remembering Santa Madalena and the somewhat primitive conditions to be found there, she found she didn't want to think of Jaime going into those areas, associating with disease at such close quarters.

'I—I—never thought about it,' she got out at last, and he moved his shoulders in a dismissive gesture.

'There is little enough done for the *indios*, but at least we try to maintain a reasonable level of physical care.'

'You mean—*you* do,' she exclaimed, and he opened the door.

'Take it easy,' he advised, and left her.

CHAPTER TEN

MIRANDA had had a sleep and was awake and restless when Teresa came to see her later in the morning.

'You see,' her mother-in-law exclaimed severely, seating herself on the side of the bed, 'I knew Jaime should have examined you.' Miranda was too weary to argue and she added: 'Thank heaven, it is not more serious.'

'It's not?' said Miranda disbelievingly, and Teresa shook her head.

'Two or three days and you will begin to feel normal again. Then you can really begin to settle down here.'

Miranda licked her lips. 'Yes, well—perhaps I ought to talk to you about that ...'

'About what?' Teresa raised her dark eyebrows. 'Settling down here? You will not find it difficult. Then, if you are happy, Carlos and I will move back to Valmonte——'

'Oh, no!' Miranda caught her breath on the words. 'That is, don't move out because—because of me ...'

Teresa patted her hand understandingly. 'I know. You do not wish to make changes. But when you and Jaime have children ...' She smiled. 'I was losing all hope of his ever producing an heir to the estates.'

If it were possible, Miranda would have felt worse. As it was she just felt even more wretched, and was almost glad when Teresa left her to see about lunch.

She didn't remember much of the next thirty-six hours. By the evening of that day she was running a high temperature, and sweating profusely. She couldn't bear the closeness of cloth against her hot skin, and kicked off the covers time and again, only to have them replaced once more.

Through the long night that followed, she was aware of cool hands sponging the moist areas of her body, and reassuring arms that held her while her nightdress was removed and replaced with another. She thought sometimes it was Teresa, or Sancha or one of the servant girls who held her, but often she was aware of Jaime there beside her, his strong fingers allowing the clutching grasp of hers.

The fever broke during the afternoon of the following day and by evening Miranda was sufficiently recovered to swallow a little of the broth Teresa brought to her. But only a little before she sank into an exhausted slumber that lasted until morning.

Jaime appeared as Sancha was helping her to wash, and the Indian woman bestowed a warm smile upon him as she left them alone together. Miranda, conscious that her hair had not been brushed for days, and that the fever had left her skin without its usual bloom of health, slid down beneath the covers leaving only the upper half of her face visible.

Her husband came down upon the bed, however, and drew the sheet back to her waist, making his usual inspections before saying: 'You're feeling a little better, hmm?'

Miranda nodded. 'Yes, thank you.'

Jaime regarded her wryly. 'That was very polite. You can't be as well as I thought.'

'I am.' Miranda realised there was no use in trying to pretend with him, and propped herself up on her elbows. 'It's just that—well, I look such a mess!'

His eyes narrowed. 'Fishing for compliments?'

'No!' She was indignant. 'I mean it. You might have let me do my hair and get on some make-up before seeing you.'

'Why? Would that erase the memories of you as you were twenty-four hours ago?'

Miranda flushed. 'Don't remind me!'

Jaime shrugged dismissingly, and then said: 'Are you hungry?'

'A little.'

'Could you eat a boiled egg?'

'Could I get one?' she asked, astonished.

'We do have chickens, you know,' he retorted dryly. 'Is that what you'd like?'

'I'd love it,' she agreed honestly. But as he made to get up, she caught his hand. 'Jaime ...'

'Yes?'

His eyes were completely detached, and she realised he was deliberately looking at her as a patient and nothing else.

'I—I—thank you,' she muttered lamely, and he bowed his head.

'No trouble,' he assured her, and left the room.

By the evening of the following day, she was able to eat normally again, and the day after that she was permitted to get up after lunch. It was wonderful to take a shower and wash the sweat from her hair, as well as her body, using Teresa's hand-drier to restore it to its usual shine.

Then she dressed in a simple cotton tunic, ankle-length, with slits up the side and a low square neckline, the amber colour of which toned attractively with her hair. But she had lost weight, she realised as she tied the cord about her waist, and saw how the swelling curves of her breasts were outlined beneath the thin material. Still, it was not unattractive, and without her pallor, the delicate lines of her face would have been quite enchanting.

Teresa came up to accompany her downstairs, and Jaime's instructions were that she could stay down for dinner but retire immediately afterwards.

Chiquita served tea in the *sala*, and the two women were enjoying the ritual when Carlos appeared. He and Julia had kept out of Miranda's bedroom while she was ill, but now he viewed her with evident relief.

'What a terrible thing to have happened!' he exclaimed, after kissing both of them. 'We should be everlastingly grateful that Jaime chose medicine as his career.'

'Indeed.' Teresa regarded her daughter-in-law ruefully and then shook her head. '*Nao importa*, she is well now, and that is the important thing.'

Carlos seated himself opposite and accepted some tea from his wife. Then he said unguardedly: 'Unfortunately, Jaime tells us that you have allowed this unhappy incident to influence you against our country.'

The unexpected accusation caught her unawares, and for a moment Miranda could do nothing but stare at him, her teacup in her hand; and Teresa, as if realising her husband's words had been a trifle careless, chose to make her own contribution:

'You must not feel that we are blaming you, *cara*, but I know Carlos feels as I do, and we hope you will put these last days out of your head and decide to stay.'

Briefly, Miranda wondered if Jaime had put his parents up to this, but these past days had given her an insight into his character too, and she was no longer so willing to jump to the wrong conclusions. Besides, she ought to thank him for putting into her hands the perfect solution to at least one of her problems.

Putting down her cup, she folded her hands in her lap and said quietly: 'Whatever I decide to do, I'll never forget your kindness to me.'

Carlos snorted impatiently. 'Kindness? Is it kindness to welcome our son's wife into his family? Is it kindness to care for her when she is sick, and ensure that she has the best medical attention available? What kind of country is it that you come from, Miranda, that considers such things a kindness? We have only done what we wanted to do, what it is our duty to do. Does your family mean nothing to you, Miranda?'

She coloured. 'I have no family,' she said carefully. 'My father died when I was a little girl, and my mother died eighteen months ago——'

'But we are your family now!' exclaimed Teresa, leaning foward to cover both of Miranda's hands with her own. 'That is what Carlos is trying to explain. We are sorry that your parents are dead, of course, but you must never feel that you are alone ...'

Miranda felt a lump in her throat. 'You're very kind,' she said again, and was overwhelmingly relieved when a maid appeared to announce that someone called Juan Vargas was waiting to speak to his employer.

Carlos grimaced goodnaturedly, and smilingly excused himself. Teresa watched him go with affection, and then offered Miranda more tea. To the girl's relief, the conversation moved into less personal channels, and they were discussing the merits of skin creams in this kind of climate when Jaime appeared. He was dressed in mud-coloured levis and a matching shirt, sweat stains visible around his arms and causing the shirt to stick to him in places.

He apologised to his mother for his appearance, then looked questioningly at his wife. 'I see you took me at my word,' he commented.

Miranda lifted her head. 'Wasn't I supposed to?'

'Of course.' His slightly mocking smile included his mother in its envelopment. 'And now, as it's obvious you're feeling much better, if you'll excuse me I'll go take a shower.'

This time it was Miranda's eyes that followed the masculine form from the room, and Teresa watched her intently before saying quietly: 'Why did you do it, Miranda?'

Her words brought Miranda's head round sharply. 'I beg your pardon?'

Teresa sighed, but she didn't back down. 'I asked why you did it, Miranda. Why you came here? After all this time?'

Miranda's composure splintered. 'I—why?' she echoed, playing for time. 'Why do you think I came?'

Teresa frowned. 'When Jaime came home and told us he had married some girl in England, we were hurt but not altogether surprised. You see, we had suspected there was someone—someone who drove him back to England time after time. For years we had been trying to interest him in girls here, but without success. At one time we thought he might enter the Church, but then his marriage to you altered all that.'

'I see.' Miranda tried to assimilate what Teresa was saying, but all that stuck in her mind were the words '... we had suspected there was someone ...' Who? *Who?*

'When you sent that telegram,' Teresa was going on, 'I began to wonder whether we had known the whole story. I even hoped that perhaps Jaime had been responsible for your absence—that you had wanted to come here, but he had refused to allow it. Then, last night, when he told us ...'

Miranda didn't know what to say. So much of what Teresa suspected was true, but not for the right reasons. And how could she explain the true facts of the case without arousing Jaime's mother's anger and contempt?

'I—well, I was very young when we got married,' she faltered awkwardly.

'Jaime told us that,' Teresa agreed. 'He said you had needed time to adjust.'

Miranda bent her head. 'I did.'

'And now?'

'I don't know ...'

And she didn't. Faced with Armageddon, she couldn't take the irrevocable step which would put her once and for all outside the circle of Teresa's affection. She told herself it was because she was still very weak, that such decisions required a cool nerve and a level head, which was what she did not have right at this moment. But deep inside her, she shrank from destroying that tenuous bond.

But if she was dissatisfied with herself, Teresa was apparently not. Whatever Jaime's mother had expected, it had not materialised, and for that she was grateful. Which meant that she approved of Jaime's choice of a wife, thought Miranda, wondering why that realisation had the ability to silence any further protests.

Jaime returned, lean and attractive, in dark green velvet pants and a cream silk shirt, with a jabot of pleated lace at the neckline which on anyone else would have looked effeminate. On him, it simply accentuated the hard lines of his face, and only his eyes showed any trace of softness. His mother raised her eyebrows at his appearance, however, and he pulled a face at her before saying wryly:

'As it's my wife's first evening downstairs, I thought I ought to distinguish the occasion.'

His mother nodded, and rose to her feet. 'I think that's an excellent idea, Jaime. You may now excuse me to do likewise.'

Miranda offered Jaime some tea after his mother had left them, but it was cool and he refused, saying he would prefer something stronger. In the event, he poured himself a glass of the raw spirit Miranda had seen the men drinking at the *estancia*, and flung himself on to the couch beside her with weary relief.

'You've been to the village?' she enquired stiltedly, feeling obliged to say something, but he shook his head.

'I've been to one of the outlying farms. The man's wife was expecting their eleventh child, and unfortunately it came earlier than was expected.'

Miranda turned to him. 'Is she all right? The woman, I mean?'

He shrugged. 'She's alive.'

'And the child?'

'Him, too. Although I doubt either of them will last the week.'

'Oh! How awful! Why?'

He sat up, spreading his legs to suspend his hands holding the glass between. 'Consuelo is too old to have children. She must be forty, if she is a day. She has already done her duty

to her husband, but still she goes on having pregnancies, each
time destroying her health that much more.'

'But why will she die? If she's come through the birth ...'

'She's lost a lot of blood. She should be taken to the hospital
at Valentes, but Vasco won't let me take her.'

'He won't *let* you?'

Jaime quirked an eyebrow at her. 'That really gets to you,
doesn't it? But here a man is master in his own home.'

'But if she's dying ...'

'He won't believe that. She's alive, the baby's alive. *Servus
et humilis*, and God will provide.'

'You sound so—cynical,' she almost whispered the words,
and with a derisive twist of his mouth he went to pour himself another drink.

'*Domine, non sum dignus*,' he quoted dryly, and then
looked straight at her. 'What was my mother saying to you?'

Miranda examined her hands with assumed concentration.
'She was—asking me how I felt.'

'Is that all?'

'What else could there be?'

'She didn't mention the fact that I had told them you
weren't happy here?'

That brought her head up, her lips parting defensively.
'Carlos—said something about it.'

'And?'

'I—said I didn't know what I was going to do.'

His eyes narrowed. 'Why did you say that?'

'Because—I don't, do I?'

He frowned, and then bowed his head in a gesture of nega-
tion. 'You are feeling quite well now, though, aren't you?'

'Yes.' She was swift to agree, and he swallowed the remainder of the liquid in his glass.

'So ...' He replaced his glass and came across to stand feet
apart, looking down at her. 'Perhaps we should talk now.'

'What about?' Her voice was breathy, but he chose not to
notice.

'You ask me that!' he commented, coming down beside
her again, closer this time, his nearness filling her nostrils
with the potent odours of soap and after-shave lotion and the
musky scent of his maleness. 'You know why you came here
better than I do.'

Miranda's breathing quickened. 'And—and you said you —you wouldn't let me go . . .' she pointed out unsteadily.

Jaime's eyes dropped to her parted lips. 'Do I take it you're holding that against me now?'

She shifted discomfitedly. 'I—I'm only reminding you what—what you said.'

'Oh, I remember what I said,' he affirmed softly, stroking the back of his hand along the curve of her jawline almost unconsciously. 'But I don't recall that you paid it a lot of heed.'

'I—I didn't. I don't!' She put her hands down to the couch and shifted her weight from one position to another. 'But since I've been ill, I've not had much time to—to consider the future . . .'

'No?' His fingers probed the neckline of her tunic, lifting the thin material away from her skin, deliberately caressing the soft flesh. 'Do you like me to do this?'

His question was as unexpected as it was incisive, and she flinched away from the look in the eyes he raised to hers. 'I— *no*!' she got out chokingly, but his twisted smile revealed his disbelief.

'So why don't you stop me?' he demanded, sliding the strap of the tunic aside to stroke her shoulder with his lips. 'Stop me . . . or join me . . .' and taking her throat between his fingers, he turned her face up to his.

She opened her mouth to protest again, but the words were never spoken against the demanding pressure of his. Instead she felt sweetness, like a wine-dark liquid, invading her whole being, turning her limbs to fluidity in his arms. Imprisoned between the back of the couch and the thrusting hardness of his body, she had difficulty in maintaining her identity, let alone anything else. His mouth was bruising hers, forcing a response that left her drained and clinging to him, unknowingly inviting more than kisses. Almost involuntarily, her hands fluttered to find something to hold on to, but all they encountered was the hard length of his thigh, and she drew back instinctively from such an intimate contact.

'*Meigo*,' he whispered, against her lips. '*Deus sabe, tu queria* . . .'

'I am sorry if I am intruding.'

Julia's coolly cultured tones fell like pebbles into a still pool, causing ripples that swelled and increased, enveloping all of them in the aftermath.

Jaime's reactions were slower than Miranda's, but while she felt the instinctive words of protest rising in her throat as he continued to kiss her, he only turned aside from her with obvious reluctance. Miranda's hands automatically sought the slipping strap of her tunic, sliding it back into position, nervously reaching for her hair as she endeavoured to seek the calmness of manner exhibited by her sister-in-law. Jaime relaxed back against the cushions with lazy resignation, regarding Julia through darkly cynical eyes.

'If you're sorry, why didn't you just get the hell out of here?' he inquired, in much the same tone that he might have used to complain about the weather, and his sister's naturally pale features flushed with unbecoming colour.

'If you must seduce your wife in full view of any of the servants who care to look, I see no reason why I should not join the audience,' she retorted stiffly.

'I was not seducing her,' Jaime corrected flatly, straightening away from the cushions, indifferent to his wife's evident embarrassment. 'I doubt in those circumstances whether even you would have dared to intrude,' he added.

Julia linked her hands before her, but their unsteadiness revealed that she was not as calm as she pretended. '*Es o porco*, Jaime!' she declared through tight lips. '*E pena sua esposa——*'

'Speak English!' he commanded impatiently, getting to his feet. 'If you must insult me, have the decency to do it in a language my wife can understand!'

Julia held up her head. 'Perhaps *she* should learn *our* language,' she retorted, her eyes shifting to Miranda. 'I called my brother a pig, *senhora*. And I was about to say that it was a pity you could not teach him better manners!'

Miranda felt obliged to rise too, her gaze darting uneasily from one to the other of them. Jaime's eyes moved over her with disturbing appraisal, and she could feel the intentness of his regard burning into her like a brand. She felt as if he had set his mark upon her, and all without the assuagement that only his possession of her body would bring.

'I—I'm sorry,' she said now, turning deliberately to Julia, unwilling to explore in greater depth the feelings Jaime could arouse in her. 'It's my fault, of course.'

'Your fault!' Julia was fast recovering her composure. 'What on earth do you mean?'

Miranda cast a discomfited look in Jaime's direction, and then said carefully: 'That I can't speak Portuguese, naturally. What else did you think I meant?'

She sensed rather than heard Jaime's amused intake of breath, but Julia was far from amused. 'Yes, I rather think it is,' she agreed coldly. 'Perhaps if Jaime had married a woman instead of a girl, she might have found it in her to suffer the privations of living here before now.'

The unwarranted attack caught Miranda unawares, but when Jaime would have made some cutting retort, she silenced him with a look. 'Perhaps that's so,' she conceded quietly. 'But your brother never gave me the chance to find out.'

She heard Jaime's sharply-drawn breath this time, but refused to acknowledge it, waiting instead for Julia's reply. And when it came, she was more than gratified.

'Is that so?' Clearly, Julia didn't for one moment doubt that she was telling the truth. Her eyes lifted to her brother's face. 'I am beginning to understand now.' A cold smile lifted her lips. 'That was your way of getting out of a difficult situation, was it not? Our mother was becoming too eager in her attempts to find you a suitable wife, no? By marrying Miranda you—how do they say it?—spiced her guns.'

'Spiked,' amended Jaime dryly, but Julia was hardly listening to him.

'I should have guessed, of course.' She turned to Miranda once more. 'My apologies, *cunhada*. It would seem you are making the best of the situation only. I congratulate you.'

Miranda accepted her good wishes without satisfaction. She was disturbed and confused by what she had heard, and she turned to her husband blankly, waiting for him to deny Julia's accusations. But Jaime's features were as enigmatic as ever, and what had begun as an attempt to hold her own with this woman, who seemed so much more Portuguese than English, became a battle with her own ragged emotions.

The reappearance of Teresa and Carlos was more of a reprieve than a relief, and Miranda spent the remainder of the evening pondering over what her sister-in-law had said and why it should have had such a profound effect on her.

CHAPTER ELEVEN

MIRANDA awakened next morning with the ominous feeling of disaster hanging over her. She lay for several minutes just staring at the shifting curtains before making any attempt to get out of bed, caring little what day or time it was.

The night before had been a total anti-climax, she admitted to herself, remembering the hours she had lain awake after retiring, waiting for Jaime to come upstairs, fully expecting him to try and take up where he had left off earlier. She had never really considered the outcome if he did, but when she heard sounds in the adjoining dressing room the full import of what she had been hoping for came through to her. Then, of course, what stuck in her throat was the realisation that in spite of everything his sister had said, she had still wanted him to come, and that was the most painful thing of all to bear.

She had expected problems when she left England. She had known from previous experience that Jaime was not the easiest man to deal with. But she had been determined to succeed, and prepared to face the difficulties when she came to them. The thing she was forced to concede with bitter honesty was that the problems she was facing now were not the ones she had contemplated on the flight out from London.

Sliding her legs out of bed, she got to her feet, relieved to find that she felt few after-effects of her illness. She was still a little weak, but that would pass now she was eating normally again, and at least she was no longer plagued by giddiness.

She padded across to the windows and looked out. Apart from the domestic sounds of cattle lowing, and hens clucking near the barns, all was quiet. While she was ill, she knew, Carlos had made the hands walk on eggshells in the yard, but now she would have welcomed their careless rowdyism.

The sun was filtering through low-hanging clouds, and she guessed it would rain before long. The ominous weather seemed indicative of her mood, and she looked mutinously towards the dressing room door.

Uncaring that she was not dressed, she went to the door and opened it. Jaime had seen her plenty of times without clothes, she thought, smiling bitterly when she recalled her initial desire to remain aloof with him. How aloof could she remain with a man who had carried her to the bathroom on those frequent occasions when her metabolism had been in danger of running out of control, or who had sponged the secret places of her body and destroyed any mystery she might have possessed?

But the dressing room was empty, Jaime's bed unmade and tumbled; witness to the restless night he had spent? she wondered. She had discovered the connecting door to the landing outside during these past days of inactivity in her room, and knew now that he could come and go as he pleased.

She closed the door again just as Chiquita appeared with her breakfast tray. 'Ah, *senhora. Como esta?* You are feeling well, *sim?*'

'*Bem, obrigado.*' Miranda had learned simple phrases. 'Er—where is my husband?'

Chiquita's sharp eyes flickered over her and then moved knowingly towards the dressing room door. Miranda guessed that it would be common knowledge about the *hacienda* that Senhor Jaime slept in his dressing room, but she refused to allow this to disturb her.

'Senhor Jaime—he is gone, *senhora,*' Chiquita answered carefully, setting the tray down on the bedside table, and Miranda found her nerves tightening painfully.

'G—gone?' she echoed faintly. Then, more calmly: 'Gone where, Chiquita? To the village?'

'The village, *senhora?*' Chiquita frowned. 'Ah, Santa Madalena? Oh, *nao, senhora.*'

'Then where?'

Miranda was finding it increasingly difficult not to give in to the impulse to shake Chiquita. Was she being deliberately obtuse? But no, Chiquita was not like that. She simply didn't understand Miranda's urgency, that was all. And she probably wondered why Jaime had not told her where he was going himself.

Now she clasped her hands together and said rather unhappily: 'Is gone to Belo Horizonte, *senhora.*'

'Belo Horizonte!' Miranda couldn't keep the dismay out of her voice. 'But—' She broke off to lick her lips. 'When will he be back?'

Chiquita spread her hands. *'Nao conheco, senhora.'*

Miranda frowned. Obviously she was not going to get anything further out of her, and with a tight smile, she dismissed her. But after the girl had gone, and Miranda had poured herself a cup of the strong black coffee, she couldn't help wondering whether this was his way of giving her freedom. Did he expect her to be here when he returned? Or not?

Although Jaime's departure had destroyed her appetite, she forced herself to eat some breakfast, remembering how easily her strength could be undermined again. Then, after a refreshing shower, she dressed in saddle-stitched cream levis and a matching shirt, and went downstairs.

It was after nine, and the house was a hive of activity, with Sancha organising the staff from the kitchen. Miranda had learned that Sancha did most of the cooking herself, and obviously enjoyed what she produced, judging by her ample girth.

As there was no sign of Teresa, Miranda asked one of the maids the way to the kitchen, and came into an enormous room at the back of the house where Sancha was sitting at a scrubbed table, enjoying a mid-morning break of coffee and cheese. Slatted wooden blinds at the long windows shaded a modern steel sink and drainers, but the huge range was wood-fired. The floor was stone and flagged, but any sense of chill was dispersed by the huge fire burning in the grate which kept the temperature bordering on the eighties.

Sancha hastened to her feet as Miranda came into the room, dismissing the two maids who were giggling together as they prepared vegetables at the sink, and bidding Miranda to take a seat all in one breath.

Miranda smiled her thanks, but indicated that Sancha should sit down also before saying awkwardly: 'I—just wanted to thank you ...'

Sancha frowned, and for a moment Miranda thought she didn't understand her. But then the old woman's fleshy features beamed, and she let out a stream of unintelligible language, which although Miranda could not understand it, was so obviously complimentary that the girl felt her face turning pink.

Shaking her head to show her lack of comprehension, she tried again: 'I—know you—helped; when I was sick.' She mimed feeling ill, and Sancha ceased her chatter to nod happily, and Miranda added: 'I am—much better now.' Again she mimed the feeling. 'Much better.'

Sancha continued to nod for some seconds after she had finished, and half embarrassed by the old woman's intense regard, Miranda got to her feet again. At once, Sancha rose too, and came round the table towards her, putting a detaining hand on her arm.

Then, with obvious difficulty, she spoke. 'You stay Monte Paraiso,' she declared firmly. 'Senhor Jaime—want you stay, no?'

Miranda gave an offhand shrug of her shoulders. 'It's very kind of you to say so, but——'

'Senhor Jaime's woman!' Sancha insisted, nodding again. 'You make many *bebes*. I know. Sancha knows.'

Miranda gasped. She couldn't help it. The idea of her and Jaime making a child together seemed as unlikely as it had ever been. And besides, she told herself fiercely, if she had any child it would be Paul's.

Managing to extricate herself from Sancha's grasp, she backed towards the door, and as she did so Julia came in. She regarded Miranda with much less hostility this morning, and frowned as she tried to gauge what had been going on.

'Is anything wrong?' she asked, but Miranda hurriedly reassured her.

'I was—just leaving,' she said, recovering her equilibrium. 'I—er—where is your mother?'

Julia shrugged. 'About somewhere. Why? Do you want her? I can find her for you.'

'Oh, no.' Miranda shook her head. 'It's not important. I—Chiquita tells me Jaime has gone to Belo Horizonte.'

Julia looked disturbed. '*Chiquita* told you?'

Miranda flushed. 'Jaime must have—forgotten,' she offered uncomfortably, and saw the other girl's scepticism. 'Will he—that is, do you know when he'll be back?'

Julia looked thoughtful. 'He should not be away more than two or three days.'

'Two or three days!' Miranda pressed her lips tightly together. 'I see.'

Julia raised an apologetic hand at Sancha and accompanied her sister-in-law along the corridor back to the main body of the house. 'I guess he did not tell you anything,' she observed quietly. 'He has gone to the university, Miranda. He lectures there sometimes.'

'I didn't know that.'

Miranda stared at her, and Julia sighed. 'You do not know very much about my brother at all, do you?' she said. 'I wonder, is that his fault—or yours?'

Miranda moved her shoulders defensively. 'Thank you for telling me anyway.'

Julia paused, and Miranda walked on, but after a moment the other girl quickened her step again to catch up with her. 'Miranda ...'

'Yes?'

Miranda hesitated reluctantly, unwilling to hear any further revelations from Julia's lips, but the other girl said something completely unexpected.

'Look,' she said, 'I know you have to take things easy for a day or so, but perhaps you would like to see something of the estate while Jaime is away.' She smiled. 'I could show you.'

Miranda was astonished. 'That's very kind of you, Julia.'

'No, it is not.' Julia spoke ruefully. 'It is my way of—apologising for—well, for misjudging you.'

Miranda's lips curved. 'I just might take you up on that.'

'Right now, if you wish,' suggested Julia at once, and Miranda, who had been dreading the long days until Jaime's return, was only too happy to agree.

That first morning, Julia took her out in the Landrover. It would be more suitable, she said, for someone only just recovering from being ill, but within two days Miranda was on horseback again, and loving the feeling of freedom it gave her.

Nevertheless, her first outing taught her she knew nothing about the actual running of the estate. Used to helping Lydia with the paper work involved in dealing the Tembury estates, she had foolishly imagined Monte Paraiso was governed along similar lines.

She couldn't have been more wrong. To begin with, Monte Paraiso was something like ten times the size, and to some extent incapable of sustaining a series of small units. Much of the land was given over to the cattle that wandered unhindered over two hundred square miles of the long grass so common in this area. There were farms, Julia explained, but they were further south, where the land was richer. Even so, there was cultivation, mostly for their own use, and Miranda was delighted to be offered a peach straight from the tree.

'Brazil is essentially an agricultural country,' Julia told her as they rode home. 'You have heard about the coffee beans, of course, but did you know we rank only third in the world for cotton production, as well as corn and sugar-cane, wheat, rye, tobacco . . .'

'I believe you,' exclaimed Miranda laughing. 'And beef, too.'

'Ah, yes. Beef.' Julia nodded towards a herd of cattle grazing nearby. 'We cannot escape them, can we?'

Miranda shook her head, by now well used to avoiding the occasionally aggressive bids of bulls in the herd, jealously guarding their territory. There was a kind of impressive rawness about the life out here, and out of sight of the homestead, alone with the horses and the cattle, and the languidly wheeling hawks which could fall on their prey with such deadly precision, Miranda had come to love it. She was beginning to understand why people born to this way of life found the confining limits of a city unacceptable, and wondered if that was how Jaime felt.

Julia had shown her the airstrip, about half a mile from the house, but the small Cessna they owned was absent. With Jaime in Belo Horizonte, Miranda hazarded, unwilling to ask his sister whether he flew himself. So far, they had avoided discussion of Jaime and his reasons for marrying her, and she would prefer to keep it that way.

One evening, the Carvalhos had a dinner party. They invited some friends from an adjoining estate, the Mineiras, whose daughter, Silvana, was the same age as Julia. Julia's fiancé Miguel was there too, and Miranda enjoyed the unusual experience of being the centre of attraction.

The Mineiras were not like Aunt Lydia's friends, whose conversation was always littered with malicious references about mutual acquaintances. Senhora Mineira was a charming woman, who confided an amateur interest in painting, and their daughter showed a sincere envy of Miranda's life in England. She envied the opportunities Miranda had for attending plays and concerts, particularly those of a popular variety, and it was strange hearing Silvana talk about groups whose records Miranda collected back home.

When dinner was over, Teresa asked whether the young people would mind if they played bridge, and in consequence, Miguel was left with the three girls to entertain. He seemed willing enough for the task, and they adjourned to the low level lounge where there was a record player and space for dancing.

Fortunately, the kind of music **they liked** did not require them to take partners, and before long Miranda was demonstrating the latest steps from England. Julia and Silvana clapped their hands, and produced their own version of a *fado*, and then it was Miranda's turn again, laughing and sinuating her limbs to the lively throbbing of the drums.

It was Silvana who saw Jaime first. Miranda was swaying in time to a particularly lilting rhythm, the folds of her gold-embroidered caftan giving tantalising glimpses of honey-brown legs between the thigh-length slits, when something about the expression the other girl was wearing caused her to glance round.

He was standing on the steps, propped against the wall, arms folded; and judging by his travel-stained appearance, he had not yet sought the facilities a bathroom offered. His brown pants and jacket were creased, and the shirt beneath was less than immaculate.

For a moment Miranda faltered, and then the curious delight in seeing him again got the better of her. Uncaring what the others might think, she maintained the rhythm of the tune and held out her arms towards him, inviting him to join her.

If he had refused, she would have been shattered, but after only a brief hesitation he descended the remainder of the steps and drew her into his arms. It was more than four years since they had danced together, but Miranda could remember that other occasion as clearly as if it were yesterday. With his arms looped around her waist and his hard body against hers, it was the most natural thing in the world for her arms to slide around his neck and she lifted her face to his without reluctance.

Jaime looked down at her, and although his nearness was intimidating, she refused to let it worry her.

'So you're still here,' he remarked in an undertone, his expression revealing none of his feelings, and she caught her breath.

'Did you think I wouldn't be?'

'Let's say, I was prepared for the worst.'

'What is the worst?' she countered tremulously. 'My being here—or my leaving?'

He drew her a little closer. 'That remains to be seen.'

She expelled her breath sharply, and then, as if needing a safer topic, she asked: 'Did you have a good trip?'

'Good enough.'

'You didn't tell me you were leaving.'

He swung her round so her back was to the others, sitting on the window seat watching them. 'I knew you'd soon find out.'

'Chiquita—Chiquita told me you had gone to Belo Horizonte, and Julia—she said you sometimes lectured at the university there.'

He inclined his head in silent acknowledgement, and then said: 'You would like Belo Horizonte. It's new and modern, with broad streets and plenty of shops.'

'What makes you think I need shops?' she countered, allowing her fingers to move against his nape, knowing that he was aware of them by the involuntary response of hardening muscles. 'I like it here. I really do. Julia's been showing me the estate, and I know all about what you grow and how many cattle you run ...'

'Do you?' His eyes dropped to the tantalising glimpse of cleavage visible above the dipping neckline of her gown. 'And do you also know that Monte Paraiso belongs to Carlos, not me?'

'I know he took it over when your father died—he told me that. But he told me that this house is yours, and the land immediately surrounding it.'

Jaime's eyes sought her again. 'What are you saying? That you'd like to live at Monte Paraiso?'

Miranda drew an unsteady breath. 'Is that not what you had in mind——' she was beginning softly, when a movement beyond Jaime's broad shoulders attracted her attention. Another man had walked to the top of the steps leading down on to the floor where they were dancing. Another man who was swaying slightly on his feet, another man whose face was extremely pale—but also extremely familiar!

'*Paul!*' Her ejaculation was choked, and she lifted tormented eyes to Jaime's face. His mouth had taken on that recognisably mocking curve, and in that moment she could have killed him.

'I forgot to add that I went to Rio, too,' he intoned almost inaudibly, but she pushed him away and went to meet the other man.

'Hello, Miranda,' Paul said, almost sheepishly, supporting himself against the handrail beside the steps, and making no move to touch her. 'I guess you thought I'd never make it.'

Miranda cast another destructive look in Jaime's direction, and then turning back to Paul exclaimed: 'What do you mean?'

'My telegram,' Paul explained, clearing his throat with difficulty. 'You did get it, didn't you? But of course, you must have done. How else would your—your—that is, Knevett have known where I was?' he finished lamely, and at that Jaime stepped forward.

'I'm afraid I'm to blame,' he remarked casually. 'I kept your telegram a secret, Courtenay. I wanted to—surprise Miranda.'

Miranda's frustration was almost tangible. She stared at her husband blindly, forcing back the tears that threatened to complete her humiliation. How could he do this to her? All her life she seemed to have been asking herself that question, and never once had she had a satisfactory answer.

Paul, obviously not well and impervious to the tensions around him, made a dismissing gesture. 'Well, I'm here now,' he said, 'and as you can see, a little wobbly on the old legs.'

Miranda licked her lips. 'You've been ill?'

'Air-sick,' inserted Jaime, with annoying candour. 'I'm

afraid—Paul, is it?' He knew damn well it was, thought Miranda angrily '—yes, Paul isn't used to our somewhat— fluctuating air currents.'

'That's right,' Paul nodded vigorously. 'I've never flown in anything but jets, until today.'

Miranda took several deep breaths, trying to gather her composure, and Julia and her boy-friend, and Silvana, came forward politely. Jaime took over the introductions, and Miranda wondered if she was only imagining the trace of humour in his voice. After all, she had no right to be so angry when in fact she should be delighted at seeing Paul again. But what had begun as only uncertainty had been made manifest when she saw Paul and her husband together. Paul's fair good looks seemed insipid compared with Jaime's dark attractiveness, and remembering her different reactions to the touch of their hands, she knew with quelling conviction that marriage to Paul was out of the question now, whatever happened.

'And now, if you'll excuse me,' Jaime was saying, 'I'll go take a shower. By the way, Miranda ...' He turned to her and she tensed automatically. 'Perhaps—Paul might like something to eat or drink. He lost the last of his lunch over Sete Lagoas!'

Her fists clenched and she glared at him, but to no avail. There was nothing she could say to penetrate his mockery, and although Julia said: 'Really, Jaime!' in rather shocked tones, he showed no trace of contrition.

After he had vaulted up the steps and disappeared upstairs, the atmosphere in no way eased. Julia was looking at her sister-in-law with evident suspicion, and both Miguel and Silvana seemed discomfited by this unexpected intrusion.

'I—would you like something to eat?' Miranda suggested awkwardly, but Paul just shook his head, visibly shuddering.

'Can we just find somewhere to sit down?' he asked softly, and feeling horribly guilty, Miranda gestured towards the window seats.

The music had stopped now, and no one was making any attempt to put another record on. Consequently their conversation was clearly audible and therefore stilted to say the least.

'So you didn't know I was coming,' Paul exclaimed, after

they were seated, making an abortive attempt to capture one of her hands.

'No.' Miranda cast a subtle glance in her sister-in-law's direction, and put a yard of space between them. 'Jaime— Jaime's like that. He—enjoys—surprising me.'

'But, Miranda——' Paul shifted towards her and then stopped abruptly when she backed off again, shaking her head pointedly. 'Miranda, what's going on?'

'Did you have a good flight out from England?' she parried, and he sighed impatiently.

'As good as these flights can be,' he retorted, returning to the attack. 'Miranda, have you told Knevett you want——'

'*Not now*, Paul!'

She was compelled to silence him then, and before he could make any further comment, Teresa appeared. She smiled rather absently at her daughter and her friends and made straight for Miranda.

'My dear, Sancha's just told me that Jaime's back.' Her eyes shifted to Paul rather speculatively. 'And that he's brought someone with him.'

'Yes.' Paul had risen politely to his feet at her mother-in-law's approach, and now Miranda joined them. 'Er—this is Paul—Paul Courtenay, Teresa. A—a friend.' Her eyes appealed to him not to dispute this. 'Paul—my mother-in-law, Senhora Carvalho.'

His face mirroring his distrust of the situation, Paul shook hands with the older woman, and then Teresa said hospitably: 'Does—er—does Mr Courtenay want some dinner?'

'Thank you, no.' Paul answered for himself. 'I'm afraid your son flew a little too recklessly for me.' He patted his flat stomach. 'I think I ought to give this a few hours to recover itself.'

Teresa's smile was polite but guarded, and Miranda guessed she had not appreciated that reference to her son's flying abilities. But at least it answered Miranda's question as to whether Jaime piloted the plane himself.

'You're—staying, Mr Courtenay?' Teresa asked now, and her tone brought a wave of colour to Paul's pale cheeks.

'I—your son invited me,' he declared defensively, and Miranda winced at the look in Teresa's eyes.

'I see.' She folded her hands tightly together. 'Then I'd

better arrange for a room to be made ready. If you'll excuse me ...'

Miranda stared after her mother-in-law as Paul sank down again weakly on to the window seat. Oh dear, she thought wretchedly, what now?

Paul succeeded in catching her hand, and she allowed herself to be drawn down beside him, almost unthinkingly. And as if Julia had seen enough, she and Miguel and Silvana mounted the steps into the hall, disappearing into the room where her parents and Silvana's had been playing cards, leaving Paul and Miranda alone together.

'Now, what's going on?' demanded Paul shortly. 'I come here at your instigation, and I'm practically treated as a leper——'

'That's not true!'

'What is true, then? Have you asked—*him* for a divorce?'

'An annulment—yes.'

'And?'

Miranda shrugged. 'He refused.' That at least was true.

Paul made a sound of annoyance. 'And he didn't say one word to me about it all the way up from Rio!'

Miranda hesitated. Then: 'What did he say?'

'Not a lot. He asked me a lot of questions about my job and my family and how long I'd known you, but that was all. And then—well, I was sick, wasn't I? After that, I couldn't say much at all. Damned lunatic!'

'What do you mean?'

'I mean your husband's not fit to handle an aircraft!' declared Paul spitefully. 'My God, if that's the quickest way up here, give me pack-mules every time!'

Miranda felt a bubble of hysterical amusement rising inside her. 'It can't have been worse than the car journey I made. I was ill for days.'

'Barbaric country!' Clearly Paul was not enamoured by its undoubted physical beauty. 'Give me England every time. There's no place like it.'

'I—wouldn't say that,' murmured Miranda reflectively, and then sensing Paul's irritation, she added: 'How—how is Aunt Lydia?'

'I didn't come here to talk about Aunt Lydia. I came to be with you. I thought you wanted me. Your telegram ...'

'Yes?' Miranda held her breath.

'Well, it was—unexpected, to say the least. I mean, I thought you said you had to do this alone.'

'Are you sorry you came, Paul?' she asked, half hoping his reply would be positive, but for an answer Paul pulled her into his arms, and she was struggling to be free of him when Jaime's voice drawled:

'I'd advise you to do your wrestling in other places. The servants gossip, you know.'

Miranda stumbled to her feet. 'That never worries you!' she declared, and he shrugged.

'As you pointed out earlier, I do own this property. I'm entitled to do as I like.'

'And usually do, I'd say,' put in Paul aggressively, and Jaime's attention shifted to him.

'Are you accusing me of something, Courtenay?' he inquired pleasantly, strolling towards them, his hands tucked into the waist-high pockets of his suede pants. 'Because if you are . . .'

'Oh, for heaven's sake, Jaime!' Miranda exlaimed, half alarmed at that unspoken threat, but Paul refused to be intimidated.

'You don't scare me, Knevett. I've met your type before. All brawn and brute force and precious little else!'

'Is that so?' Jaime halted in front of him. 'And what type are you, I wonder? You've got a nerve, I'll grant you that, coming here with the declared intention of taking my wife away from me——'

'She asked me to come here——'

'Correction—I asked you to come here!' retorted Jaime harshly. 'I sent that cable myself.'

Paul looked at Miranda in astonishment. 'Is that——'

'Paul, I——'

Their half-spoken conversation was never finished.

'I do not lie!' Jaime averred coldly. 'I sent the telegram because I wanted to see for myself the kind of swine who has been making free with my wife!'

'*Your wife!*' Paul's voice was filled with scorn. 'What kind of husband are you?'

'You want to find out?'

Miranda could hear the hardening tone in Jaime's voice

and responded to it. 'Please!' she cried. 'You're both behaving like—like——'

'I told you your vocabulary was sadly lacking,' remarked Jaime in an aside that brought the whole situation into ludicrous focus, and she gasped in horror.

'You're only pretending to be jealous,' she told him in shocked tones. 'Paul, for God's sake, stop letting him make a fool of you! Can't you see? He doesn't mean it. He doesn't mean a word of it!'

And with a broken sob and a despairing look at both of them she ran from the room, passing Teresa without even seeing her.

In her room, she flung herself on the bed, panting breathlessly. But the tears which had been so precarious downstairs had deserted her now, and all she could see was Jaime's cruel humour in a situation he had created.

When he had first appeared, she had been so *glad* to see him, ridiculously glad. She had made him take her in his arms because that was where she had wanted to be, and for a few minutes she had known supreme contentment in the knowledge that she could arouse him as he aroused her. What she had not considered was that it was purely a physical reaction to her woman's body, and that any woman might have had the same effect on him. And when Paul appeared behind them . . .

She shuddered. It had been terrible. He was the last person she had expected—or wanted, she admitted—to see, and his presence there was like an intrusion into that very special world she had succeeded in making for herself.

She plucked miserably at the silk coverlet. So what was she saying? she asked herself helplessly. That she wanted to stay here? That she didn't care if she never saw Paul—or England—again? That if Jaime would make her his wife in every sense of that ill-used word she would be happy to accept him?

She rolled over on to her back. And why? she thought, staring blindly at the ceiling. Because she didn't flinch when he touched her? Because he could arouse her in ways she had not known a woman could be aroused? Because she loved him with every fibre of her being . . .

She heard the Mineiras leaving and sat up abruptly. How

rude Jaime's parents would think her. How rude the Mineiras would think her. But how could she go down there again and face Paul—and Jaime? She needed time to compose herself before she faced the decision she would have to make, and besides, there was always the chance that her husband might come to find out whether she was all right ...

But Jaime didn't come, and when nervous exhaustion sent sleep to claim her she was still wearing the gold-embroidered caftan that she would never be able to dissociate from the awful events of this evening.

CHAPTER TWELVE

CHIQUITA awakened her as usual, her eyes widening curiously as she took in the other girl's dishevelled appearance, and Miranda sighed.

'It's all right, Chiquita,' she said calmingly, '*esta bem!* I—I must have fallen asleep as soon as I came upstairs.'

'*Sim, senhora.*'

But Chiquita looked sceptical, and who could blame her, Miranda thought wearily.

'*Quer me correo bo banho, senhora,*' Chiquita suggested, obviously hoping that Miranda might confide in her, but she was refused the opportunity to run a bath.

'I—I'll just take a shower,' said Miranda, sliding off the bed. 'You know—*chuveiro,* shower?'

'Ah, *sim, senhora.*' Chiquita gave a faint smile, and with another regretful look, left her.

After she had gone and Miranda was pouring herself some coffee, however, she guessed the presence of another male in the house was arousing some curiosity among the female members of the staff. Particularly an Englishman, who might or might not have made some statement in the presence of a servant that was worthy of anxious speculation. She couldn't help wondering how Paul was feeling this morning, and wishing with all her heart that his indisposition had kept him in Rio just a little longer.

She forced herself to drink the fresh orange juice which she always enjoyed at this hour of the morning, and ate a roll without butter. Then she took off her clothes and walked naked into the bathroom.

She ran the shower hot and then cool, shivering a little as she towelled herself dry. She wondered where Jaime was this morning, and whether he had said anything more to Paul after she had gone to bed. Why did he persist in behaving like an irate husband when it was obvious she was nothing more than an embarrassment to him? He had wanted a shadow wife, as Julia had said, but not the substance.

She dressed slowly, choosing black jeans and a purple shirt. The outfit was more sophisticated than any she had worn so far, and then, unable to put off any longer, she went downstairs.

There was no one about and she walked through the mesh door and stood for a few minutes on the verandah, breathing deeply. At this hour of the morning the air was crisp and invigorating, and attracted by the mare and her foals in the paddock, Miranda crossed the yard to speak to her. She wished she had some sugar or an apple to offer her when the mare nuzzled her hand, and the foals, learning quickly, came to push their soft noses against her fingers.

'*Bom dia,* Miranda.' It was Carlos who had come out of one of the store-sheds to speak to her and she turned to him eagerly.

'Good morning.' She managed a smile. 'It's a beautiful morning, isn't it?'

Carlos looked skyward for a moment and then nodded. 'Did you sleep well?'

Miranda wondered if she imagined the undertone in his casual question. 'Reasonably so,' she admitted. 'I—I'm sorry if I offended your friends last night——'

'*De nada.*' Carlos shook his head quickly. 'We were—concerned about you.' He paused. 'This man Courtenay—who is he?'

Miranda swallowed with difficulty. 'Didn't—didn't Jaime tell you?'

'He said he was someone you had known in England.'

'Oh.' Miranda didn't quite know how to take this. 'Was that all?' she asked faintly.

Carlos sighed now, scratching his head as if finding what he wanted to say difficult. 'Miranda,' he began, and she stiffened at his tone. 'There—well, there was some trouble last night, was there not? Between Jaime and this man?'

'Trouble?' Miranda hoped she didn't sound as shattered as she felt.

'Yes, trouble.' Carlos hesitated. 'Look, I know it is not really my business, but these past two weeks we have come to care for you, and we would be sorry if you felt you could not confide in us.'

'Confide in you?'

'Yes.' Carlos drew a deep breath. 'I know that things are done differently in England. I know that it cannot have been easy living there, married to someone several thousand miles away. But was that truly Jaime's fault? If you felt you could not share his life here, you should not have married him. And I suggest this is what this man Courtenay feels also. Am I not right?'

Miranda didn't know how to answer him. She didn't know what else Jaime might have said. And until she did, how could she explain?

The sound of horses' hooves brought both their heads round together, and it was almost with relief that Miranda saw her husband riding into the yard. She looked round, wondering whether Paul had been riding with him, but he was alone. He saw his stepfather and his wife standing by the fence, and urged his mount in their direction.

'*Ola*, Jaime!' Carlos greeted him good-naturedly. 'Did you see them?'

Jaime swung down from the horse's back. 'Yes. They're out by the Rio Rosado. About three hundred of them altogether.'

Guessing they were discussing the cattle, Miranda turned away, only to have Jaime's arm descend across her shoulders. Of course, she thought tautly, this was for his stepfather's benefit. Why? To reassure him that all was well between them? That Paul's advent meant nothing of importance?

Without caring too much what Carlos thought just then, she turned mutinous eyes up to her husband and asked tautly: 'Where's Paul?'

'I was just about to tell you,' Carlos interposed before Jaime could say anything. 'Julia has taken him riding this morning.'

'It was my suggestion,' remarked Jaime lazily. 'There's nothing like God's good clean air to brush away the cobwebs.'

Miranda felt resentment rising inside her. 'You're so clever, aren't you?' she said through clenched teeth, but Jaime only laughed.

'You see,' he said to Carlos, 'what more could any man want? A loyal *and* admiring wife.'

Before Miranda could make any cutting retort, Jaime drew

her away across the courtyard towards the house. Carlos, obviously relieved by what he thought he had seen, turned back into the store-shed, and only then did Jaime release her, saying dispassionately:

'I hope you haven't been confiding in Carlos. He knows nothing about your relationship with Courtenay.'

'He knows there was trouble last night,' she flared, but Jaime merely pulled a wry face.

'My mother did not like the way he talked about me, that's all.'

Miranda hunched her shoulders. 'Your flying, I know.' She looked doubtfully at him. 'What was wrong? Were the air currents turbulent?'

Jaime stifled his mirth. 'They usually are over the mountains,' he agreed.

Miranda watched him closely. 'And you flew low over the mountains, didn't you?' she exclaimed angrily.

'Let's say we did a bit of contour flying,' he replied, with evil humour, and although she was furious with him, she felt an uncontrollable surge of laughter overtaking her.

Determined he should not see that she found it at all amusing, she went ahead of him into the house, schooling her features before facing him again. But when he went past her towards the stairs, she had to speak to him.

'Where are you going?'

'To take a shower,' he informed her dryly. 'Want to come with me?'

Her cheeks flamed, but she didn't rise to the bait. 'We have to talk,' she declared firmly. 'Please.'

Jaime shrugged, and continued on his way upstairs, and after a moment's hesitation she went after him, following him along the landing to the door to the dressing room. He opened the door and went inside, but Miranda hovered uncertainly on the threshold.

'Are you coming in?' he demanded, beginning to unbutton his shirt, but she shook her head and closed the door and walked further along the landing to the door leading into the bedroom.

When she stepped inside, however, he was standing at the open door to the dressing room.

'That was a bit pointless, wasn't it?' he asked mockingly.

'All roads lead to Rome, as they say.'

'What are you doing in my room?' she demanded.

'Our room, to all intents and purposes. And I was going to take a shower, if you remember.'

'You don't normally use this bathroom.'

'No,' he agreed, 'but I see no point in not using it as it's vacant at the moment.'

Miranda felt exasperated, as he took off his shirt and tossed it on to the floor behind him. 'Will you stop taking your clothes off and listen to me?' she exclaimed.

'I can listen to you just as well ...' he drawled, but he baulked at the zip of his pants and contented himself with taking off his belt. 'Go on, then. What do you want to say?'

He strolled into the bedroom as he spoke, and Miranda, who had been holding the door slightly ajar, closed it and said: 'Why did you really send for Paul?'

Jaime halted in the middle of the floor and bent down to pull off his socks. He had shed his boots earlier, but barefooted he was still tall enough to intimidate her. Then he straightened and looking straight at her, he said: 'That was what you wanted, wasn't it?'

Miranda drew an unsteady breath. 'There was no need to bring Paul here.'

'Why not? Wasn't I entitled to weigh up the opposition?'

'Opposition!' Miranda echoed the word harshly. 'You don't consider Paul to be any opposition to you!'

Jaime's eyes narrowed. 'What makes you say that?'

Miranda flushed. 'Oh, stop playing games, Jaime! You brought Paul here to make a fool of me! To make fools of both of us, Paul and me! You get some kind of perverted amusement out of making people jump to your bidding, and as you've told me a dozen times that you're not prepared to agree to an annulment, I see no point——'

'Perhaps I've changed my mind,' Jaime interrupted her quietly, and she was shocked at the wave of faintness that swept over her at his words.

'Wh—what?' she whispered.

'I said, perhaps I've changed my mind.'

'Yes, yes, I know. But what do you mean?'

'What do you think I mean? Surely it's obvious. I'm considering giving you your freedom. That is what you want, isn't it?'

Miranda turned aside to grasp the post of the bed with trembling fingers. She felt physically sick, and she wondered if it was possible to have a relapse after a dose of fever. But deep inside her she knew that her physical condition had never been better, and that what had knocked her sideways was the thing Jaime was saying.

Almost unaware, he had come to stand beside her, and she started when he reached out and took hold of a strand of her hair. He allowed the living threads to slide through his fingers, and then raised them to his parted lips.

It was more potent than a caress, more intimate than a kiss; as if he had taken hold of her, taken possession of her. Breathing shallowly, she lifted her eyes to his and saw that all the derisive mockery had disappeared.

'Your hair tastes good,' he murmured huskily. 'Do you want me to see what the rest of you tastes like?'

Miranda hardly knew what she was saying. 'We—we can't,' she protested, but it was a half-hearted denial. 'It—it's eleven o'clock in the morning. Someone might come in ...'

Heavy-lidded eyes were shadowed with sensual persuasion. 'No one will,' he assured her softly, unbuttoning her shirt as he spoke and sliding it off her shoulders. 'Come on, Miranda ... You want this as much as I do.'

She knew he spoke nothing less than the truth. When he bent his head to caress her shoulder with his lips, her hands went involuntarily to his chest, spreading against the hard nipples that nudged her palms, sliding down to where his body hair disappeared below his navel into the waistband of his pants.

His lips moved over her shoulder to her neck, moving up along her jawline to the corner of her mouth. His hands at her waist urged her against him, but she needed no further persuasion to arch her body against his.

When his mouth found hers, her lips parted eagerly, greedy for his demanding possession, and what had begun probingly soon became hard and passionate.

'You're not going to stop me, are you, Miranda?' he breathed against her mouth, and the urgency of her response gave him his answer.

'Don't talk,' she moaned sensuously, and with a sound of extreme satisfaction, he lifted her on to the bed ... and joined her.

CHAPTER THIRTEEN

MIRANDA had always believed that the kind of physical assuagement she had read about, the consummate joining together of two bodies to make one whole and wholly satisfying experience, never actually happened in real life. Her own unfortunate experience with Mark had soured the natural awakening of her emotions, and since then she had avoided close contact of any intimate nature. Only with Jaime had she begun to suspect that there was more to making love than the plain possession of her body by a male of the species, but even then, when faced with the simple fact of what was expected of her, she had panicked.

But not for long. Jaime was not Mark—or Paul. He knew exactly how to play on her senses so that not only did her fears dissolve but her inhibitions too, and slowly and sensually he took possession of her until the final barrier was no more than a moment's anguish in a mounting tide of ecstasy.

When it was over, she came down from the heights with real reluctance, clinging to him achingly, realising his skin like hers was moist with sweat.

'Well?' she probed nervously, making no attempt to move away from him, and his hands moved to imprison her face between his palms.

'So I was the first,' he murmured huskily.

'Did you doubt it?'

'Oh, yes,' he said softly, nodding his head. 'All the time.' His thumbs explored her lips. 'Did I hurt you?'

Miranda's nerves forced a choking gulp to her lips. 'Did I hurt you?' she countered tremulously, and his wry smile aroused all the loving adoration she felt for him.

'I guess I can stand it,' he assured her gently, and she buried her face against his chest.

'I love you ...' she whispered, unable to suppress the words, her breath escaping on a sigh as his mouth covered hers again.

Some time later, Jaime propelled her away from him and got up from the bed. 'I guess we should go down for lunch,' he murmured, looking down at her tenderly, and Miranda propped herself up on her elbows to reach out and touch him.

'I'm not hungry,' she breathed, and he smiled.

'I am,' he declared. 'But not for lunch!' and before she could detain him further, he walked purposefully into the bathroom.

Miranda remained where she was, listening to the shower running. She was reluctant to displace the languid inertia of her limbs, unwilling to start really thinking about what had happened and what it might mean . . .

Jaime came back, his lower limbs swathed in a towel, and crossed the bedroom to the dressing room. She heard drawers being opened and the bang of the wardrobe door, and then he came back to the open doorway again, changed into navy blue fitted pants and a matching silk shirt.

'Are you getting up?' he inquired lazily, and she was tempted to invite him to join her again. But it was midday, and her face burned when she considered what construction other members of the household would put upon their absence. Not least—Paul!

'Jaime . . .' She didn't know how to broach the subject, but it had to be said. 'Jaime, what about Paul?'

Just for an instant something flickered in his eyes, and then was gone. 'What about Paul?' he returned, and there was a trace of hardness still in his tones when he spoke the other's man's name.

Miranda's tongue appeared to moisten her upper lip. 'Will you—that is, do you want me to speak to him?'

There was silence for so long that she thought she had said something wrong. Then at last Jaime shook his head.

'No,' he said firmly. 'No. I'll speak to him.'

Miranda shifted restlessly. 'What will you say?'

His eyes narrowed. 'What do you want me to say?'

She faltered. 'Do I—do I have to tell you?'

Jaime covered the space between them in a few strides. 'Put some clothes on!' he told her huskily.

Miranda's apprehension disappeared. 'All right,' she said a little breathlessly, and with a parting caress he opened the door and left her.

When Miranda came downstairs about half an hour later, she found Paul and Julia sitting with Jaime's parents on the verandah. They had been having a pre-lunch cocktail and Miranda herself accepted the same. But there was no sign of Jaime, and she looked round in surprise.

'Jaime's not here,' his mother said, as if anticipating her question. 'He's gone to Valentes.'

'*Valentes!*'

Miranda was shocked. Valentes was all of a hundred miles away. Why had he said nothing of this to her?

She saw Paul looking at her, and guessed he was wondering what she was thinking. Obviously Jaime had said nothing to him either, judging from the smugness of his expression.

'What have you been doing, Miranda?' he asked, coming to take the seat beside her that Carlos had vacated to go and get her drink. 'Julia and I have been riding, but we've been back almost an hour.'

Miranda lay back in her chair, wishing Paul would not talk to her. She needed time to think, to try and understand what it was Jaime was doing to her. Why had he not told her he was going to Valentes? Why hadn't he spoken to Paul before he left? Didn't he care that the other man was still here, still believing Miranda wanted a divorce?

Turning to her mother-in-law, she said: 'How—how long will Jaime be away?' and saw the look Teresa exchanged with her daughter.

'I——' The older woman was obviously discomfited. 'I— I'm not sure,' she got out at last, and Julia gave a faint nod in agreement.

'But you must know——'

'There you are, Miranda!'

Carlos was back with her cocktail, and his advent interrupted them so that when Miranda would have spoken to Teresa again, she was already speaking with her daughter. Was it her imagination, Miranda wondered uneasily, or were Teresa and Julia deliberately avoiding holding a discussion with her? Had it anything to do with Paul? Had he said something? Oh, why wasn't Jaime here to sort it all out?

Lunch was a subdued meal with Miranda responding only desultorily to Paul's sporadic attempts at conversation. But after it was over, he cornered her in the drawing room, closing the door despite her anxious protestations and advancing on her determinedly.

'Now,' he said grimly, 'you're going to give me some explanations!'

'Oh, Paul!' She twisted her hands together helplessly. 'I—well, I wish I could have saved you the journey!'

'The *journey*!' Paul stared at her. 'What do you mean?'

'I'm not divorcing Jaime, Paul, and he's not divorcing me!'

'Are you crazy?'

'It's true, Paul. We—I—I love him. I think I always have.'

'You're out of your mind. You don't love him!'

'I do. I do!'

'And what about him? Does he love you? Is that why he cabled me to come out here? To take the woman he loves off his hands? Grow up, Miranda, for God's sake!'.

'It's not like that, Paul. Before—before you came, I wasn't sure——'

'And now you are?'

'Yes.'

'What made you change your mind, I wonder?' His eyes narrowed maliciously. 'That tumble on the bed he gave you before he left for Valentes?'

'What do you know about that?'

The horrified admission was out before she could prevent it, and Paul's lips curled in a sneer. 'What do I know about it?' he echoed. 'You don't imagine your husband didn't tell me, do you? My God, he couldn't wait to make it clear that whatever happened between us, I'd only be getting second best!'

'I don't believe you!'

Miranda had turned deathly pale, but Paul was merciless. 'Please yourself. It's your decision.'

She drew an unsteady breath. 'When—when did he speak to you?'

'When do you think? Before he left for Valentes, of course.'

'And—and did he say why he was going? To—to Valentes, I mean?'

'No. But my guess is that he's hoping I'll persuade you to do the honourable thing and leave before he gets back.'

'That's the *honourable* thing!'

'Well, let's face it, Miranda; you're flogging a dead horse here.'

She caught her breath. 'You know nothing about it.'

'I know quite a lot. I know for instance that you've become something of an embarrassment to him.'

'An embarrassment!'

'Surely. Look, Miranda, he never wanted you out here. He only married you to get his mother off his back. I gather she was eager to have him marry some girl——'

She gasped. 'How do you know that?'

Paul shrugged. 'I could lie and say your husband told me. But I don't have to. No, as a matter of fact, his sister supplied the information. I gather she made the situation plain to you, too.'

Miranda put a confused hand to her head. 'I can't take this in ...'

Paul came towards her. 'You don't have to. Not right now, anyway. Honey,' his tone became wheedling, 'you don't belong here. You know that and I know that, and it looks like the Carvalhos know it, too. Come home with me—back to England. Back to sanity!'

Miranda put some distance between them. The last thing she wanted right now was for Paul to try and offer her sympathy. Sympathy was something she could do without. She didn't love him; she never had. And now she didn't think she liked him much either.

'I—think you ought to leave,' she said at last, with slow deliberation.

'What?'

Paul was obviously astounded, but she stuck to her guns. 'You heard what I said.'

'And what are you going to do?'

'Me?' She held up her head. 'I shall stay here.'

'You're a fool!'

'Possibly. But you forget, I'm Jaime's wife. Nothing can alter that. Not now.'

'You think not? Don't be too sure. He's a Catholic, I know that. But they have their methods, particularly here where the Church is all-powerful. You came here for an annulment, remember? And if Knevett wants one, he'll get it, believe me.'

Miranda's hands balled into fists. 'I think you'd better go.'

'And how am I supposed to get back to the coast?'

She thought hard. 'I believe Carlos's manager flies the Cessna. He can take you.'

'What? Get on board that pigeon-carrier again? No, thanks!'

'Then you'll have to drive down. I'm afraid I know nothing about river sailings.'

Paul stared frustratedly at her. 'And you're really staying?'

'Yes.'

'Why?'

'I've told you—I love him!'

'Oh, Miranda . . .'

She turned away, however, and didn't look round until the door had slammed behind him. Only then did she walk on rather unsteady legs across the floor and follow him into the hall.

Carlos was just coming out of his study, and now he looked doubtfully at her. 'Miranda!' he exclaimed in surprise. 'Is something wrong?'

She took a deep breath. 'Not exactly. But Mr Courtenay is leaving. Is there any way he can get down to Rio?'

Carlos stared at her blankly for a few moments and then gathered himself with obvious difficulty. 'He is—leaving? Alone?'

Miranda's face flamed. 'Yes.'

'I see.' Carlos shook his head rather confusedly. Then he blinked and sought for words. 'I—Juan can fly him to Belo Horizonte. He can get an internal flight from there.'

Miranda hesitated, but flying to Belo Horizonte was not like flying all the way to Rio. 'I'll tell him,' she said firmly. 'Thank you.'

She would have turned away, but Carlos caught her arm and drew her round to face him. 'Miranda . . .' he said wonderingly. 'But—we thought——'

'I'm staying!' she declared tremulously. 'You can't make me go!'

'Child, child!' Carlos was quite choked. 'We do not want you to go. Whatever gave you that idea?'

Miranda's lips trembled. 'At lunchtime——'

'At lunchtime?' he prompted.

'I felt—my presence wasn't wanted.'

Carlos sighed heavily. 'I am afraid that was Julia's fault. You see, she went riding with—with Courtenay this morning and ...' He spread his hands. 'She told her mother that he and you were—well, connected. He must have said something. I cannot believe that Julia——'

'Oh, no.' Miranda shook her head, feeling immensely relieved. Now she only had Jaime to face. 'Paul would—talk. And—we were—friends, more than that even. But not lovers. Never that.'

'And your visit here? Was not that instigated by this man?'

Miranda bent her head. 'Oh, yes. Yes.' She looked up at him. 'But after I saw Jaime again ...' She lifted her shoulders expressively. 'Can you understand?'

A faint smile lifted the corners of Carlos's mouth. 'I am not so old that I have forgotten what it is like to be in love.' He shook his head. 'So many words, so many misunderstandings. But you are so young. You have all your life ahead of you.'

Miranda felt the prick of tears behind her eyes. 'I don't know what to say ...'

'Leave it to me. I will tell Teresa—and Julia. You will see, they will be as delighted as I am.'

And Jaime? she thought silently. But the words were left unsaid.

Paul left in the afternoon after agreeing to the flight to Belo Horizonte instead of facing the long drive down through the mountains. He and Miranda had no more private words before he left, but he did hand her a letter which he said Aunt Lydia had sent her. Miranda thrust the envelope into her trousers' pocket and concentrated on shaking hands with him and bidding him a good journey. It wasn't easy destroying her only lifeline with England, but her life was here and if Jaime turned her out she would face that problem when she came to it. Brazil had not been civilised by women who turned back at the first obstacle. And she nurtured the memory of Jaime's lovemaking with an aching obstinacy that eschewed any sentimentality. She could arouse him, couldn't she? she told herself fiercely. And marriages had been built on frailer foundations.

Even so, as night drew in and Jaime had not returned, her determination faltered. Joining his parents and Julia for the evening meal was not easy either, and she bravely spent some time in front of the vanity mirror, restoring the colour to her cheeks and accentuating the colour of her eyes with a deeper eye-shadow. Her dress, too, was a deliberate choice: black chiffon, it gave her skin an amber glow, and newly washed hair swung softly about her shoulders. The only jewellery she wore was a gold coil about her throat with matching pendants suspended from her ears.

'My dear!' exclaimed Teresa, when she appeared. 'You look—beautiful!' She surveyed her with real admiration. 'We're so glad you decided to stay.'

'We are,' Julia echoed behind her. 'I'm sorry if I upset you at lunchtime, Miranda, but Paul Courtenay——'

'I know, I know,' Miranda nodded. She licked her dry lips. 'Did—did Carlos explain ...'

'... that you and Paul were friends? Yes.' Teresa smiled. 'We guessed he was no friend of Jaime's. They hated one another on sight.'

Miranda's answering smile was nervous. Had they? Had they really hated one another on sight? Or had that been another of Jaime's little humiliations? She seemed to have spent her whole life recovering from his humiliating.

'Never mind,' Teresa added, 'it's over now. He's gone. And you are here.'

If only it were that simple, thought Miranda, pushing iced melon round her plate. But she had made her bed. Now she had to lie in it.

No one mentioned Jaime during the course of that long evening. Perhaps they felt that Miranda's personal affairs had suffered enough at their hands. At any rate, she was spared that embarrassment, even though she would have liked to have asked when he was expected to return. Not today, evidently, she thought, as she prepared for bed, tossing her gold necklace carelessly on to the dressing table.

It was a hot night, and turning out the light, she opened the long windows on to the balcony. Leaning against the window frame, she breathed deeply of the night air, closing her eyes against the thought of the morning and Jaime's eventual return.

A curious sound broke the stillness suddenly, a loud whirring sound, like an aircraft yet not like one. She blinked and looked up frowningly into the night sky, and saw the lights of some craft descending rapidly on to the home paddock in front of the house. A helicopter, she realised with some astonishment. And then, more anxiously: *Jaime!* Only Jaime would fetch a helicopter in over those mountains after dark.

The engine was cut and silence ensued for several minutes until a dark figure detached itself from the trees surrounding the paddock, and strode swiftly across the courtyard and into the house.

She tensed. She couldn't help it. Likely he would go straight to the dressing room tonight, but there was always the chance that he might check to see if she had gone. She heard the footsteps coming along the corridor and shrank into petrified stillness against the wall as the door crashed open and the main light was switched on.

She could not have been more shocked if he had crept up on her in the dark. The unexpected explosion of light was an invasion of her innermost feelings, and she sank behind the curtains, watching him from between their enveloping folds.

She saw the way his eyes went first to the bed and how his expression hardened when he saw she was not in it. But was 'hardened' the right word, she wondered, as with an anguished sound he sagged against the door frame, raking his long fingers through his hair in a strangely defeated gesture. Then, before she could summon the courage to step out from her concealment, he came right into the bedroom, closing the door before sinking down on to the side of the bed and burying his head in his hands.

And then she knew, knew it as surely as if he had written it out for her—he thought she had gone with Paul! Somehow he thought she had left with the Englishman! And he was shattered!

She straightened away from the wall, and as she did so an enormous furry insect, attracted no doubt by the light from within, whirred past her ear. She shuddered in horror, letting out a startled cry, and precipitated into the room without ceremony. She slammed the windows shut behind her, and as she did so, Jaime rose to his feet to face her.

'*Miranda!*' he said disbelievingly. Then: 'Miranda!' more coldly, and she wondered if she had only imagined his torment.

'Hello, Jaime,' she got out jerkily. 'I—I heard the helicopter ...'

His lips curled. 'Is that why you chose to hide yourself on the balcony? Did it give you a kick to watch my reaction?'

'To watch your—*no!*' She stumbled into words. 'I—I was waiting for you to come back. When you came in ...'

'Yes?'

She expelled her breath on a small sigh. 'If you must know I did want to see how you'd react——'

'You said not!' His voice was harsh. 'My God, how did you expect me to react? I thought you'd left me!'

Miranda gathered her defences and took a step forward. 'Why—why did you tell Paul about us, if that's how you feel? Why did you let him think you wanted me to go?'

'*What!*' She could have sworn his astonishment was genuine. 'What the hell are you talking about? I haven't spoken to Courtenay since he went riding with Julia this morning.'

'You haven't?' Miranda's heart leapt and then subsided again. 'Then—then how did he know about—about us?'

Jaime tugged off his jacket and his tie and tossed them carelessly on to a chair. He looked utterly weary now and compassion for him overwhelmed her.

'Jaime ...' she whispered. 'Did you really want me to stay?'

She had thought he might come to her then, might take her in his arms and show her exactly how much he wanted her; but he didn't. Instead, he kicked off his boots and socks and flung himself full-length on the bed, one arm across his brow shading his eyes.

'What damn-fool kind of question is that?' he demanded, not looking at her. 'Miranda, I'm too tired to make any sense of this.'

Anger flared within her. 'You're too tired!' she snapped. 'How do you think I feel?'

Jaime dropped his arm and regarded her through narrowed lids. 'Look,' he said flatly. 'You're here, and for now that's all that matters.'

'It does matter to you, then?' she demanded.

Jaime closed his eyes for a moment. 'Of course it matters to me,' he said wearily.

'Well, you have a funny way of showing it.'

'Why?' His eyes opened again. 'Miranda, I've just had one hell of a day, do you know that? And what happens at the end of it? I arrive back at the airport to find the Cessna's gone, and to be told that the Englishman left this afternoon. I ask—was he alone, and no one knows. Can you believe that? *No one knows!* How do I know what he might have told you? Might have persuaded you to do? So I come back here like a bat out of hell, and what do I find? Your bed empty, and you playing hide-and-go-seek on the balcony! Well, okay, Miranda. You got your pound of flesh. Thinking you had gone really finished me. But don't ask me to fawn around you tonight, thanking you for saving my sanity, answering stupid questions about how Courtenay knew about us! *In nomine Patris*, how could he not know about us? You're my wife!'

Miranda trembled. 'Do you love me?'

Jaime groaned, but with a sigh he got up from the bed and came to her, his hands sliding from her shoulders, down her bare arms to imprison her wrists at her sides. 'I loved you when your eyes spat venom at me across the width of a party table,' he told her quietly. 'Now come to bed and stop playing damn silly games.'

Miranda lifted her face wonderingly to his. 'You—you can't have done.'

'Why not?' he asked patiently, his fingers finding the long zip at the back of her dress and propelling it downwards, and she shivered in delight as the night air ran over her heated flesh.

'You—you never said ...' she faltered, and his expression grew wry.

'Circumstances haven't contrived to make things easy for us,' he averred, drawing her unresisting hands to his body. 'You undress me,' he commanded, his voice thickening, and with eager fingers she did as she was bidden ...

Hours later, the moonlight was flooding in through the open curtains, illuminating the shadowy line of beard on

Jaime's jawline.

'You need a shave,' she told him drowsily, and he rubbed his rough chin teasingly over her soft shoulder.

'Now?' he murmured, but she shook her head and snuggled closer to him. Then he sighed, and said: 'Tell me about Courtenay. I have to know.'

'It doesn't matter,' she breathed, but he lifted her chin and forced her to look at him.

'Come on . . .'

Miranda sighed. 'Paul—Paul told me you had—well, told him that we had—that this morning we had——'

'Made love?' he suggested tenderly, and she nodded.

'Yes.'

'You thought I'd do a thing like that?'

She pressed herself closer to him. 'What else could I think? How else could he know?'

'Why? What happened?'

'I went downstairs for lunch and you had gone.'

'They told you I had gone to Valentes, didn't they?'

'Well, yes. That was why I was so ready to believe the worst. Why didn't you tell me you were going?'

'Why didn't I——' He broke off to prop himself up on one elbow, looking down at her. 'My God!' he exclaimed. 'They did tell you why I'd gone, didn't they?'

Miranda blinked and shook her head. 'No.' She frowned. 'Oh, it was awful! Lunch, I mean. Your mother and Julia were hardly speaking to me.' She stopped suddenly. 'I suppose that was why I wasn't told.'

'Miranda, Miranda!' he said impatiently. 'You're not making sense. Why were my mother and Julia not speaking to you?'

'You don't know, do you?' She put up her hand to touch his face, and he caught it and drew the palm to his mouth. 'Mmm, don't do that.'

'Why not? Don't you like it?'

'Too much,' she confessed breathlessly, and with a groan he bent his head and covered her mouth with his. Then he drew away again, much to her disappointment. 'Must we talk?' she asked rather plaintively, but he inclined his head and reluctantly she went on:

'Paul—Paul had told Julia that he and I—that we had an

understanding . . .'

'Or words to that effect,' remarked Jaime dryly, and she nodded.

'I suppose so.'

He sighed. 'I'm beginning to understand. So you never found out why I left?' He pulled her close to him again. 'Remind me to compensate you for what I said earlier. What in God's name can you have been thinking all day?'

Miranda's laugh was breathy. 'That was part of it, anyway.'

'But why the hell didn't they tell you later? Or are they still not speaking to you?'

Miranda shook her head. 'It wasn't that simple. You see, after lunch Paul told me that you had—well, what you were reputed to have said to him, and that—that you expected me to be gone before you got back from Valentes——'

The epithet Jaime used at that point Miranda would not have cared to repeat, but it was not inappropriate considering what Paul had tried to do.

'Go on,' he said, when he had got control of himself again, and she continued:

'I told him I didn't care. That I was going to stay anyway. I—even if you had said what he maintained, I still wanted to hear it from your lips. After—after what had happened between us, I couldn't believe I didn't have a chance of making you change your mind . . .'

'Some chance,' muttered Jaime unsteadily, burying his face in the hollow between her breasts. 'If you'd left with Courtenay, I'd have killed you!'

Her breathing almost stopped. 'Would you?'

She heard his muffled groan of protest. 'I'd have wanted to.'

'So I stayed,' she got out breathlessly, after another disturbing interlude. 'Carlos—your stepfather—he believed me when I told him there was nothing between Paul and me and he told the others. But, as you can imagine, dinner was quite an awkward occasion.'

'And no one mentioned me?'

'I think they just steered clear of personal topics,' she admitted honestly. 'And after all, they didn't know what Paul had said.'

'No,' Jaime nodded thoughtfully. 'A man scorned is much

the same as a woman, I guess.'

'It was what he said . . .'

'What did he say?'

'That you had—had just tumbled me on the bed.'

A reluctant smile touched Jaime's lips. 'And I had.'

She pressed her balled fist into his shoulder. 'Swine!' she declared affectionately, and he grinned. 'But how did he know?'

Jaime shrugged. 'I can think of a number of ways. We'd been absent together for a significant length of time, one of the servants might have told him they'd seen us going into the bedroom together.' He paused. 'And when I left here, you did have a—a certain look in your eyes . . .'

'Oh, Jaime!' Miranda's lips twitched. 'You don't know what an awful day I've had!'

'Hasn't the night made up for it?'

She raked her nails down the supple skin of his back. 'You're mean . . .'

He kissed her again, and then drew back to say more soberly: 'I haven't had such a great day myself.'

'Of course.' She frowned. 'I still don't know why you went to Valentes.'

Jaime sighed. 'Do you remember me telling you about Consuelo?'

'The woman who had the baby?' exclaimed Miranda at once.

'That's right. She died today.'

'Oh, Jaime!' She stared at him compassionately. 'That was why . . .'

'Vasco came for me just after I left you. He was in a terrible state. She was haemorrhaging pretty badly, and I only had time to go to Santa Madalena and send for the helicopter from the base at Valentes.'

Miranda stroked his cheek. 'I'm sorry.' She hesitated. 'And the baby?'

Jaime shrugged. 'He may live. He's in the hospital now. Ironically, even if he does, Vasco won't be able to keep him. He will probably be sent to the mission home along with half a dozen of his brothers and sisters.' He released her for a moment to turn on to his back and stretch his arms, his face mirroring his frustration. 'If only he'd let me take her away a week ago . . .'

'It's not your fault,' Miranda ventured gently, and throwing off his melancholy, he turned to her again.

'I know. But waste in any form appals me.' He smiled. 'That's why I live here and not in England. Lydia can handle the estate. She's had plenty of experience. It doesn't need me. Santa Madalena does.'

'And me?' she probed tentatively.

'Oh, you need me,' he assured her huskily. 'Which is good, because I need you, too.'

'Why didn't you ever tell me?' she protested.

'When? When I came back to see you, only to find you were on the point of marrying Mark?'

'You came back to see me . . .' She was disbelieving.

'Didn't you know it? Didn't you feel it, as I did, when we danced together?'

Miranda remembered dancing with him all too well. 'I—I'd never felt like that with anyone before . . .'

'Nor had I,' he muttered roughly. 'And believe me, I didn't like it one bit. Not when I found out exactly why you were marrying Mark!'

Miranda sighed. 'I was a horror, I know . . .'

Jaime smiled. 'I'd have to agree with you.' Then he sobered again. 'Seriously though, I grew close to hating you then. Until I saw you after Mark had—I think you know what I mean.'

'Did you believe that he hadn't—touched me?'

'I had to. Or I'd have gone out of my head.'

'But you were so horrible!'

'So were you.'

'When my mother had the stroke——'

'I took care of her, didn't I?'

'At a price!'

'It was the only thing I could think of to protect you from some other moron like my cousin!'

'But you left me! Immediately afterwards.'

'Would you have had me then? If I'd demanded what was mine?'

Miranda hesitated. 'I could say no, but I don't know. When you touch me . . .'

'You were too young, and it was too soon. You'd have

fought against it. I wanted you to experience the life you
were prepared to barter yourself for. I wanted you to grow up.
Then Lydia was to send you to me ...'

'Lydia was——' She broke off to stare at him. '*What?*'

'You heard. Didn't she do it? She told me she did.'

Miranda gasped. 'Well, yes. It was her idea that I came
out here to see you and ask you for—for the annulment ...'

'Not quite what I had in mind, but it served the purpose.'

She gave a helpless cry. 'You really are a beast, aren't you?'

'But you love me?'

'Oh, yes.' She pulled his face down to hers and for several
minutes the silence was only broken by their tortured breathing. Then she drew back from him again, her brows drawn
together. 'But only yesterday you said—you said you were
considering letting me go.'

'I had to be sure you wanted to stay. So I gambled ...'

'Dangerously, as it happened,' she breathed.

'Agreed,' he murmured, his voice thickening. 'And
now ...'

It was late the following morning before Miranda remembered Aunt Lydia's letter. They had overslept, but now
Jaime had gone to help Vasco with the funeral arrangements for Consuelo, and she had showered and put on a
silk robe, and was sitting at her dressing table brushing her
hair when she saw the envelope projecting from the pocket
of her jeans.

Reluctantly, she slit the seal and pulled out the sheet of
monogrammed notepaper. But as she started to read, her lips
curved into a smile. The letter read:

My dear Miranda,

*I expect by the time you get this Jaime will have told
you why I suggested you went out to Brazil to see him for
yourself. But just in case he hasn't, let me explain. We
knew, Mark and I, that Jaime was attracted to you. He
had written and admitted as much, but he was waiting
until he had finished his training before coming back to
England to see you. Unfortunately, Mark was always a
little jealous of his cousin, and when he saw you for himself, you know what happened. You knew I never approved*

*of your relationship with my son. That's no secret. And I
wrote and told Jaime what was going on.*

Miranda gasped at this point. So Mark had been right
about something—his mother had used Jaime to try and
separate them. She read on:

> *Afterwards, all that mattered was that Mark was dead
> and I was dependent on Jaime's benevolence. He was
> always a generous boy, but he knew I would do anything
> to stay on at the Hall. We were sorry when your mother
> had the stroke, but it did give Jaime a lever, and as you
> know he used it. He used me, too. I tell myself I would
> not have been a party to it, if I had not been sure he loved
> you, but I have been practising self-deception for years, so
> I could be wrong.*
>
> *However, I do want you to know that your husband is
> a fine man, while Paul Courtenay, is, I regret, too much
> like Mark to ever make you happy. There is a small
> animal you may encounter in South America, called a
> scorpion. No doubt you have heard of it. It's got the
> reputation for being quite an unpleasant character, but I
> like to think that nothing is ever as black as it's painted.
> Its sexual habits are unusual, though. The male and
> female indulge in what scientists claim to be a courtship
> dance, which entails quite a lot of manoeuvre and per-
> suasion. Considering the dangers each of them offers to
> the other, I think they're rather courageous for going on,
> but nothing worth having is easy to come by. Perhaps you'll
> remember that when you have to choose between Paul
> and Jaime.*

She signed herself: Sincerely, Lydia Sanders, but Miranda
wondered if she had ever been sincere about anything in her
whole life.

She gave Jaime the letter to read that evening as he came
out of the bathroom after taking a shower before dressing
for dinner. He fastened the cord of his bathrobe about him
and frowned, but he sat down on the side of the bed and
read it while she watched him.

Then he looked up, a humorous expression on his face. 'Well, well!' he drawled. 'I don't have to wonder which of us she considers the scorpion—Courtenay or me!'

Miranda's fingers toyed with the sash of her dressing gown. 'Why do you think she wrote the letter?'

He pushed it back into its envelope. 'Why do you?'

Miranda shrugged. 'She wanted to be sure I knew what a wonderful husband you were.'

Jaime grinned, reaching for her hand and drawing her between his legs. 'Do you honestly believe that?'

'I know it,' she breathed, bending to caress his temple with her lips.

'No. I mean the bit about Lydia wanting us to be happy.'

Miranda straightened, frowning. 'What do you mean?'

'Shall I tell you?'

'You'd better!'

'Well, it's like this,' he murmured, starting to unfasten the sash that kept her robe in place. 'I told Lydia that if she let any other man lay a hand on you, she'd be out of the Hall so quick her feet wouldn't touch the ground. I should think when I phoned her from Rio when you had disappeared she would need a whole bottle of librium to recover from the things I threatened her with when she admitted there was someone else.'

'Jaime!'

Miranda stared down at his bent head, scarely aware of his hands inside her robe, propelling her closer to him.

'Mmm?' His lips caressed her midriff. 'You smell delicious. Can I eat you instead of dinner? Why the hell did my mother have to invite the family to meet you tonight?'

'Jaime!' she said again, less convincingly now as her senses began to betray her, and he took pity on her.

'All right.' He looked at her through lazy lashes. 'Let me see—her brief was to look after you, to give you a good time, but no serious attachments, right?'

'And ... and she knew if I went back with Paul ...'

'Precisely,' he grinned. 'I told her to get you out here, and I'd do the rest.'

'Oh, you ... !' She glared at him in mock indignation, and his humour disappeared as he pulled her down beside him on the bed.

'You want to change your mind?' he demanded, shedding his bathrobe, but Miranda didn't even bother to answer him in words.

EYE OF THE STORM

MAURA SEGER

A powerful
portrayal of
the events of
World War II in the
Pacific, *Eye of the Storm* is a riveting story of how love
triumphs over hatred. In this, the first of a three-book
chronicle, Army nurse Maggie Lawrence meets Marine
Sgt. Anthony Gargano. Despite military regulations
against fraternization, they resolve to face together
whatever lies ahead.... Author Maura Seger, also known
to her fans as Laurel Winslow, Sara Jennings, Anne
MacNeil and Jenny Bates, was named 1984's
Most Versatile Romance Author by *The Romantic Times*.

An epic novel of exotic rituals
and the lure of the Upper Amazon

THE
TAKERS
RIVER
OF GOLD

JERRY AND S.A. AHERN

THE TAKERS are the intrepid Josh Culhane and the
seductive Mary Mulrooney. These two adventurers
launch an incredible journey into the Brazilian rain
forest. Far upriver, the jungle yields its deepest
secret—the lost city of the Amazon warrior women!

THE TAKERS series is making publishing history.
Awarded *The Romantic Times* first prize for High
Adventure in 1984, the opening book in the series
was hailed by *The Romantic Times* as "the next
trend in romance writing and reading. Highly
recommended!"

Jerry and S.A. Ahern have never been better!

TAK – 3

Harlequin reaches into the hearts and minds of women across America to bring you

Harlequin American Romance ^{T.M.}

Get this book FREE!

Harlequin American Romance

Twice in a Lifetime
REBECCA FLANDERS

PASSIONATE!
CAPTIVATING!
SOPHISTICATED!

Harlequin Presents...

**The favorite fiction
of women the world over!**

Beautiful contemporary romances that
touch every emotion of a woman's heart—
passion and joy, jealousy and heartache...
but most of all...love.

Fascinating settings in the exotic
reaches of the world—
from the bustle of an international capital
to the paradise of a tropical island.

**All this and much, much more
in the pages of**

Harlequin Presents...

Wherever paperback books are sold, or through
Harlequin Reader Service

In the U.S.
1440 South Priest Drive
Tempe, AZ 85281

In Canada
649 Ontario Street
Stratford, Ontario N5A 6W2

**No one touches the heart of a woman
quite like Harlequin!**